Keisha & Trigga

A Gangster Love Story

3

LEO SULLIVAN
PORSCHA STERLING

JOIN OUR MAILING LIST!

Text **LEOSULLIVAN** to **22828** to join our mailing list!
To submit a manuscript for our review, email us at
submissions@leolsullivan.com

READ MORE ON THE LIT READING APP!

Read more books like this one **for less**! Check out some other new releases on the LiT Reading App. Go to www.litreadingapp.com to learn more!

© 2015
Published by Leo Sullivan Presents

This one is dedicated to the readers and to every author signed to Sullivan Productions & Royalty Publishing House. We appreciate every one of you and are humbled by your unwavering support.

PROLOGUE

ONE MONTH LATER

"Okay, take your time and look closely," Detective Burns coached with an eager grin on his face.

He was finally about to get one step closer to closing out one of the biggest cases of his career. It wasn't the big kahuna...of course, that was Lloyd. If he could get Lloyd nailed down, he would most certainly get the fat ass raise and corner office that he'd been coveting for years; but locking Maurice Bivens down for the murder of Kenyon St. Michaels and one of Lloyd's EPG gangsters was nothing to look down on.

On top of that, if he could get Maurice to talk, he might find out some of what he needed to know in order to lock Lloyd up too. Life was looking good for Detective Burns. His wife had been so happy about him arresting Maurice that she'd almost let him sleep back in their bedroom the night before. If this eyewitness correctly identified him as the man who had murdered Kenyon St. Michaels and agreed to put her testimony on record for the trial, it would seal the deal for his career—and he might even get a bit of celebratory sex from the Mrs. Sweeeeeet!

"Okay Ms. Simon, do you see the man here that you testified you witnessed running from Kenyon St. Michael's home the night of his murder?"

Burns watched as the eyewitness took a deep breath, hesitating as she looked through the glass at the black men of various shapes, sizes, and skin-tones in the room ahead of them. He almost wanted to point directly at Maurice Bivens and ask her frankly, "IS THIS THE GUY?!" but he knew then that his case would most definitely be shot to hell. The witness continued to hesitate, and he heard someone clear his throat next to him. Burns turned and came eye-to-eye with his captain, who was giving him a disappointed look. Burns began to get anxious.

"Look really hard...REALLY hard, Ms. Simon. Do you see anyone who looks ANYTHING like the man you called us about when you heard about Mr. St. Michael's murder?"

Sweat beaded up at the top of Burns' brow. He gave a look of desperation at his captain and sent him a silent plea for more time. To Burns' absolute chagrin, his captain shook his head solemnly and moved towards the witness.

"Ms. Simon, I know you've been through a traumatic experience...you've just been released from the hospital after nearly losing your life. I wish I could have asked you sooner so your memory would be sharper, but I couldn't. Now, I understand we can't expect you to be able to remember back to that night—"

"But I do remember," the witness said finally.

Burns' ears perked up instantly as a ray of hope shot through him like a firework. Finally, alas, his case might be saved. Rushing to the witness with a grin on his face and furrowed brows, he forced himself between her and his captain, then grabbed onto her shoulder.

"You see him? Do you see the man?"

The witness wrinkled up her face and turned to look him square in the eyes. Her brown eyes focused in on him, and he could see from her expression that her thoughts were crystal clear, and she was firm in whatever she was about to say. *Please God...let her be about to say what I need.*

"No," she said. Instantly, the breath left out of Burns' lungs. His shoulders slumped and his face damn near hit the ground, but he had to try one last time. Maybe she was mistaken.

"Are you sure? You don't see the man here...the man you called us about and said was Maurice "Trigga" Bivens. You don't see him here?"

"No," she said again.

"BUT HE'S HERE! You don't see him?" Burns said desperately. He felt his captain's hand on his shoulder, but he ignored it. "Did you suffer an eye injury? A head injury? Could it be that you don't remember correctly?!"

"NO, NO, NO! I was mistaken. Maurice is not the man who I saw...he's not the man who killed Kenyon St. Michaels. He's the man who saved my life!"

Burns' mouth dropped wide open.

"WHAT?!"

Tish bit her lip and shook her head vigorously as she looked through the glass at Trigga. He was standing straight up with his jaw clenched tightly, and his gray eyes staring straight ahead. On his face was his normal pissed off scowl. With each second that he was made to continue standing there, he was getting visibly more and more annoyed until finally, he just crossed his arms in front of his chest and looked straight through the glass at where Tish was, as if to say 'hurry the fuck on!' Tish shuddered and backed away from the glass. It almost felt like he could see her.

"Can he see me?!" she shrieked.

Burns furrowed his eyebrows in confusion. "What?" He then turned to look through the glass and saw that Trigga seemed to be staring straight at his only eyewitness. When he turned back to Tish, he noticed that she had a look of pure terror on her face.

"Ms. Simon, if this is not the man who killed Kenyon and he's actually the man who saved you...why do you seem so afraid?" he asked her slowly.

"I'm not afraid," Tish lied as she tried to gather her composure and stand straight. She shot a wary glance back over to Trigga, who was now looking down at his feet as he shifted from foot to foot.

But the truth was she was still afraid. If Trigga ever found out that she was the one who was behind him getting arrested for murder, she wasn't sure what would happen. All she knew now was that she had to correct her wrong decision. He'd saved her life. She couldn't possibly move forward with being the sole reason he would be locked away forever for a murder after that. All she had been trying to do was get him away from Keisha; she'd never thought that it would spiral this far out of control.

When Keisha was gone one day to class, she went into her room and got the number for the detectives out of her room. She had seen the card on Keisha's dresser for days, and convinced herself to use it after Queen and her men had tied her to the bed and threatened to kill her if she made a sound. For whatever reason, she knew that Keisha wouldn't leave Trigga alone, no matter what new bullshit he wrapped her up in, so Tish decided to call the detectives to solve the problem for her.

She lost her nerve until she saw on the news that Kenyon St. Michaels had been murdered. She knew from working in the club that Kenyon was Lloyd's cousin. Once again, someone connected with Trigga's situation was harmed, but Tish didn't think anything of it until the day she'd almost walked out of her room and stumbled upon Keisha holding a baby and talking to Trigga. Keisha had thought that Tish was gone, but she was home. Her car wasn't in the yard because she'd allowed Luxe to use it. After hearing everything that Trigga told Keisha about killing Kenyon and the baby that she was holding, which belonged to Dior and Keisha's ex-boyfriend Lloyd, Tish knew she had to call the police because Keisha was being pulled in even more into Trigga's web of crazy criminal activity and murder. If she didn't do anything, the next time it could be her or Keisha dead and on the news.

"Um...hello?" Tish whispered as she held the phone to her ear.

Although she knew she was in the house alone, her eyes darted around the room to make sure no one was around. The paranoia that she felt was for good reason. She didn't know exactly who Trigga was or the power he had, but she did know that she'd almost lost her life just by being associated with someone who was connected to him. Whatever he was in was not only affecting Keisha, it was affecting her too, so she had to get rid of him for her and Keisha's sake.

"Yes? This is Detective West. How can I help you?" the voice said on the other line through the loud cacophony of background noise. The detective sounded rather short-tempered at the moment, and angry about something. Tish hesitated and contemplated hanging up the phone.

Suddenly Tish heard some ruffling, and the background noise was muffled as if he'd placed his hand over the receiver.

"Burns, turn down that fuckin' music! I got someone on the line!"

"Oh shit...my bad. You ain't gotta be so fuckin' mean, West—"

"SHHHH!!! I'm sorry, I'm here. Now how can I help you?"

Tish took a deep breath and sat down on the top of her bed as she held the card between her fingers and stared at it. She bit her lip softly as she felt a shiver rise up her spine. She was from the hood. She knew that snitches got stitches. But hell, apparently innocent bystanders got caught up in shit too, which was why she needed to go through with this call.

"Hi, I have some information on Trigga—um, I don't know his actual name. You questioned him at the hospital a few months back. He was there—"

"I remember. Mr. Maurice Bivens, aka Trigga," West said slowly with a smirk on his face. He shot a look at Burns, who was shoveling blue peanut M&Ms in his mouth; he separated them by colors and ate them all together, a habit he'd developed as a child.

At the mention of Trigga's name, Burns frowned and looked at West with a curious expression on his face. They were sitting outside of one of Lloyd's properties to see if they could pick up his where-abouts. His cousin had been brutally murdered, his wife was in the hospital, and their child was missing. They had reason to believe Lloyd had something to do with it, but they needed to locate him first and gather enough information to nail his ass once and for all.

"Yes...that's him. Trigga, I mean Maurice. I saw a murder on TV last night and Trigga—"

"You mean Mr. St. Michael's murder? You're saying Maurice Bivens had something to do with that?" West exclaimed as he clutched the phone in his hand. He was beyond excited, and he could feel Burns' eyes on him as he held on to the phone like it was his lifeline.

"Yes, he did—"

"How do you know?" West pressed her. He licked his lips as he waited for her to respond. When she didn't say anything right away, he asked her again, "How do you know?"

"I saw him—"

"YOU SAW HIM?!" West nearly shouted at the top of his lungs. He turned to his partner, who was dancing in his seat with his hands up; one of his fists were closed as he shook the blue M&Ms in his hand.

"Can you come into the precinct and tell us what you know? We need to get all of this down on paper to make it an official statement. I need your full name and number!"

Tish swallowed hard and closed her eyes as she tried to settle the feeling of unrest in her body. Something was telling her that she needed to hang up the phone and forget all about trying to protect Keisha. Keisha was a grown woman. What she needed to do was just pack up her own shit and move away so she wouldn't get hurt, and leave Keisha to make her own mistakes.

"Hello? Are you there?" the detective asked.

Tish pulled the phone away to hang it up, but when she tried to press the red button to end the call, she couldn't. It was a fault of hers that she was sometimes too protective of those she loved and considered friends. Being the oldest in a big family of over twenty cousins, it was just the way she was raised. She had no siblings, so she felt like she was the big sister and the protector of all her younger cousins. She'd made a life out of taking care of her loved ones. She couldn't just leave Keisha alone when she knew she was making a mistake. If anything happened *to her because she'd left her here with Trigga, she would never forgive herself.*

"Hi, I'm here," Tish said with more confidence. "Yes, I'll come down and make a statement."

Now Tish was standing in front of the glass next to the detective who had arrested Trigga, and he was staring at her with pleading eyes full of desperation. He wanted so badly for this to be his moment of victory, and the only thing standing between him and that moment was her. Now his hopes were dashed to shit, because she wasn't going to implicate Trigga in Kenyon's murder. She couldn't.

"I'm not afraid," she repeated. "He's just not the man who did it. He's the one who saw me dying and called for the ambulance to come get me."

"Yeah, but why did he leave you there to die if he's so chivalrous?" the detective asked, stepping back and crossing his arms in front of his chest. He had a skeptical gaze as his superior stared at him uneasily for a minute. He didn't like the way that it seemed like Burns was trying to push his witness.

"He probably left because he was trying to find the person who shot me. Lloyd Evans," Tish said matter-of-factly. "He also took with him my roommate, Keisha O'Neal. Tri—Maurice was trying to save her before you stopped him."

Burns' face dropped and he turned sharply to look at his captain, who was giving him a look that said 'you have officially fucked up again'. Burns knew then that his ass was grass. He'd arrested the wrong man. As they originally thought, Lloyd was the one behind everything and they would have to let Trigga go once again.

"Okay, Ms. Simon, I hear you." Burns pulled a card out of his jacket pocket and handed it over to her. "I want you to take my card in case you hear anything. Stay close. We may need you again once we bring in Mr. Evans. Do you know anything that can help us find out where he may be?"

With her eyes down, she thought about anything that could help him as she stared down at her pink manicured toes peeking out the front of her open-toe black boots. Finally, she sighed and shook her head.

"No, I don't. But if I hear anything, I promise that I'll call," she told Burns.

Burns held her stare for a minute without saying anything, and then exhaled and stepped to the side to allow her to walk by him. He followed behind her in silence down the hall until she exited out the door that led to where they were, in the restricted area. Running his hand through his hair, he cursed under his breath as he thought about his horrible luck.

This was beginning to be the most fucked up game of cat and mouse that he'd ever played; but obviously, it was because he was chasing the wrong mouse. Trigga wasn't squeaky clean, that he was sure of, but Trigga had a way of covering his ass so that Burns would probably never be able to catch him.

Burns was nearly to his cubicle when he felt like someone was watching him from down the hall. He lifted his head and came eye to eye with his captain, who had a firm, threatening and extremely serious look on his face. Burns knew right away that he was in for it.

"Listen here," he started as Burns watched him with a straight face. "I don't want to hear anything else about you arresting this fuckin' Maurice aka *Trigger* character anymore!"

"You mean Trigga—"

"Do you think I give a fuck?!" His captain's face turned apple red with anger, and his breathing grew heavier. Burns was unsure as to whether he should answer the question, or if it was rhetorical. When his captain didn't answer right away, he shifted his feet and opened his mouth to let out a sheepish reply.

"Um, no Captain McGuire, I don't think you give a fuck."

Captain McGuire gawked at him incredulously for a few minutes, which made Burns feel like it might have been a good idea not to answer his captain's question; then Captain McGuire lifted his hand and began poking Burns in the chest as he spoke, slightly pushing him backwards from the force.

"This entire investigation you've led concerning Trigger, Lloyd, and whoever else has been a complete fuckin' embarrassment to the entire precinct! I want you off the case for good! I don't care if you see Trigger murder someone with your own fuckin' eyes! You better walk the other damn way! I don't want to hear shit about you arresting this man ever again, or I will have your ass working in the fuckin' mailroom!"

With that, Captain McGuire stormed off behind Burns to his office. With a face redder than the scarlet letter and a disposition just as shameful as the woman who wore it, Burns trekked to his desk and sat down, completely aware that every ear in the area had heard what the captain had said, although his co-workers were trying their hardest to pretend to be busy.

Burns dropped his head in his hands and tried to erase the happenings of the morning out of his mind. There was no mistaking it. This was the worst day of his life.

CHAPTER ONE

A FEW WEEKS LATER...

A BABY CRIED IN ONE OF THE ADJOINING APARTMENTS AS Trigga trudged down the long, desolated hallway and up three flights of stairs. The rancid scent of piss combined with the funk of somebody taking a shit lingered in the air. He was in search of apartment 313, and ironically, the date happened to be Friday the 13th. Trigga hoped that would somehow be a good omen instead of bad.

The notorious Bankhead Projects were a deadly war zone riddled with guns, violence, drug, poverty, and enough homicides per year that a cemetery was constructed out of an abandoned junkyard two streets down to accommodate the sudden surge of murders in the area. Trigga had thrown caution to the wind when he made the bold decision to go on a 'seek and destroy' mission in search of Keisha.

The first place he started was with Lloyd's trap houses, after he had ambushed one of his foot soldiers that was part of some fake ass 'Ground Patrol' part of Lloyd's organization. Trigga pistol whipped him unmercifully, and the guy told him where several of Lloyd's trap houses were right before Trigga shot him in the head—execution style. He needed to send a clear message to Lloyd that he was not to be fucked with.

The idea of going into the projects to hunt down Lloyd's crew would have been brilliant had it not been for the daunting fact that nearly all trap houses were located in the heart of the hood—in the most dangerous high crime areas that not even police went into without armed back up. But Trigga was a hood nigga, so he took hood nigga chances.

Strapped with a .9mm and a Mossberg shotgun under his hoody jacket, in the wee hours of the morning just before dawn began, he was on a mission. He was determined to find Keisha, and fast!

With his head slightly bowed and eyes cast down, just enough to conceal his face, he bounced right by a few goons posted up in the archway building entrance, selling drugs. There was a bone-chilling cold in the air that morning. The temperature was in the single digits. A tempest wind whistled against his hoody as he walked. Someone called out to him; the sound seemed to echo in drones across the barren concrete walkway. Was it a drug dealer or a dope fiend trying to get his attention? It didn't matter; he just kept it moving as nonchalant as possible, with his hand on his nina and the shotgun in his pants. There was no doubt in his mind that if he was confronted, he was going to set both weapons blazing.

A HUGE COCKROACH scurried across the door on apartment #313 as he shifted the shotgun in his pants and prepared to knock. For some reason, he was filled with trepidation...like someone was watching him.

And there was.

He just happened to glance down the corridor and saw a skeleton face with hollow, pale cheeks ensconced with sunken eyes. It was a dope fiend; the same one he had spotted when he entered the complex. Trigga played off his suspicion as he mustered the heart to do what he came to do next.

Vaguely, he could hear a Drake song coming from the other side as he knocked softly on the door, then rubbed his hands together anxiously as if warming them from the cold. In reality, he was preparing himself for action. He stole another glance down the hall, and the figure was gone.

"Who da fuck is it?!" a deep baritone voice bellowed from the other side of the door.

For some reason, his heart somersaulted in his chest, and his hand absentmindedly eased towards the strip in his pants' pocket.

"It's Mook. Shady Grady sent me over," Trigga lied as he shifted his weight from one foot to the other. He paused when he thought he detected movement down the corridor.

He knew if the occupant on the other side opened the door, all hell was going to break loose. He also knew that earlier, right before he violently pistol-whipped Shady Grady and shot him, dumping his body in a nearby dumpster. He gritted his teeth and tried to ignore all distractions in his mind, which was swirling with thoughts about Keisha. Before Shady Grady met his end, he told Trigga that there were sometimes up to four or five people in this trap house, and the crew spent most of their time getting high and tricking with hood rat bitches.

But he'd also said there was a good chance Keisha would be in there if Lloyd had her.

"Fuck you want?" the voice asked, and Trigga heard the door push with a clink, like someone was pressing their body against it. Instantly, he was conscious of the peephole in the center of the door. He had not noticed it at first because of the dirt and graffiti smeared all over the door.

"I came to get some work, my nigga. I got a stack, na'mean?"

Trigga gestured with both hands as he squinted at the tiny peephole. The entire time, his heart beat like a bass drum. It was always part of the adrenaline rush he got when he was about to bust his gun, like fire bursting through his veins.

He stole another glance down the corridor and saw not one person, but three dope fiends this time, and they were all headed his way. Each one was disheveled and dirty-looking, and one of them walked with a severe limp. Trigga was reminded of the *Walking Dead* movie as he scrutinized the scene.

"Fuck!" he cursed under his breath.

He already knew what the business was. The first junkie must have left and got his buddies for reinforcement. This was the ecology of the ghetto. Trigga was perceived as a lone sheep and they were the predators, determined to make him their unwilling prey.

Or so they thought.

"Yo, my nigga, we ain't doing nuttin' and when you see dat nigga Shady Grady, tell dat nigga to answer his fuckin' phone!" the voice grumbled from the other side of the door.

Trigga's heart sank as his plan failed right before his eyes.

But he wasn't prepared to walk away. He needed to find Keisha, and he couldn't give up so easily after coming so far. Then suddenly, he heard what sounded like a woman's scream, or perhaps it was a dry cackle. Whatever it was, it came from the other side of the door. A timorous shiver ran up his spine while his fifth sense whirled like a silent alarm.

Keisha was in the apartment. He could feel it in his soul. His mind churned as he hesitated to walk away and glanced down the hallway. The junkies were fast upon him. One of them was tall, about 6'4 with a puckered face and a weathered, swarthy complexion. He wore a green, tattered army jacket and a scowl on his face that showed he meant to cause serious bodily harm. He was definitely the aggressor of the bunch. Trigga immediately decided that he would shoot him first, a headshot to the dome. The others didn't look too brave and after their buddy was shot, they would most likely take off running.

Just as Trigga was about to come up with his strip, he heard the rattle of the door's metallic security chain being pushed to the side, and the knob turning. Then the door opened and music blared from inside, along with a billow of smoke.

"Yo, what you say your name was again? You got some smoke?" a guy asked, with scruffy dreads askew and partially cascading down his shoulders.

He eyed Trigga and scratched at his armpit, puffing on a Black & Mild cigar wedged between his bulbous lips and all-gold grill. Trigga peeped the big .44 Desert Eagle tucked in his sagging pants and then fell right in line with his performance. It was time to get the party started.

"Nigga, is a pig pussy pork? Fuck you mean? Damn right, I got some smoke. I got some loud and some Afghan gas, my nigga! My name is Mook," Trigga said, going into his impromptu act.

Then he reached his hand into his baggy pocket like he was grabbing the weed, but it was the .9 mm. The dope fiends had stopped in their tracks at the exchange of words. Trigga had said the key words to pique their interest when he mentioned his supply. They were all ears as they waited for what was about to happen.

With a shrug, the guy opened the door wider, allowing a halo of smoke to form a ring around his face, which still held a stern grimace and tight frown.

"Come in, and dat shit better be some fuckin' gas. We don't smoke mid up in dis bitch," he said, his harsh expression falling just a bit as he moved to let Trigga in.

As soon as Trigga stepped into the cluttered apartment, full of tables and a few chairs scattered throughout, he moved with speed and timed agility just as dude turned to lock the door behind them. Trigga came up from the waist with his nine and struck him so hard with the pistol that his head hit the door and he keeled over backwards, landing on the floor with a loud thump. Trigga moved fast, turning him over to strip him of his gun. There was a trickle of blood, like a small stream coming from his head where the deep gash lay that Trigga made.

Up and moving with his heart racing, he began to enter into the living room and walked carefully with his ears trained on catching even the smallest sound. Suddenly, he heard the sound of a woman distressed. She was crying, sobbing profusely.

Keisha? his mind raced. He reached down and secured the Mossberg shotgun from his pants, placing it in one hand and holding the nine steady in the other.

"Ohhh, G--God your hurting me," the female wailed, then Trigga heard a loud slap.

"Ouch!" she cried out again.

It was dark and quiet except for a TV blaring, which cast a dim light in the room. Willowy shadows danced on the wall. Standing at the entrance, Trigga could make out the silhouette of three people immersed in one, like snakes slithering altogether, but he couldn't make out their faces. Then he heard a man's voice, coarse and brutal.

In another part of the house, the Drake song crooned loudly, "*You used to call me on my cell phone, late night when you need my love....*"

"Bitch shut up and take all this!"

There was another slap, and the female cried out in pain. Bodies shifted like flesh on flesh. Trigga couldn't see shit, causing his imagination to run wild. He tried to steady his anger at what he thought was going on, but it was proving to be one of the hardest things he'd had to do in his life. He grinded his teeth together as he listened to the man's voice demanding once again that the woman stop hollering and take every bit of him. The voice sounded familiar to Trigga, and it started to fuck with his mind.

Lloyd? Trigga thought to himself.

The voice belonged to Lloyd! It took everything in Trigga's power not to start blasting through the darkness, shooting everything that moved with both weapons wielded as he had originally planned. As he groped around, nearly blind as a bat, he occasionally bumped into something and struggled not to make a sound loud enough to alert his prey, as they continued their sexual assault on the defenseless female. When he got close enough, he peered in and was able to make out a couch and an entertainment center as he moved stealthily, palms sweaty with his finger on the trigger. He sidestepped around the couch, and the painful sobs got louder. The female was being punished.

Keisha! His thoughts merged in his mind at her voice.

Then it happened. His foot hit a glass of some type. The noise resonated with a loud cling, like glass striking glass.

"Damn Steve, you done knocked over the muhfuckin' Cîroc and broke the bottle," one of them said.

Then suddenly, the light came on in a flash and like a horror movie, the guy that Trigga had struck over the head with the pistol walked into the room behind him, staggering and wavering on wobbly legs like he was drunk, blood streaming down his face. His wavering presence alerted everyone in the room of Trigga's presence.

The woman screamed loudly, and one of the men raised a chrome-plated .38 that shined brightly even in the dim room.

But he was too slow.

K-Boom! K-Boom!

Trigga fired the Mossberg shotgun. The sonic boom sounded like a canon erupting in the living room. The impact from the weapon tore a hole in the man's chest the size of a softball as the impact from the bullets lifted his body across the room.

"Don't nobody fuckin' move," Trigga shouted as a latent cloud of gun smoke curled from the barrel of the shotgun. Frozen like store mannequins in a clothing store, three sets of petrified eyes stared back at him, and he couldn't believe what he was seeing.

Astounded, Trigga had to do a double-take, causing his jaw to drop as he stood dumbfounded.

"What da fuck?" he muttered as he tried to come to grips with what he was seeing. "I said, don't nobody move! And don't look at my fuckin' face!"

Keisha?

CHAPTER TWO

In the buck, ass up, face down with a huge dick nearly the size of a baseball bat in her ass and another shoved in her vagina, she was sandwiched between two men. She looked up at Trigga with a painful scowl. It wasn't until she wiped away a ringlet of hair partially covering her face that Trigga realized it wasn't who he thought it was. She looked almost identical to her in the smoked filled hue of the ambient light. His pulse raced, throbbing in his chest.

He thought he heard movement, somebody at the front door. There was a gun on the carpet about three feet away from them, just close enough to reach if its owner wanted to. Close enough to get shot if he was daring enough to die trying.

"Where da fuck is Lloyd?" Trigga barked, waving the guns threateningly. His mind must have been playing serious tricks on him. He could have sworn that he heard both Lloyd and Keisha inside the apartment.

"I...I...dunno, man. We ain't seen Black in a minute—"

The man took a quick timid glance up at Trigga's face, but he didn't say anything. The chick with a round, fat ass was awkwardly mounted atop him when Trigga struck him upside the head with the butt of the shotgun.

Whack!

"Didn't I tell you don't fuckin' look at my face?"

"I...I'm sorry," he stammered with a fresh lump on his forehead.

"FUCK DAT! Look up again and I'ma murk err'body n' dis bitch," Trigga growled as his eyes surveyed the place. He didn't want to get shot by some fool that just happened to stumble out the back room with an AK-47.

"I heard Lloyd in here," Trigga said again, looking around and taking in the apartment cautiously.

"Man, Lloyd ain't here," the fat guy said with his head bowed down, afraid to look up at Trigga. A trickle of blood ran from the golf ball-sized lump on his head. The chick was still on top of him, as still as a statue. They were all too afraid to move.

"Ouch! I'm catching a cramp in my leg! Can I get down?" the chick whined as she looked back at Trigga.

She had a caramel complexion with flawless skin, and a bodacious body with a full sleeve tattoo on her left arm, and a piercing on her right bottom lip and eyebrow. She had a big, round ass with wide hips and thighs. She was doing some type of acrobatic act of balancing herself, teetering with both dicks inside of her as she squatted on the balls of her feet. The sight of it intrigued Trigga for a second, but he shook it off and focused on his reason for being there.

"Move. But if you look at me again I'll slump yo' ass too, bitch," Trigga threatened softly to her. She careened over on her back as he walked over and kicked the gun laying on the floor out of reach, and closer to the door he'd entered through.

The guy that had been lying underneath her was skinny, with tattoos covering his entire body. He resembled the singer Trey Songz. His body was chiseled like an athlete or a guy that had spent years in prison working out. His hair was cut short with a high top dyed red, and he seemed to be in his early 20's. His face showed defiance balled up in an angry scowl of disdain. Occasionally, he would glance over at the gun lying out of reach on the floor near the door, but not at Trigga as he had been told.

"I'ma ask y'all niggas one last time, and you better answer because I ain't got all fuckin day! Where is Lloyd?" Trigga asked with an even tone, but his eyes gleamed like he was ready to wreak havoc. He was trying not to show his anxiety.

The big chubby nigga who he had struck upside the head seemed to have some type of speech impediment as he struggled to answer.

"I—I w-w-was trrrrrr...trnya ta t—tell you, we ain't s-s-s-seen Black!"

As he stuttered, his enormous penis began to shrivel up until it was lying fully flaccid across his thigh. He was shaking like drugstore jelly; so bad that his fat blubber, rotund potbelly heaved like a miniature earthquake as he struggled to breathe. He was panting and wheezing for air like he had a bad case of asthma, with fear etched across his face. But his fear was nothing in comparison to the female; she was utterly terrified as she cried hysterically.

On the coffee table next to them was a pile of money, stacks of about two hundred grand, an AK-47, and an Uzi. There was also about an ounce of Molly and a purple Styrofoam cup with deep purple liquid inside, better known in the hood as 'Lean'.

Trigga saw he had walked in and caught them sipping, trickin' with a bad bitch and getting high, just as Shady Grady had told him. Only thing he had been wrong about was Lloyd.

"Y'all gon' die today fa sho', but I can either make that shit fast or I can make it slow. Choice is yours."

"Nigga, dis EPD! East Point Gangsta for life! You outta bounds comin' up in here with dat Rambo shit, expecting a nigga to tell you sumptin'," the fake ass Trey Songz said with a brazen shrug, face scowled with seething contempt as he clutched his nuts. His brawny muscles flexed and his taut abs knotted up, showcasing his eight pack as he turned his head, as if to symbolize that the conversation was over.

Click!

Trigga rushed over and jammed the barrel of the Mossberg to his leg so hard the guy flinched in pain.

"Fuck nigga, say dat again? Rap slick and I'ma squeeze on yo' fuck ass!"

The girl panicked and started shaking violently as she cried, "Oh God! Oh God! Oh God! Pleeeeaaase don't kill me, don't kill me!"

Trigga noticed that her eyes were rolling around in her head. She was high as fuck, and the terror of what she was experiencing had her buggin' out like she was about to lose it.

The skinny guy, still defiant, tried to scoot back but his back was against the couch. He looked up and frowned, staring Trigga right in the face. By doing so, he had just signed his own death certificate. Closed casket.

"How in da fuck you think you gon' make it out of here. It's death before dishon—"

K-BOOM!

The impact from the shotgun blew a large chunk of his leg off, severing it in half, along with a hole in the floor the size of a basketball, causing dust and debris to rise to the ceiling like a small typhoon.

"Ohh, shit! Oohhh, shit!!!! Ooohh shit, you fucking shot me. You shot me!" the skinny guy cried in agonizing pain as he held on to what was left of the lower portion of his leg.

It was nothing more than a nub right beneath the knee, with the bone fully exposed. Blood was pouring from it like a blown faucet. The lower portion, the calf and foot landed on top of the girl's lap. She looked down at it on her naked thigh and completely lost it. She screamed frantically as her body spasmed, jerking animatedly as she ran in place while still sitting on the floor, her legs thrusting like she was the one who got shot. She knocked the body part off, causing blood to splatter her face and chest.

He aimed the gun at her. "Bitch, shut the fuck up!"

"I don't know where he is! I swear to God. Can I go?" the female babbled. By then, she was on the precipice of a mental breakdown.

The guy with the missing leg continued to moan in excruciating pain. Trigga felt a pang of empathy for him and focused his attention on the fat, chubby one. The clock in his head screamed a warning that it was past time for him to exit the premises and keep it moving.

Trigga aimed the Mossberg's barrel at the chubby guy's nuts.

"Talk or I'ma castrate your fat ass with dis here shotgun, nigga!"

"Y-you can probably find him at Pink Lips, the strip club! The last time I heard he was hittin' the stripper, Luxe. Or try his baby mama. He tried to kill her sh—sh—she didn't die so he lookin for her t —t—too."

Trigga nodded his head.

Damn, this nigga ruthless as fuck, he gon' murk his own baby mama.

Trigga finally felt he was getting some place.

"What about a caper about a year ago in New York? Lloyd and some of the crew touched some niggas for twenty bricks of cocaine, killed them and dumped their bodies in the river. I know one of you niggas had something to do with it."

The fat guy began to wiggle his head from side to side. He exclaimed, "NO!" causing his jaws to bounce.

"You talkin' 'bout Queen's brotha! I had n—n—nothin' ta do with dat. That was them!" he gestured, pointing to his partner scowled on the floor writhing in pain with the severed leg. The man began to moan louder into a crescendo, like a high-pitched wail.

"So you tellin' me this nigga had something to do with it?" Trigga asked with a raised brow.

The fat guy began to stutter so bad that Trigga couldn't understand what he was saying. He had to lean close and press the shotgun down hard on his nuts. He nodded his mammoth head up and down to signal 'yes' as his beady eyes looked accusingly at his buddy.

"He's lying!" the skinny dude managed to yell as he squirmed on the floor with blood gushing from his leg.

He would bleed to death if Trigga didn't kill him first.

"Who else was there?" Trigga yelled.

"Ke...Kenyon, Day-Day and him!" the fat one blurted out.

Trigga checked off two of the names in his head. Kenyon was dead, and so was Day-Day; he had personally killed them. Day-Day was the guy he had shot and ran over with the car the first night at the club when he encountered them in an ambush.

Trigga whirled onto the skinny guy and pressed the shotgun onto his one good leg and with a gloating grin; he spoke like Lucifer himself.

The skinny kid talked a mile a minute. His allegiance to Lloyd and his East Point Gangstas went out the window when he saw that he was about to lose his other leg. He admitted that he had indeed been a part of the crew that robbed and killed Queen's brother. He claimed that all he had done was pistol whip her brother and tie him up. He said that he wasn't the one that shot him in the head and tossed the body in the river.

"Nigga, dats it?" Trigga asked with a sinister sneer after the guy finished talking.

"Wait! And there was somebody else," he blathered.

"Hurry up so yo' mama can dress yo' punk ass up," Trigga muttered, growing increasingly annoyed.

"Man, you said you wasn't goin' kill—"

"No, I said if you didn't talk, yo' mama wasn't going to have to waste money on pants and a long casket. So if you want to leave here with the rest of ya limbs in place, you better talk!"

"Dior—Lloyd's wife..." the guy hesitated suddenly.

"Fuck nigga, talk! I ain't got all day!" Trigga shouted as he looked around at the bloodshed and carnage. His ears jumped when he thought he heard something at the front door.

"...Dior.... she helped plan the lick. She was the mastermind. She was playing both Kenyon and Lloyd."

Trigga's mind went blank. It took him a moment to recover, for his mind to digest what he'd just heard.

Dior masterminded it all? he thought to himself.

Then in the distance, he heard it. It was the shrill of police cars approaching. He glanced over at the window. A beacon of dawn's early light was starting to peek over the horizon, igniting a pale blue morning sky.

It was time for him to go!

He placed the nine in his pocket to free his left hand and scooped up the money off the coffee table. There was a duffle bag on the floor. Grabbing it, he placed the guns that were on the table inside, along with the money. The female with chatoyant, tearful eyes continued to cry pensively as she watched him with apprehension and dread. He would have to kill her too. It was unfortunate, but she'd seen his face so there was nothing he could do.

Trigga rose with the quickness. He was suddenly moving fast, purposefully, like a man on a mission. He needed to get out of there.

"I got some bad news," he said to no one in particular.

"What?" they all said in chorus.

"I gotta put y'all to sleep. This is for Queen, to avenge her brother's death," he said with the cadence of a ghetto priest doing a eulogy. Leveling the shotgun, he aimed just as both men began to squirm and plead for their lives.

K-Boom! K-Boom!

He shot both men. Blood and brain matter splattered the walls and upholstery. The chick screamed like reality had claimed the last iota of her drug induced sanity. For some reason, Trigga didn't have the heart to shoot her.

Then just as he aimed his weapon, he looked up when he heard a noise. The dope fiends that he had encountered were in the apartment. They were blocking the doorway like they weren't afraid to get shot, but this time it was too many of them. Trigga took notice when one of them picked up the gun off the floor.

Just then, he heard the screeching of cars coming to an abrupt stop. What looked like neon lights blue and white strobed the window in a kaleidoscope of colors, as the sirens blurred.

"Man whatcha doin' in here?" the one with the army fatigue jacket on said in a deep throaty voice. His eyes were deep in the sockets of his head, and too close together. He looked like a lunatic set loose from an asylum.

With no choice, Trigga gave them his full attention. The chick seized the opportunity and hopped up from the floor, then darted across the room. Trigga flinched like he wanted to shoot her. He watched as she stood by the window with her eyes on him.

Boldly, one of the junkies rushed over and picked up the ounce of Molly that was on the table. Two others began to ravage through the pockets of the dead man Trigga had first hit when he entered.

"Fuck," he muttered under his breath as he watched the scene. The police were outside, and he was cornered.

CHAPTER THREE

"Man, give us a hit or something to get high off," the junkie wearing the army jacket said as he eased closer. His greedy eyes held Trigga's with something Trigga was all too familiar with: desperation. The kind of desperation that could make a man do a foolish thing like rush a dude that was strapped with not one, but two bangers.

Suddenly, Trigga had an idea. He reached into the duffle bag and began to toss money in the air like it was graffiti. The junkies all went into a frenzy like a pack of hyenas on a kill as they dove at the money.

In one quick leap, Trigga jumped over the couch only a few feet from the panic-stricken girl. He startled her and she began to flip out, thinking that she was next up to meet her maker.

With three quick steps, she ran and jumped out the window head first into a full swan dive, causing glass and metal to shatter. She screamed a bloodcurdling howl all the way down three stories, which ended with a calamitous thump of flesh hitting concrete, serenaded by the sound of sirens and the clamor of startled voices that had witnessed it.

Trigga tucked the shotgun and the nine back in his pants and slung the duffle bag over his shoulder as he moved quickly to exit the apartment. He bumped into several junkies moving at a brisk pace.

To his dismay, out on the corridor there was nothing but chaos as people gawked with their doors open. Others rushed around, being nosy while trying to steal glances inside apartment #313.

He saw the stairway up ahead and sprinted to it. As soon as he made it to the stairs, his phone chimed. He started not to answer it as he proceeded down the stairs. His breath fogged in the air around him. There was a frigid chill in the air, along with the smell of piss and stale garbage.

He stepped over beer cans and discarded trash, but his phone continued to go off. For some unknown reason, his mind beckoned him to answer it. He looked back up the stairs and adjusted the duffle bag on his shoulder. His pulse raced; in the distance, he could hear the police sirens.

The caller ID read, 'Keisha'.

"Keisha?" his voice echoed as he answered the phone. He slowed as he repeated her name, causing his chest to tighten with anxiety. His breathing became jagged as perspiration glistened off his forehead in the cold. He spoke into the phone.

"Keisha! God, man, where are you? Are you okay? I'ma come get you, baby. Where dat pussy ass nigga Lloyd at? He better not have laid a hand on you!"

"Trigga...I love you...I love you...."

Trigga stopped in the middle of the pissy stairwell and tried to make out what she was saying. Then his heart clenched in his chest when Keisha began to talk strange, like she was high or something, just before the phone went dead. The last thing he'd thought he heard was some type of popping sound.

"Fuck!" he scoffed, banging his fist on the concrete wall. His voice echoed like he was standing in a tunnel. He took off down the stairs faster this time, with purpose.

Trigga walked out the side entrance of the building and there was a sea of police cars, ambulances, and fire trucks congested everywhere.

Coming straight for him was a platoon of police.

"Hey, you!" a cop called out.

Trigga slowed his pace. He suddenly had the urge to toss the duffle bag with the guns and money in it, but it was too late. Instead, his hand reached for the banger in his waistband. It had all come down to this, an infinite moment in a fragile time.

He was about to have trial on the streets, rather than wait for a judge and jury to decide his fate.

Things were about to get worse.

Much worse.

CHAPTER FOUR

MAJESTIC PALM TREES SWAYED IN THE BACKDROP OF CERULEAN BLUE skies as a balmy sun shined bright. The pacific oceans ebbed and tide rushed ashore, tickling Keisha's pedicured pink toes as she laid on the white sands, giggling girlishly. She was in bliss as Trigga messaged her clitoris with nimble fingers as a blunt simmered, dangling from his perfectly pursed lips.

This is my heaven on Earth, she thought as she looked down at Trigga's bulging manhood print. His erection was long, hard, elongated all the way across his thigh. For some reason she was giddy, high off being next to him and his sexy, brazen body. She managed to conceal the erogenous moan that threatened to erupt from somewhere in the back of her throat as he stroked her faster, stirring her passion with his fingers.

"I love you Keisha," Trigga cooed with the most serious face. She caressed his angular jaw with a delicate hand, and felt her juices about to cream all over his fingers.

"I love you...too. Oomph...that feels good," she purred in a sultry voice as she nibbled at the corner of her bottom lip.

Keisha was semi-nude, wearing only a one-piece thong bikini

bathing suit, and topless in the hot tropical sun, causing a sheen of succulent perspiration to sparkle on her ample breasts like sweet honeydew. They were all alone, isolated on some beautiful exotic island with a name hard to pronounce, in a distant part of the world far away.

"I want to make love to you right here," Trigga whispered in a husky voice, lisping with his sexual need that turned her on.

Instantly, she could feel herself getting more wet, about to erupt like a dam. She reached out and caressed the tip of the mushroom head of his manhood through his shorts, and he rewarded her with a subtle sigh that segued into a lustful groan.

Again, he repeated, "I wanna make love to you, put all these twelve inches inside of you."

"And what if I let you...how would you do it?" she teased in a sensuous, breathy tone that made them both blush with sex faces.

"I'd eat your pussy like a gourmet meal; ass first, for an appetizer. Lap up the cum like it was sweet honey, then lay the wood like you were the last woman on Earth and I loved you with every fiber, every sinew of my masculine being," he said like a melodic poem, then eased two fingers deeper inside her vagina, causing her to squirm and momentarily pinch her eyes closed then open.

"Humph....shit...." She squirmed and thrust her pelvis at him as she felt her pussy lips jerk uncontrollably and her legs spread wider, involuntarily like they had a mind of their own. His fingers began to delve deeper, making that loud, wet gushy sound. She threw her head back in the white sand, savoring the moment as an ardent sun bathed both of them in its sumptuous glow.

Then with tacit consent, she nodded her head, "Yessss!" It was her confession to lovemaking.

She was his for the taking.

Without being told, he eased her bikini down across her curvaceous thighs, to her ankles as she lifted her hips and legs to oblige him. He bowed his head and began to lick at her erect nipples. His tongue trailed saliva down her body, then he nibbled on the pink morsel of her love...

Suddenly, like an eclipse of the majestic sun, the sky grew ominously gray. A cold chill dominated the air. The tempestuous wind began to blow sand and water, then out of nowhere, the sky erupted with a belt of lightening, ricocheting and striking the sand right next to them.

Then one after the other, lightning struck. More ocean water washed to shore; they were engulfed in rain and water, as if the once gentle ocean had turned brutal and was determined to engulf them, to swallow them whole. She was being pulled out with the tide as Trigga called her name frantically. He held her hand for dear life, then his grip slipped and she was going under.

She couldn't swim. She was drowning....

Then she awoke.

Again, Keisha had been dreaming. It was her only escape from the grim, dreary reality of her cruel confinement. For weeks perhaps, she had been confined to a five-by-five wooden shipping crate. It was about the size of a dog house, not big enough for her to even stretch her legs. The space was so cramped she could hardly turn from one butt cheek to the other when she slept in pitch black darkness. There was a plastic bucket for her to release her bodily functions in. The stench of her unwashed body was unbearable. No human being was supposed to be treated like this.

A piece of PVC pipe was hooked up to the crate; it served as a ventilation device so she would have fresh air to breathe, barely.

Someone had called her name. She awoke in the stifling heat, and found herself once again feeling like she was suffocating with her body scarred, battered, black and blue from the beatings. She was emaciated and frail from starvation. Hunger was her constant companion, but that wasn't the worst part. She had an addiction so strong it was as if forty demons from the pit of hell had consumed her body. Her withdrawals were so severe that if she didn't get the drugs, she could die.

Why wouldn't he just kill me? Why would he torture me like this? Why?

Her mind screamed in the darkness. She was a shallow husk of her former self, and losing her sanity fast.

She welcomed death if that would be her only way to escape the pain, her only refuge from the anguish of his wanton brutality, along with the constant gnawing pang of hunger that consumed her gut in the tight, small cramped space. Not to mention, the addiction that was worse than anything she could imagine. He kept her medicated, sedated in a way that she had become a slave to the euphoric high of opium, better known as heroin.

Her hands were bound but shaking, tied tight in front of her. Some type of cloth bag was placed over her head. There wasn't even a blanket or pillow for comfort. The only thing she had was a worn, tattered carpet that smelled like mildew and pure funk. She was completely nude.

"Yes," she responded meekly in the darkness; the quaver in her voice gave way to just how panic stricken she was.

The door to the crate was opened. She could make out the sound of feet shuffling along the old wooden floor. The stench of her own body appalled even her as suddenly fresh air filled the interior of the crate and she inhaled as a sliver of light illuminating under the hood she was wearing.

"Ohhhhh, weeeee, goddamn bitch you stink!" Lloyd said.

A female giggled in the background. He snatched the bag off her head, the light coming from a window somewhere hurting her eyes. Keisha frowned and placed a hand over her face to shield the light.

"Please, let me go. Please let me go," Keisha cried.

"Bitch, you know you want this, don't you?" Lloyd challenged as he held the hypodermic needle up in the air, the tips of the syringe gleaming as a trickle of the potent fluids inside rose and shimmered down the needle.

"Don't you bitch? You want it!"

"I wanna go home! I wanna leave here...pleaaaase," Keisha cried.

Her lips were severely cracked and ashen; her skin was pasty with dirt caked in the creases. Her face was gaunt with hollow eyes and sunken cheeks. She had deep, dark circles underneath her eyes. She was so skinny you could count each of her ribs.

Luxe giggled some more and took a step forward. She crossed her arms over her breasts and with a haughty grin, she watched as Lloyd untied her hands then wrapped a belt around her arm and inserted the needle, injecting the heroin in her vein. Satiated, Keisha's eyes rolled back in her head as her body went limp, and she expelled what sounded like a guttural, deep throaty sound.

"You ain't give her too much, did you Black?" Luxe asked with an arched brow creased with concern.

"I dunno, maybe," Lloyd responded with a hint of concern, and watched Keisha's face start turning blue.

"Looks like she stopped breathing too," Luxe said with a grim expression as she walked over, looking down. She held her nose from the rancid stench of the body as she checked Keisha's wrist for a pulse. She then looked at Lloyd with a grim expression.

"This bitch better not die." He hauled off and slapped the shit out of Keisha, leaving his handprint across her face. She barely responded as he struck her again and again.

"Oh, fuck!"

Lloyd rushed over to the other side of the basement and picked up the large bucket of water he had been planning to let Keisha bathe with. He doused the water on her face.

It worked.

Keisha responded. Inaudibly, she blurted out some words, spat out water, and ran her hands through her nappy, coarse hair.

"Dayum...I'm high ass fuuuuuuuuck," Keisha muttered, monotone, with a slur as her head began to bob. A sliver of slob dangled from her mouth as she scratched her private area, then her neck. Her fingers lingered and stalled as she nodded again.

Wham!

Lloyd slapped her again.

"Don't hit me no muhfuckin' mo'," she slurred as her head rolled around on her frail, skinny shoulders.

With anorexic fingers similar to talons, she made a feeble attempt to hit Lloyd. For some reason the dope always emboldened her, and secretly Luxe got a kick out of her bold antics. Junkies were fun to watch.

"Bitch, that pussy ass nigga of yours is runnin' round here robbing my trap houses, killing my niggas! He costing me hundreds, but I have a trick for his ass. I want to you to do me a favor. Do you wanna go home? Do you wanna leave here?" Lloyd asked with a mischievous smirk on his face.

"Yes...Yes...I'm hungry. I'm so hungry. I need a bath...I wanna go home...please..." she cried plaintively as her head rolled around on her shoulders.

"Just do what I say. I see you got that fuck nigga's phone number in your phone. I want you to call Trigga. Tell him you're okay—"

"But I am not...okay! I'm hungry...I'm tired. W—why you doin' this to meeeee?"

She erupted in tears again, and began to rock back and forth in the crate to a drug-induced rhythm in her head.

For the first time, Luxe looked at Keisha with sympathy; even though she at one time despised the girl, she saw something in her she had not seen before.

"Bitch, I'm tryna help you! All you have to do is call the nigga Trigga, tell him to come get you. Tell him I'll text him the address where."

"You gon' kill him! You want me to set him up...noooooo, don't make me do that. I can't do that—"

"Bitch, you gon' die right here in dis muhfuckin' crate. In this fuckin' basement. Is dat what the fuck you want? Or you want a bath, some food to eat, some clothes, and the heroin you can get high off of, and to walk yo' ass out dat door?"

"Ye—yes..."

She sniffled and tears fell melancholically down her cheeks as suddenly, the thought of food infused her mind and yes, she was high and the drugs could only mask the hunger cramps in her aching stomach for so long.

"Call him then, bitch. Tell him you're okay. Tell him you're going to text him an address to meet you at to pick you up in Bankhead."

He dialed a number and thrusted a phone in her face. The speaker phone was turned high. She hesitated and her pulse quickened as she waited for Trigga's voice to erupt on the line. The entire time Luxe, with abated attention, watched the volley of words between the two of them like it was a deadly confrontation.

If Trigga took the bait, he would literary be walking in front of a firing squad of over twenty of Lloyd's most trusted goons. The Ground Patrol would be waiting with deadly assault weapons to plow him down before he even knew what was about to happen.

Fuck ass punk bitch! You steal a nigga's muthafuckin' dope and money, then betray me by fuckin' one of my worst enemies, and now da' nigga terrorizing my fuckin' business. I'ma kill this fuck nigga. Then I'ma go and make sure I get rid of Dior and that ugly ass baby this time for sure, Lloyd thought, seething mad.

Nothing had been going right. Recently, he had learned after all he had done to murk Dior and the baby, they still managed to live. Well, he was going to see about that. The only bright spot was his rat ass cousin Kenyon had mysteriously gotten murked, and not even he knew how that happened. But for now, he was focusing his attention on Trigga and Keisha.

With his jaw clinched tight, he waited as Keisha cradled the phone in her trembling hand.

Trigga's phone continued to ring, then he finally answered it.

"Keisha! God, man, where are you? Are you okay? I'ma come get you, baby. Where dat pussy ass nigga Lloyd at? He better not have laid a hand on you!"

Lloyd's body went rigid, stiff at the threating tone of Trigga's raspy voice, and instantly his hand went for his strap as if Trigga was standing right there.

Trigga was talking a mile a minute, speaking with heightened urgency. He sounded winded. Keisha could make out the echoing sounds of footfalls in the distance, like he was walking fast down a stairwell. She could also hear police sirens in the distance.

Her heart sank.

Trigga was in trouble. She could sense it...feel it. The feeling was palpable, like a second layer of skin.

"Trigga...." Keisha spoke in a hoarse voice with dry cracked lips, as she swallowed the lump in her throat. Her face was etched with desperation and dread. She looked up and saw Lloyd smiling with a feral grin. He nodded for her to continue as he gestured with his hands. He needed for her to walk him into the ambush.

"I love you...I'm okay. I love you...I love you...." she said breathily in a singsong voice as she began to sob pensively out of control.

"I love you too bae. Everything is going to be alright. Just tell me where you at...please?" he asked with his heart on his sleeve.

As she cradled the phone in her hands shaking, she glanced up at Lloyd. With a frown, he gestured for her to talk. He wanted her to tell Trigga she was okay.

Keisha press her lips tight across her face as they trembled. A thin line of mucus ran from her nose, and she looked again at Lloyd.

"Where you at? I'ma come get you. Is everything okay, baby? Are you safe? Baby, don't cry please," he said continuing; his words were coming fast and pain-stricken. It broke his heart to hear her crying.

Keisha looked up at Lloyd with a repugnant stare.

"Bitch talk!" Lloyd mouthed silently, egging her on with a stern expression.

"Tell me the address, Keesh. Tell me where you are. I'll come get you now. I promise, Keisha, I can feel something is not right, something is wrong. Please," Trigga said like he was moving down a flight of stairs, the gallows to his own hell.

She couldn't do it. She couldn't lead Trigga to what she knew would be his demise, no matter what that meant for her.

Keisha tore her eyes away from Lloyd and closed them tight as a single tear cascaded down her ebony cheek, and dangled on her chin as she purposely escaped to her safe place. She began to smile as her hand trembled with the phone in it.

"Okay, this is where I'm at..." She smiled some more with her eyes closed as the vision erupted behind her closed lids. Lloyd and Luxe exchanged wary glances as another tear slid down her cheek.

"It's a beach with white sand, a glorious sun, and I am free. And you're handsome and your beautiful face is close to mine...you're holding my hand about to make love to me. And it's the happiest day of my life." Her voice shivered and cracked in a singsong overtone as she smiled, while the maudlin tears soaked her face.

Lloyd glanced over at Luxe as if to say 'do you belief this shit' but Luxe had tears in her eyes as she looked at Keisha with a sad expression on her face.

Lloyd instantly became furious.

"Whaaaaat da' fuck!!" he exclaimed, exacerbated, and reached back into the back of his pants to remove his nine.

"I will make love to you, Keisha. Baby, I'll hold your little hand on the white sands, but first you have to tell me where you are at? PLEASE!" There is a poignant plea in his voice as it echoes like he is in running in a tunnel.

Click!

Lloyd cocked the gun to her head, right above her eye socket, causing Keisha to flinch and close her eyes tightly. He was about to kill her. Luxe squirmed and looked like she was watching a horror film where she was a captive participant.

"Bitch, you better tell 'em what I told you to say or I'ma put one in your fuckin' brain," Lloyd whispered. His caustic voice was like sandpaper raking across a chalkboard.

With her eyes still pinched tightly, she was smiling as more tears spilled down her cheek. Keisha had a deep, dark secret place to retreat to in the abyss of the darkness of her reality that had become her sheltered home. She didn't mind dying; in fact, she welcomed it. Dying would take the pain away, the hunger cramps that made her stomach churn from starvation, the craving for a drug that had become her master and made her the slave.

She welcomed death. The dying part was easy; she was already dead in her mind. She'd rather be dead.

"Bitch, talk!" Lloyd repeated more coarsely.

Her lips trembled with no words coming out as Lloyd held the gun pressed hard against the bridge of her eye. His face was a mask of an angry scowl as he waited for her to say anything wrong. Luxe watched petrified, with her mouth forming an incredulous 'o'.

"Trigga...baby, if you come..." she hesitated, swiped her moist tongue across her chapped, cracked lips and exhaled her courage while inhaling her waning fear. Her words were languid but lethal to her listeners, however, potent to hers. This was her freedom.

"If you come...if you come...Lloyd is going to kill you—"

Wham!

BLOCKA!

A shot is fired.

Keisha's body keeled over.

The phone is disconnected.

Luxe screams!

CHAPTER FIVE

"Don't you fucking move!"

Trigga looked up from his hoody as he held the cell phone tightly in his hand, with grief and pain all over his face. The cops were headed straight for him, trotting with bulletproof gear, helmets with plastic eye shields, helmet protectors, and batons ready to bludgeon him with. Just when he was about to come up blasting, ready to have court on the street and go out with a banger blazing, he noticed in the frenzy of his panic-filled brain that these were riot police. They were there to hurt and harass, to make him guilty until proven innocent.

A vagabond woman next to him was shoved to the ground as several people ran; a bottled was hurled at the cops, and obscenities were yelled as people watched them manhandle the defenseless woman.

Trigga was violently pushed against the wall and punched in his stomach. A baton came down hard across his shoulder blade, causing him to yell out in pain.

Black people impoverished in the projects had no rights.

Then, like a small tornado, the cops moved in practiced sequence, marching past him in militant style, on to wreak more havoc onto the people they were paid to serve and protect.

The sun was an orange haze as it peeked over the mauve-colored horizon. Even though it was early, the streets were teeming with people, dope fiends, hustlers, and slovenly dressed prostitutes headed home to escape the sun like vampires.

Trigga staggered past clutches of people and saw the girl who jumped out the window. A white sheet covered her chalk-outlined body as police surrounded her, some of them talking and laughing with each other over her dead body, as if they were at a festive barbecue.

Trigga moved through a gate with a hole cut in it for easy access, and passed across a yard. A muggy, spotted dog barked as he bent a corner and found his car at the Shell gas station across the street. Once inside, he checked his phone. His breathing was jagged, filled with desperation. He couldn't dial Keisha's number fast enough. She was in trouble, serious trouble, and the reason he knew was because his gut feeling told him so.

No answer.

He replayed the conversation in his head.

"Fuck!" he banged his fist on the steering wheel and happened to look up. The Arab-looking man inside the gas station was peering through the window, watching him as police cars streamed by.

He tossed the duffle bag in the backseat as his mind ruminated over what had happened. At least he had a plan. He needed to go back to the club he had first met Keisha at, but first he did something that may have been done more out of habit than rationale. He dialed Keisha's phone and his mind took a trek down memory lane as he drove off, turning in the opposite direction of the streaming police cars.

He remembered the time he was posted up outside her apartment in his car. He was supposed to be her security, but he had dozed off and fell asleep, then she came and banged on his car window and surprised him with breakfast. A smile tugged at his lips.

"Please answer your phone, baby...please..." he silently prayed.

To his dismay, the phone went straight to voicemail.

His heart sank.

He turned on the I-285 expressway with his mind still percolating, evaluating what he was going to do next. It didn't take long to figure that out when his phone chimed. He reached for it off the passenger seat and was shocked at the caller ID name.

"Nigga, what you want?" Trigga growled into the phone

"Man, I'm in a little bit of trouble." The call belonged to Mase, Trigga's twin brother.

You can say that again, Trigga thought to himself. *Because the next time I see you, I'm going to kill you like you tried to do me.*

"What kind of trouble?"

"This man and those people got a gun on me, talkin' 'bout I walked out without payin'. I swear to God on Mama, on err'thang I love, I forgot the money and left it at the homeless shelt—I mean, hotel I'm staying in."

Just then there was a commotion, like a struggle, the ruffling of clothes, a body being slammed. Mase cried out in pain. Someone else got on the phone; they sounded winded.

"Listen man, if this yo' damn brother, he comes up in here in our family restaurant, Ms. Mays, and ordered all this damn food. He got collard greens, fried chicken, candied yams, macaroni and cheese, peach cobbler, fried shrimps, then tried to sneak out the door without payin'."

"I told'cha I was going to pay for it!" Mase hollered. It sounded like he was in some kind of chokehold; there was a scuffle.

"Then why did you run?" an elderly woman's voice shouted from the background.

"I was running to go get the money!"

WHAM!

Mase cried out in pain.

The person on the phone continued. "Mister whatever yo' name is, me and my four brothers help our elderly mama run this business, and we all good Christians. But like the Bible says, mama taught us to never spare the rod."

"Spare the rod?" Trigga repeated, baffled.

"Yep, we finn'ta beat his ass black and blue with this here rod, unless you gon' come up with the thirty-seven dollars and forty-two cents to pay for his meal. Mama don't believe in calling the police. The Bible speaks against that too, 'Thou shalt not snitch-ith'!"

With that said, Trigga had to scratch his head, befuddled as to what to do.

"Tie 'em to the back of the dishwasher and beat his ass good with the water hose. Teach 'em bout coming into Ms. Mays' restaurant thinking he gon' get a free meal. Son, God help you but you 'bout to get a free ass whippin'," she said like she was about to get a kick out of watching her sons beat Mase.

"Trigga, help me! Come on, man," Mase screamed. There was more tussling in the background.

"Okay, I'll be there with the money," Trigga said, and mopped at his face with a weary hand.

He was weary with fatigue and growing more tied. He hadn't slept in days. He had run up in three of trap houses, and finally he was getting somewhere. He needed to go back to Pink Lips, but first he needed to deal with his brother's betrayal. It would be an easy task and take no time at all, to lullaby his punk ass to sleep and get back to the business of finding Keisha. That was, if she was still alive.

"Thanks, man! Thanks, man. I got'cha, my nigga," Mase said in a high-pitched tone of gratitude. He was thinking that it was over because his underdeveloped mind hadn't yet put two and two together to figure out that Trigga knew of his disloyalty; but the harsh reality was it was just beginning. What Trigga had in store for Mase, he would need a body bag and a casket when he was finished.

Trigga was about to murder his own flesh and blood, his once beloved brother, and oddly he felt no remorse. All he had to do was think about Keisha, or the innocent homeless couple that had been murdered in cold blood. One thing did trouble him though—why?

Perhaps Mase would take that secret to his grave with him. Perhaps Trigga would have the nerve to ask him before he sent him to meet his maker.

"I'll be there in a few minutes," Trigga said reluctantly. They gave him the address. The restaurant was located in Stone Mountain on Memorial Drive, near the hub of the city's ghetto.

MS. MAYS' restaurant was located right on a corner. The streets were teeming with pedestrians, the homeless, children frolicking in store parking lots, and general innocently people commuting from work or school, some traversing by foot, others on cars and buses. Trigga was instantly reminded of his city, the Big Apple, New York. Just as he tucked his nine in his pants and hopped out his whip in the parking area, he peeped several hooligans stationed out front of the restaurant. Of course, they were clocking him, watching his every move.

"Yo my nigga, I got some loud," one dude said. He sported a long goatee beard with a round, shiny bald head.

"You fuck with that molly, my nigga?" another dude said, and flashed what looked like an ounce plastic bag of colorful Skittles candy.

"I'm good, yo," Trigga said, and swung the door to the restaurant open.

THE PLACE WAS PACKED and instantly, the delicious aroma of frying foods and baked cakes were mouthwatering. It was ambrosia to his starving stomach.

"Heyyyy, handsome, with your fine ass," a table full of hood rats caroled.

They looked like off-duty prostitutes to him. He nodded and

mobbed right up to the counter, where food was on display. There were two females that were taking orders from customers. Trigga was tempted to order something as he waited, until a guy with a durag on his head walked from in the back of the restaurant. He wore an apron with a wife beater t-shirt underneath. He couldn't have been much older than Trigga.

"May I help you?" the guy behind the counter asked.

"Yeah, I'm here to get my brother."

"You talking about dat shark mouth ass nigga that tried to eat and leave without payin'?" the guy said with humor. The two girls behind the counter with him laughed and turned looking at Trigga.

Trigga nodded his head 'yes'. For some reason, the guy was talking loud and the hood rats at the table behind him began to giggle. Before the guy could continue, Trigga reached into his pocket and peeled off a hundred-dollar bill, and tossed it on the counter. He just wanted to get his brother and bounce.

"That's yours. Sorry for the inconvenience."

The guy's eyebrows raised as he reached for the money on the counter.

"Thanks," he smiled coyly. "Follow me in the back."

The back of the kitchen looked nothing like the front. It was hot and damp, with a malodourous smell of bleach and stale, rotting garbage. The floors were cluttered with large pots and kitchen utensils. A radio blared gospel music from somewhere.

As they walked on the slippery, wet floor, Trigga could barely keep his balance. Up ahead, he saw people huddled around a dishwasher and a little old lady seated in a chair. She had on a white chef's hat and some type of matching cooking apron that looked more like a smock, with her restaurant's name spelled across it in bold letters.

"Ma, this the dude that's gon' pay for the meal. This his brother. He gave me this right here." He passed the old lady the hundred-dollar bill. She looked up and beamed at Trigga broadly.

"Child, bless yo-heart, we was just finna kill'em," she said with gaiety, and laughed heartily. So did her sons and some other people in the kitchen.

Mase stepped away from the dishwasher. His sleeves were rolled up. At the time, the old lady had him washing pots.

"Trigga, man, I thought you wasn't gonna come," he said with a snaggletooth grin. He was sporting a black and purple shiner, like somebody punched him in the face with a baseball bat.

"Let's go!" That was all Trigga said with steel in his voice.

Mase had lost a considerable amount of weight since he had seen his twin brother last. It would be easier to dispose of his body.

TRIGGA RODE in silence as Mase rambled on, talking like nothing had happened. For some reason, he was ecstatic to see his brother again. It wasn't until Mase blurted out something that caught Trigga's attention, as he reached into the ashtray and retrieved a partially burnt blunt then reared back in the seat and fired it up, that Trigga finally responded.

"Man, I thought I would never see you again," Mase was talking melancholically.

"Why did you feel like that?" Trigga asked with his eyes full of something his brother should have been able to read: his simmering, murderous rage.

Unbeknownst to Mase, Trigga was driving him to what would be his final resting place, a makeshift gravesite, an abandoned building he remembered from back when he had Keisha in the car, and she had been shot and presumed dead. There was a location where he was going to dump her body; it was also the same location where he met the homeless couple that Mase had murdered.

"I... I...I just felt like we have been through so much shit. When you came up missing, I figured I wouldn't see you again," Mase said, and puffed on the blunt.

Trigga turned off the main road into the dilapidated part of town, and eased his banger out his pants without Mase noticing him.

"I never came up missing, it was you. The last time I saw you was when we agreed to meet up. What happened? You never showed up," Trigga responded as he drove to the abandoned building that was just up the block.

"Oh, uh...s'umthin' came up," Mase said nonchalantly, and took another deep pull off the blunt as if savoring the taste of good weed.

Dis gotta be Queen's weed, he thought to himself.

Trigga placed the nine on his lap in full view with his finger on the trigger, his mind ruminating, concentrating on what he was destined to do next—murder his own brother. The entire time, he kept his eyes straight ahead as he stopped in front of the abandoned building.

Mase licked on the blunt paper that was starting to unwind. He mended it back with his saliva and forefinger, then suddenly asked, "Whatchu stop here for?" Mase leaned forward as smoke curled from his lips and nose.

"Remember when we was shawties, I fought for you and made sure you was straight, no matter what?" Trigga asked as if in a trance. Before Mase could answer, he continued. "Then when we got older, shit got harder. The first person I shot was that Crip dude for beating you and taking them Air Nikes I gave you for your birthday, remember?"

Mase nodded his head. "Then I killed my first man over Mama and her drug habit. I took the dude's dope, gave some of it to you, and we stayed in the trap hustling. Remember that?"

Mase nodded his head again as he looked at Trigga perplexed.

"I would have given my life for you and Mama...my only family... everything I loved."

"I know man, and you did all that shit while you was in school getting good ass grades in shit. We was living in the projects and you was handling it all." Mase puffed on the blunt, eyes glassy with nostalgia.

Trigga then cocked the banger, placing one in the chamber,

causing Mase to jump in his seat from the formidable sound he knew all too well. He looked at his brother with the gun aimed at his rib cage.

"Man, stop...stop playin'," Mase said.

"You went into my hotel room and shot them people...innocent people, thinking it was me and Keisha. Why?"

"No, man. No, I would never do that to you. You my fuckin' brother," Mase said, dropping ashes on his leg and the floor of the car as he raised his trembling hands.

"Nigga, put yo' muthafuckin' hands down."

Mase obliged. "You taking this too far. You don't even know what happened."

"You tried to kill me. Tried to kill your own fuckin' brother, that's what happened. I don't know why, but you're rotten to the core and you know what? I've always had my suspicions that your rotten ass had s'umthin' to do with Mama's death too, nigga," Trigga said with an icy glare as he turned and glowered at his brother.

"No! No! No! No, man you trippin'! You got it all wrong. It's wasn't me. I swear on err'thang I love. I didn't have nothing to do with Mama's death and it was Lloyd. Lloyd and his crew did it...they set you up to be killed at the hotel. Not me. You gotta believe me."

"Well, if Lloyd was the one that tried to kill me and he set me up, how did you know? Most importantly, why you just now telling me?"

"Ohh, ohh...uhhh..."

"And how in da' fuck did they know what room I stayed in and what time I was supposed to be there? How they know Mama's birthday was the code to get up to my room? You were the only muthafucka dat knew that!" Trigga snapped, his face a ball of anger.

Mase was cold busted!

"Man, I dunno but you making a big mistake. I don't know, man... please...we supposed to be brothers. Don't kill me!" Mase began to cry in plaintive pleas that fell on deaf ears, because Trigga wasn't trying to hear nothing he was saying.

"Get out the car. I don't want your ass fuckin' up my seats,"

Trigga gritted with his jaw clinched tight, and his eyes trained on his brother.

Just as Mase was about to reach for the for the door handle, a car drove by and suddenly stopped, its brake lights flashing as the car went into reverse, backing up quickly.

"Fuck!" Trigga scuffed.

He had made one mental blunder in coming back to the abandoned building. He didn't take into consideration what precinct the cops West and his partner Burns worked in.

Instantly, Trigga tightened his grip on the gun. He happened to look over at Mase, who was puffing on the blunt hard like he was trying to send the cops smoke signals.

"Nigga, put dat fuckin' blunt out!" he barked. Mase mashed it between his fingers and groaned in pain. He was moving too slow for Trigga's liking.

Secretly, for the first time in his life, Mase was happy to see a cop car. They had possibly just saved his life. He actually thought about getting out the car right in front of them, and making a run for it.

Trigga glanced in the backseat and realized that he had made his second blunder. The duffle bags with the guns and money that he had robbed Lloyd's trap houses with were on the floorboard, in clear view. Sleep deprived and fatigue riddled, Trigga was slipping badly.

The cop car reversed and idled, sitting side-by-side with Trigga's car. The dark tinted window slowly descended, and low and behold, there were the homicide detectives West and Burns. They both had been assigned back to duty due to the recent spike in homicides and the decrease in policemen trained to join the homicide unit. Trigga let down the passenger window. The cops were on his side of the car.

"Well, if it ain't Mr. Nine Lives himself and his crocodile mouth brother, Mase. What a coincidence to find you two on this side of town, especially since recently there has been a rash increase in gun violence. It seems somebody has been robbing and killing off some well-known dope boys. You wouldn't by chance know anything about that, now would you, boys?" West asked sarcastically.

Trigga nodded his head 'no', and to his disbelief, he looked over and saw Mase nodding his head 'yes'. It was like he wanted the cops to bust them.

"You saying yes, you know something?" the cop shouted from the other car.

"Nigga, these police can't save yo' fuck ass. I'ma bust your ass right here and that's on Mama, now try me," Trigga muttered under his voice as he turned to Mase.

"I... I... I...heard about the murders too is what I was sayin'." The tremor in Mase's voice alerted the police that something was wrong, but it wasn't until Mase fully turned facing them that the cops really thought something was up.

"Gotdamn boy, who hit you in your eye, Sasquatch Big Foot?" Detective West chided. His partner roared with laughter.

"Naw'll man, I fell," Mase said, and hung his head begrudgingly. In doing so, he stole a glance at his brother. The gun was still aimed at him, hidden from the detectives' sight by the car door.

"Yea, you fell alright! Fell on somebody's big ass fist!"

More laughter as Mase cowered.

The cops conferred with themselves as their police radio blared from inside the car, and Trigga thumped his foot impatiently on the floor of the car. People walked by gawking at the police harassing black folks, which was the norm on this side of town.

Then the cops began to exit their car.

Trigga braced himself for what was to come next. One thing for sure, he wasn't going back to jail. He prepped himself for a fierce gun battle, but he knew no matter what happened, he would shoot Mase first. For some strange reason, he thought about Keisha. He would never see her again if he failed her now. All his efforts would be futile. No, he had to leave Mase for last. His dumbass was an easy target anyways.

Trigga prepared to bust his gun with a headshot to the first cop that stuck his head inside of his window.

CHAPTER SIX

THE SOUND OF SHOES STRIKING ON THE LINOLEUM FLOOR echoed and vibrated, causing Keisha's heart to lurch in her chest as she lay face down in a puddle of blood and urine. She was immersed in darkness and barely alive. Dried saliva was matted to the side of her face. She was in so much constant pain that every now and then, her mind would just shut down, causing her to pass out just as she hoped death would come soon.

The footsteps she heard in the crevice of her mind vaguely sounded like she was dreaming, but they were real. Terror gripped her soul. She wanted to get up, she wanted to fight back, to scream even; but every meager ounce of strength she had was gone, dissipated. She was melting down to skin and bones.

The craft box door opened with a whoosh of fresh air. A limpid light shined bright from above.

Lloyd was back with more torture, more brutality, to finish what he had started.

Why won't he just kill me? her mind churned.

A hand touched her naked shoulder, causing Keisha to shiver, then a gentle voice cooed as she was being turned over onto her back.

"Ohhh, God, have mercy! I'ma help you. I'm so sorry. I never meant for him to do you like this. I brought something for your leg," Luxe said as she turned Keisha on her back. The stench of her unwashed body was overwhelming. Luxe almost puked.

"Why...won't...he...just ... kill me?" Keisha croaked. A tear distilled down her right cheek.

"Girl I dunno, but your guess is good as mine. I know I didn't sign up for no psychopathic crazy bullshit like this. This nigga done lost his muthafuckin' mind." Luxe pulled at something on Keisha's leg, making her wince in pain. "Shit, he got yo' ass chained and shit too."

For some reason, Luxe was whispering as she worked diligently. Keisha could hear water being wrung from a sponge as she began to bathe her with warm water.

"Kill...me, please," Keisha gasped.

"You crazy too, if you think I'ma kill you. I brought you some alcohol and cleaning stuff for your gunshot wound. You lucky the bullet hit the fleshy side of your thigh and just went in and came out. Other than all this damn stinky blood you lost, you gon' be okay. You hear me girl?" Luxe spoke with tears in her voice.

"Noooo." Keisha wagged her head from side-to-side as she looked up to watch Luxe bathe her body with the warm sponge. The smell of some type of Jasmine perfume and soap was soothing to her.

"Here is some food. A hamburger, French fries, and a Coke to chase it down with. I got it from a Burger King down the street," Luxe said in hushed tones as she reached in her oversized purse and pushed the contents towards Keisha. "You need to hurry and eat it before you get us both killed."

Luxe then opened a package she retrieved from a Walgreens bag. She applied the medicated salve to Keisha's leg.

"Ouch! Shit!" Keisha screamed, and squirmed like she had been hit with an electric rod when Luxe dapped the solution onto her raw, sensitive leg.

"Bitch, shut up! You gon' get me fucked up too. Lloyd is upstairs sleep and drunk. Your dude Trigga been giving him the business.

That shit driving him crazy; plus, his baby mama Dior didn't die. He thinks she was the reason for a bomb that was placed in his car."

Keisha raised her brow, then flinched in pain as Luxe worked on her leg.

She continued, "His dumb ass crazy. That baby look just like him and he tried to kill both of them, his baby mama and the baby."

"Who?" Keisha said.

"Lloyd tried to kill Dior," she whispered, and shoved some French fries into Keisha's month. Despite her pain, Keisha devoured the fries like she had not eaten in weeks. Truth be told, she hadn't.

"Trigga been busy...doin' what?" Keisha asked in a small voice, and chewed on the fries with her eyes closed as she grimaced in pain.

"That nigga a beast. He must really love you. That nigga turned up on some real gangsta shit."

"Ouch!" Keisha cried out in pain.

"This is ugly, real ugly," Luxe frowned, crinkling her nose as she wiped at the wound.

Keisha ate the food, focusing her eyes on the ceiling as a tear slid down her face.

"Why you helpin' me?" Keisha groaned.

Luxe stopped what she was doing, and the sponge pulsed in her hand along with the rhythm of her sharp breaths.

"I ain't gon' even lie, ain't gon' front. I never liked your ass, but that shit you did with Lloyd...that nigga had a gun to your head, threatening to kill you, and all you had to do was betray your man. You didn't do it. You were going to take a bullet for that nigga. I swear to God, you're a gangsta ass bitch. I'd flip on niggas for a little loose change. It would be nice to be that in love with someone," Luxe said with her eyes looking off into the distance, as if she were thinking about someone. Then a sad look crossed through her eyes, and she shook her head sadly before turning her attention back to Keisha.

Keisha just looked at Luxe and mouthed, "Food."

"Oh, my bad." Luxe unwrapped the burger and held it up to

Keisha's mouth, as she chewed ravenously. She waited for her to chew a little longer, then held the cup of soda to her thirsty lips.

"I want to help you, but Lloyd would kill me. I'm scared," Luxe's voice quavered.

"Well...if you can't...help me...out...kill...me," Keisha said in a lilting plea to her.

"Why would I do that?" Luxe screeched with alarm as she batted her long, fake eyelashes.

"Because...I think I'm pregnant," Keisha said while blinking back the tears brimming in her starry eyes.

"Pregnant?!" Luxe repeated, her eyebrows raised tight across her on forehead.

"I ain't seen...my period."

"How long?" Luxe eased closer to hear her; at the same time, she was listening out for Lloyd. If he awoke and came down in the basement and caught her, she would be punished, and he'd already made a good example out of Keisha of how he punished a bitch.

"Two months...? I don't know...I haven't seen it since I been here."

"Oh, muthafuckingodamnsonofabitch!" Luxe exclaimed full of shock and dismay.

Keisha just continued to chew on her food. Occasionally, she would give Luxe a distant stare as if she wasn't all there. Who would be after all Keisha had been through?

"Ah, ha! I got it!" Luxe said, finally with the snap of her fingers. "We can go upstairs and kill Lloyd while he's asleep, and take all his dope and money then get ghost."

Keisha nodded her head vigorously for the first time.

Luxe turned, giving a deadpan expression and said somberly with a pouting bottom lip, "The only problem is I ain't never killed nobody. I'ma a stripper, bitch, not a murderer."

"Lemme do...it."

"You can hardly breathe, much less walk, with your ribs and shit showing and your leg fucked up; plus, you might be pregnant. Besides, I got a brother in prison. I don't want to join him."

"I...can do it!"

"No. I'm going upstairs to get some of my clothes, you're about my size so you should be able to fit them. Then I'll sneak you out the house," Luxe planned out loud.

"Then what you gon' do when he wakes up and finds me gone?"

"When he wakes up and finds me gone, his money and drugs gon' be gone too. My ass going back to Miami to dance. Fuck him. I don't like the shit he did to you. His punk ass deserves it."

For the first time in what felt like years, a smile curled at Keisha's lips. She was about to be set free.

"Girl, wait right here. I gotta get something to unchain you. I'll be back."

"I promise, I ain't goin' anywhere," Keisha said as her eyes fluttered drowsily.

GINGERLY, Luxe walked back upstairs with her mind racing a mile a minute. She needed to find the key that Lloyd had for the chained lock on Keisha's leg, then grab his money and dope, gather her few belongings, clothes for Keisha, and hightail it out of there.

Easier said than done.

As Luxe crept towards the master bedroom where most of her stuff was, along with Lloyd's, she removed her shoes and padded over towards him. He lay atop the king-sized bed with his mouth slightly open, snoring lightly. On the nightstand, there was an open sandwich bag of weed, several rolled blunts, a Rolex watch and a roll of money, an open bottle of Cîroc and a purple cup half full of lean, and Keisha's iPhone. She took everything except the bottle of Cîroc and lean.

Instantly, she hurried about gathering her clothes as her heart pounded so hard in her chest that she felt like she was going to vomit. Her stomach rumbled like she needed to go to the bathroom to do number two. Lloyd was sleeping, but he still scared the shit out of her.

As she looked under the bed, she spotted a black and gold Gucci duffle bag.

Bingo!

Her heart pounded in her ears. Her breathing started to shorten with each breath, like she was having an anxiety attack.

She slid the duffle bag from under the bed, inch-by-inch. Time was an infinity of moments as fragile as a cracked hourglass, and just when she had the large duffle bag fully in her clutches, Lloyd must have heard a sound or something. He stopped snoring and stirred like he was about to get up.

Is he awake?

Luxe's stomach erupted like the sound of bodily fluids shifting from hunger cramps, but it was actually fear ripping at her gut. She froze, perfectly still, holding the Gucci bag full of what she hoped was money and dope inside. One thing was for certain; if Lloyd got up out of bed right then, she would have a lot of explaining to do once he saw her clothes packed outside the door in the hallway, and her hands on his duffle bag.

A few seconds lingered like eternity on hold. The bed shifted again.

Was he about to get up?

For some reason, she held her breath and her stomach boiled with fear, causing her to do something she hadn't done in a long time. She prayed for God to spare her life.

Soon, she heard soft snoring again. She expelled a sigh of relief and peered inside the duffle bag. Her eyes bucked wide; she started hyperventilating, causing her stomach to do a flip-flop. The Gucci bag was full of money, racks of money, all big face hundreds, and a couple kilos of cocaine. For some reason, her heart beat faster and her hands began to shake as she pulled the heavy bag over her shoulder and tiptoed back out the room.

On her way back down the stairs, something dawned on her mid-way. She still didn't have the key to free Keisha's shackles. After thinking for a brief two seconds, she remembered the key was on Lloyd's keychain. The only problem was, where was the damn keychain?

The last thing she wanted was to go back upstairs. For a fleeting second, she thought about leaving Keisha and getting a rental car and hauling ass back to Miami; but Keisha was pregnant. She couldn't leave her like that. She would have bad luck for the rest of her life knowing that she'd been able to help her, and instead did what she normally did, which was look out for her own greed.

Luxe exhaled heavily and crept back up the stairs and into the room. Lloyd was still snoring, so Luxe took the opportunity to search the room for his keys.

Nothing.

Panicked and distressed, she turned towards his sleeping body, as if attempting to mentally coerce him to tell her where the key was hidden. Then she noticed what looked like a print in his pants pocket and, upon close examination, she could see the partial key ring visibly hanging out the opening of his pocket. *If I move slowly, I could ease the entire key ring out*, she thought. She'd have the key for the chain and his car keys to get away.

Luxe padded back over and delicately eased her hand into his pocket, as fragile and gentle as someone who was handling a live grenade. With two fingers she grabbed them, then began the difficult process of taking them out without waking him.

Slowly...Slowly...Slowly...

She eased them out and just when she had them in her hands, Lloyd's eyes opened with a start.

"Fuck you doin'?!" he grabbed her arm in a vice grip.

The keys hit the floor, and she damn near screamed. Finally, her stomached erupted long and hard, causing her to pass gas like a burst balloon at a child's party. She probably needed to check her panties.

"I...I—I wanna suck dat dick, papi. You been nappin' for a minute, bae," she stuttered, trying to coo in a sexy voice, but her breath caught in her throat, creating a jagged high-pitch tone instead. She reached for his zipper, attempting to take his dick out.

Lloyd hesitated for a minute as he watched her. He loved the way she gave head and swallowed his babies, but he wasn't for it this time. He batted her hand down.

"Man, fuck wrong witchu? A nigga tired as fuck. I thought I heard yo' ass creeping round and shit, messin' up my sleep. Lay yo' dumb ass down, and go check your draws. Got the damn room smellin' like you done shit on yaself," he said and adjusted the pillow he was sleeping on.

Underneath, she spotted the chrome plated .9mm. He had been sleeping with it ever since Trigga had went on a rampage.

Before she could think twice, Lloyd reached up and yanked her in bed. She wasted no time and cuddled up right next to him in a spoon position, and prayed he went back to sleep. Soon enough, she heard the sound of him snoring again. She counted backwards from one hundred in her head, then she crept out the bed, grabbed the keys, and tiptoed back down into the hall where she picked up her belongings she had stashed there, and took them out to the garage.

Lloyd had two new whips there. One of them was a candy apple red Maserati, and the other was a dark blue BMW. Barefooted, Luxe wasted no time padding over to the BMW and opening the trunk with the remote on the key. She put all her luggage in the car and for an instant, she thought once again about leaving Keisha shackled in the basement and dipping with the coke and money. She hurried to the front of the car, hopped in, and placed the key in the ignition, ready to smash out.

Then it hit her.

Greed is a terrible thing, she thought to herself.

She held the key in the ignition so tight the radio turned off. The reserve shattered. If it hadn't been for the fact that Keisha may have been pregnant, Luxe probably would have left. She was gangsta as hell for her nigga too. She actually wasn't afraid to take a bullet for her nigga and stand up to Lloyd like a damn dude. Luxe felt like she didn't have a choice but to go back inside and get the poor girl, even though her first instincts were telling her 'no'. With a sigh, she jumped out of the car and walked stealthily back towards the house.

CHAPTER SEVEN

"Bitch, you lucky I like yo' gangsta ass. I was thinking about leaving you. Plus, my grandma always told me if you follow your first instinct, you'll never lose. Well, my first instinct was telling me to leave your ass. So since I'm goin' against that, you need to hurry and you better be able to walk."

Keisha grimaced as she nodded her head, looking down at Luxe wrestling with the key in the lock. Keisha frowned painfully. The shackles had cut into her ankle, leaving raw deep cuts. Luxe continued as she worked with the lock.

"You almost got me killed."

Click!

The lock opened.

"Wow...thank God," Keisha muttered weakly as she rubbed her bruised ankle and asked, "What...happened?"

"That nigga woke up while I was going through his pockets getting the keys. Here, your phone was on the dresser." She passed Keisha the phone.

"Thank you. Is he sleep now?" Keisha managed to ask, and continued to rub her ankle.

"He took his drunk, high ass back to sleep. Now get up, let's go!" she said in a hushed voice while helping Keisha put on a pair of her Nike running shoes she had brought to work out in, but hadn't had a chance to wear.

Luxe hoisted Keisha to her feet. She teetered and wavered like a baby learning to walk, and suddenly poised herself with correct posture. All was looking good until Keisha took one step and fell into a crate, knocking over the metal pan of water Luxe had used to bathe her with. Keisha cried out as quietly as she could in agonizing pain. The noise was maddening.

"You gon' get us caught making all that damn noise. I hope you can walk," Luxe hissed, her face was a scowl of desperation and fear.

"I'm...s—sorry..." Keisha lay on the floor panting, rolling back and forth, gripped with torrent pain.

"Come on, girl. You can make it. I'ma help you. Get up, let's go —" Luxe stopped short when they heard a noise at the same time.

"Was that a door?" Luxe asked with her eyes spread wide, like she was about to jump out her skin as she froze in place.

Keisha raised her head off the floor as she looked at the ceiling, where the sound had come from.

"I dunno, but you gotta go. Leave me, just get me some help..." Keisha could barely talk as she lowered her head back on the hard floor.

"I'm not leaving you in this bitch. We leaving together. Besides, if he's up there woke and walking around, if you with me when he catches us, you can help me wear some of the ass whipping too. You better at it than me. I would have been dead after all this shit you been through."

Despite their dreary circumstances, Keisha managed to roll her eyes at Luxe.

They waited some more for any sound to signal that Lloyd was awake.

Finally, Luxe said with a deep sigh, "Maybe it was this old ass house settling down. That's what the sound was." She glanced down at Keisha, still sprawled out on the floor for approval. Keisha gave her a blank stare.

"Bitch, you could at least agree with me. Dayum!" she huffed, disconcerted.

Luxe bent down again to help Keisha up and it was like lifting dead weight, but still she was determined to get Keisha out of the house with her.

"Grab my neck and hold on, but don't fuck my weave up, okay?"

Keisha nodded her head 'yes', despite the fact her leg felt like it was on fire and she was so nauseated and weak she was seeing stars. It felt like she was going to pass out any minute.

Together, they trudged up the stairs. It was a rigorous, long struggle for both of them but when they made it to the top of the stairs, Keisha held on to the doorframe with wobbly legs as Luxe smiled. She was bent over, breathing hard like a two-pack-a-day smoker. A sheen of perspiration gleamed on her forehead.

"We gon' turn up after this," Luxe said with a sheepish grin then added, "that is, if you ever come to my city, Miami. But don't come there looking for nobody named Luxe. I'm goin' by my real name, Andrea."

Keisha closed her eyes and wobbled, trying to keep her balance as she gritted her teeth; she was still feeling faint. Luxe must have read her demeanor, because she reached out and grabbed her arm, holding it tight.

She exclaimed between laborious breaths, "Bitch, if you fall back down them stairs, I promise you I'ma leave yo' ass right there, spread eagle."

For some reason, Luxe's facial expression and slick mouth made her smirk, as a smile threatened to pull her lips into a curve upwards. Keisha felt giddy, and a surge of energy went through her as they continued to walk. That was, until they both heard it at the same time.

Somebody was coming down the front steps. Keisha and Luxe were in the back of the house on the other side of the stairs, a mere wall section away. There was no doubt in their minds that it was Lloyd, but when Lloyd called out for Luxe, the sound of his voice made them both shiver.

"Bitch, where the fuck you at?"

"Oooh, shit!"

Luxe snatched Keisha's arm so hard it made her neck snap back as she took off, pulling her behind her. There was something about hearing Lloyd's voice that gave Keisha newfound strength that not even she knew she had, as Luxe towed her through the living room and kitchen, straight out the adjourning kitchen door into the garage.

"Get in the car!" she said, swinging open the door and shoving Keisha in, not paying attention when she collapsed face first onto the front seat.

Just as Luxe rushed around to the driver's door, she heard Lloyd's halting voice; it sounded like rolling thunder from hell with acoustics and all.

"Fuck you think you doing? What's going on?" he held his chrome plated .9mm at his side.

"N—N—nothin'! I thought I left my tampons out here—"

She passed gas again.

"Tampons? Bitch, ain't no muthafuckin' tampons in the fuckin garage. Where dat fuckin' Gucci bag at full of my money and dope?" Lloyd asked, and slightly wobbled on his legs as he took a step towards her

"I'on...I'on...I'on know what you're talking about—"

From the inside of the car, Keisha sat up, horrified, and watched the whole thing like a grisly cinematic horror film. In the dim lurid light in the garage, Lloyd had not spotted her. Yet.

Before Luxe could finish her sentence, he reached out and grabbed her by the throat, violently, with one hand in a chokehold. Then he slammed her head against the wall so hard the gardener's tool rack fell off the wall with a crash.

To Keisha's surprise, Luxe began to fight back as he choked her. It took everything in her power to watch and not jump out the car and help or do something. Luxe was putting up a good fight being that Lloyd was faded off both alcohol and lean.

Luxe shoved him back, even though he continued to hold on to her throat. She managed to strike him in the face with her fist, landing several good punishing blows. She bloodied his nose and had him staggering, making his knees nearly buckle as she screamed like a crazy mad woman while striking him.

At first Luxe's words sounded gurgled, like she was submerged under water, trying not to drown in his brutality. Then it dawned on Keisha what she was saying.

"Go, gurl, GO!!! Leave! The keys in da car. GO!"

Luxe slugged Lloyd some more. She was getting the better off him. Luxe had damn sure earned her respect. Keisha frantically looked around and spotted the car keys and luggage, along with the Gucci bag.

Then in what looked like a slow, surreal motion, Lloyd tried to place the gun to her head, aimed it, cocked it and like a wild cat. Luxe jumped into his chest, arms flailing, kicking, scratching like a bat out of hell. She bit him in the face. Lloyd howled like a wounded animal; blood squirted as they tussled over the gun. They both toppled over, hitting the hood of the car with Luxe on top, then they fell onto the concrete floor in a thump.

Keisha strained to see over the dashboard. What was going on as her heart pounded in her chest? She could hear Luxe still yelling, screaming, telling her to, GO!

Then.

BLOCKA!

The gun exploded. The sound resonated in the small space.

Keisha hoped that Luxe was alive. That the girl that had risked her life wasn't shot.

Suddenly, there was the hum of silence as Keisha's heart beat so fast in her chest she struggled to breath, struggled to gain clarity in her head. What had happened? Keisha held on to the steering wheel, knuckles paled, as she held her breath.

A head bobbed from the front of the car as she strained to see over the dashboard and the fog in her mind. To her dismay, Lloyd's grotesque face appeared, sanguineous as blood streamed from a teeth mark gush. He had a fiendish look in his eyes. She couldn't be sure if he saw her yet. She started the car. His eyes bucked wide and at point plank range, he aimed at the windshield and fired. She ducked.

BLOCKA! BLOCKA! BLOCKA!

The seismic sound of the windshield shattering in a hell storm of spraying glass and bullets was deafening from inside the car. Keisha blindly ducked with her eyes closed, placed the car in gear, and punched the gas pedal causing the large locomotive to leap forward, running over a body with a crunch. Lloyd was barely able to escape and not receive the full force from the impact of the car, because his body was positioned in front of the garage door's entrance. Still, the impact sent him sailing backwards into the dining room area's table and chairs.

With the quickness, Keisha placed the car in reverse and plodded through the aluminum garage door, hitting a parked car in the street. She corrected the wheel and drove off.

CHAPTER EIGHT

TRIGGA BRACED HIMSELF AS THE COP GOT OUT AND WALKED over to his side of the car. Trigga was prepared to start blasting as he gripped the gun, concealing it under his thigh. As soon as the cop stuck his head in the window, he was going to shoot, then he'd kill his brother and there would be a fierce gun battle with the last officer.

For some reason, the detective was smiling when he strolled up to the car. He wore a clean, tailored brown, two-piece suit with a wide brim hat, an ensemble you might see the entertainer Steve Harvey wear. His sloth eyes bounced around the interior of the car and settled on the duffle bag back in the back seat, as he shielded his eyes from the ardent sun by cuffing his hand.

"How has it been going, Maurice? What have you been up to? I see you're enjoying our city; you must be thinking about living here permanently—"

"Naw'll, I'ma leave as soon as I finish up some business," Trigga said, placing a toothpick in his mouth, seemingly reserved and relaxed, but the tension was as tight as a fat lady walking a rope. They both knew after the song and dance, what question would come next.

And the question would have severe consequences.

"If you don't mind, I would like to search your car," the detective said while still shielding his eyes from the ardent sun.

"Sure, I don't have a problem with that," Trigga said, prepared for the detective to stick his head in the car so he could blow his wig back with the .9mm.

Detective West smiled, until the next words caught him completely off guard.

"You can search my car as soon as you show me a search warrant, or let me know what the probable cause is. Have I broken any law?"

Fucking asshole. Smart ass thug criminal knows the law. That was a cop's worse nightmare. The smile faded on West's face, and turned into an irate frown.

"Punk, I don't need to show you shit. I'm tired of playing your little games. You're a suspect in nearly a dozen homicides as far as I'm concerned, and this shit has got to stop. It's only a matter of time before you get caught. We know for a fact it's you robbing the drug dealers and shooting innocent people."

"What I know is you should have been a writer, a fiction writer at that. You have a great imagination. I'm simply here on vacation. I don't know nuttin' 'bout no murders or none of dat other bullshit, so miss me with dat!"

"Bullshit, and you and I both know it. Now stop playing these fucking games with me."

For some reason, the cop was furious—angry as hell. Just as he was about to reach for the door handle and attempt to pull Trigga and possibly lose his life in the process, Mase hopped out the car. The other cop reached for his gun, about to shoot him.

"Fuck you think you doing! Where you think you going?" Burns asked.

"Man, if I'm being placed under arrest, please take me to jail but if not, I need to go. Ain't it a law or some shit for cops harassing you and detaining you against your will without arresting you?" Mase said, agitated as his chest heaved. He was visibly nervous.

"You better get your ass back into that car," the other cop said.

Just that fast, things were starting to get out of hand as Trigga looked on in disbelief. Mase was trying to make the cops take him to jail, or possibly kill him, rather than let his brother end his life.

More people started to gather around. This was the hood, and the normal activity in the naked city. Just like all gangs, in the hood, the police were perceived as a gang too, because they were at times just as crooked as the criminals with their corruption.

"I'm going to ask your ass one more time, get the fuck back into that car," the detective said with steel in his voice.

Mase nodded his head emphatically as he waved his hands in the air, "Naw, ain't happenin'. I'm not getting back into that car. My life might be in danger. You can kill me like y'all do everybody else, or you can take me to jail."

"Let that man go. Y'all always coming here fuckin' with people," a crackhead said. She was skinny with gaps of missing teeth; several other people championed her words. Things were starting to heat up.

"You and your brother beefing?" Detective West asked with an arched brow, like he was on to something.

"Just get out of here. I don't want to see this car around here no more," West said to Trigga just as his phone chimed with a text message. He didn't bother to check it, because what happened next blew his mind.

"And you, buck-mouthed one with the shiner, start walking. I don't wanna see you around here either. Is that understood?" he said to Mase.

Mase nodded his head 'yes' and stole a glance at his brother, seeing nothing but death in his eyes. He knew he was lucky to be alive. He had escaped hell wearing gasoline draws.

Mase took off in a trot with long, lilting strides. Trigga made a mental note to follow as he pulled off, but Trigga wasn't the only person that had found interest in Mase; so did the cops. There was friction between the brothers, and it was as obvious as a crack in a glass bottle.

As soon as Trigga pulled on the main street, his phone chimed again. He wanted to keep his eye on Mase, to follow his direction. Then the damn phone chimed again. He looked down then looked back up, but just that quickly, Mase was gone.

"Fuck!" Trigga scuffed, then happened to glance in his review mirror. The cops were right on his bumper. He needed to give them the slip. They made him uncomfortable. He turned the corner, unsure where he was going. The cops continued straight in the direction where Mase had been headed.

Trigga made it to a red light across from a QuickTrip gas station. As the car sat idle, he couldn't help thinking about how close he had come to dancing with death. He was about to kill a cop—no, a couple of cops. For an instant moment, his mind wondered if this was his destiny...would this be his legacy? He had even been ready to murder his own precious twin brother. His heart sank as he slouched down in his seat. His conscious was getting the best of him.

I can't do this much longer, he thought to himself, crestfallen. Then a horn blew behind him. The light had changed to green. He drove off, again thinking about Keisha, her smile, the sway of her hips, her sensuous lips. The times he had made love to her endlessly and could never get enough. He turned to head towards Pink Lips, back on his mission to find her. Mase would just have to wait.

Glancing back in his rearview mirror, he reached down to check his phone once he was certain that no one was following him. When he saw the name on his screen, his heart almost stopped in his chest. It was Keisha.

Trigga swerved to the side of the road to check the message. A feeling of déjà vu passed over him when he saw what was on the screen. Keisha's message had no words, but it told him exactly what he needed. She'd sent him a similar message, months ago when Lloyd had her and she needed his help. It was only right that she did the same thing this time.

She'd used her iPhone to send him her location. Trigga tapped on the location and sent it to his phone's GPS. As soon as it calculated the distance and the directions to his love illuminated on his screen, he snatched the wheel, pulled the car back onto the street, and took off in the direction of her location. A nagging in his mind told him to heed her warning from earlier and not take the bait. It could be an attempt from Lloyd to bring him to his death, but he couldn't bear the risk of ignoring the message if it was in fact her, beckoning for him to save her.

Fuck everything and everyone. He was going to get Keisha.

CHAPTER NINE

WITH TEARS LOCKED INTO THE CORNERS OF HER EYES, LUXE placed the phone down next to Keisha's body while she slept peacefully in the hospital bed and kissed her on her forehead. She said a prayer to God that He would spare her from Lloyd until Trigga was able to get here and protect her. That was all she could do. She had to go. If she didn't, Lloyd would certainly find her and she would meet her grisly demise at the end of the barrel of his gun. He was hurt but he wasn't dead, and Luxe knew as soon as he was able to get himself together, he would come looking for her.

Tucking the duffle bag under her arm, she slid the handle over her arm and walked out of the room, taking one last wistful look back at Keisha as she lay in the bed, breathing evenly. For the first time in weeks, her coloring was returning to normal and she was no longer the ashen pale color that she'd been while Lloyd held her captive. Luxe walked out of the room and down the hall, leaving her luggage with Keisha, along with a few stacks she'd peeled off from the stash in the duffle.

Her plan was to get to Miami, and make the money she had left stretch as long as she could. Her uncles and cousins were all hustlers, so she knew she could get rid of the dope easily. She just had to get there first and make sure she wouldn't get caught. So the first order of business was to get rid of Lloyd's, car and get lost as fast as she could.

Tossing the duffle bag into the passenger seat, she sat down and gazed up at the calming blue hues of the plumose clouds in the sky. For the first time in her life, she had done something she was proud of. Although it had almost cost her life, she'd gotten Keisha to the hospital and stayed with her until she was able to get the help she needed. Once she was in the clear, Luxe knew she had to leave before the cops were called to ask her questions, or before Lloyd found her. She'd thought of another person more than herself, for once in her life.

For a fleeting moment, she thought about Tish, the last person she'd betrayed for the sake of a few dollars. Truth was, the emotions that she had for Tish were the closest she'd ever come to actually loving someone; but in the end, when it came to money, she'd betrayed her trust as well.

Pushing the ignition, Luxe bit her lip and listened as the engine came to a roar. She placed the car into gear and pulled out of the parking spot. She wanted to get far enough away to a place where she could call a cab and dispose of the car. There was no way that Lloyd didn't have a way to track down a car as expensive as his brand new BMW. If she didn't get out of it fast, Lloyd would be able to come right to her.

Luxe pulled out of the entrance of the hospital and hit the turning signal to pull out of the parking lot. When the coast was clear, she lifted her foot from the brake and prepared to press the gas, but the sight in front of her made her stop right in her tracks. There was a car speeding towards her at top speed. The car was bobbing and weaving past a few cars that lie in between them, but the motion did nothing to suppress its speed. Frozen beyond the ability to scream, Luxe's mouth fell open when the vehicle turned at the very last minute to avoid a head-on collision and swerved right in front of her, obstructing her movement from where she sat at the entrance of the hospital.

The ardent sun high in the sky blinded the face of the person who jumped out of the driver's side of the car, making Luxe raise her hand to shield her face as she made a feeble attempt to catch the identity of the person approaching her. His body was massive and muscular, and in his hand was a banger, his finger on the trigger.

Was this one of Lloyd's men who hadn't yet had his life claimed by Keisha's beau? Was he here to do Lloyd's dirty work for him and end Luxe's life in his absence?

Before Luxe could begin to open her mouth to utter fear-filled pleas for her life to be salvaged, the driver's door was ripped open so hard that it nearly came loose from the hinges, and the assailant in front of her grabbed at her upper arm and drug her out of the car. Luxe's mouth opened in horror as she reached out in vain for anything that her fingers could reach to protect herself with. There was nothing.

"Where da fuck is she?!"

Luxe's head rattled like a ragdoll as massive hands shook the shit out of her. Saliva flew from her lips and slapped the side of her cheek as she rattled helplessly in the hands of the man who held her.

When the shaking stopped, Luxe's head fell back as she tried to gather her bearings. She was disoriented and slightly nauseated. She felt a rough hand grab the side of her face and snatch her face upwards, so she was able to look into the eyes of the man ahead of her. Fear crippling her; she squeezed her thighs tight to stop the sliver of liquid that had begun to seep from between her legs. Her terror brought on the urge to pee, and even when she was able to identify the person who held her, it did nothing to quench the emotion that was steadily rising up in her.

"Trigga?" she whispered finally.

His face was pulled into a snarl as he clutched her around her neck, raw from Lloyd's earlier assault. He squeezed tighter and bit down on his bottom lip as his eyes bore into her, completely oblivious to the small group of people walking by who were stealing curious glances at the sight before them. However, the crowd seemed to be well-versed in the rules of the streets and walked on steadily, minding their business less they become next on Trigga's murk list.

"BITCH, you betta fuckin' speak!" Trigga pressed the gun in his hand against her ribcage. The sight of it was cloaked in between their bodies as not to alert onlookers who thought him and Luxe were having a lover's spat in the middle of the street.

"Sh—she—she's in the hospital! I brought her here!" Luxe said finally, fresh tears pooling in her eyes. "I snuck her out to get her help. Pl—please, you gotta let me go 'fore Lloyd gets here! I texted you… room 614. She's in there!"

Thoughts beckoning him to complete competing tasks, Trigga tried to decide which murmurs in his mind to listen to. Should he let her go or should he drag her ass with him? He'd granted enough mercy already for the day, though accidentally, when Mase walked his ass away from the bullet sitting in the chamber of Trigga's gun which already had his name on it.

"I heard her talk to you…she risked her life for you and I couldn't let her die. I snuck her out…please, you gotta let me go. Lloyd has a tracker on this car! I gotta dump it and skip town," Luxe pled with her eyes rolling around frantically in her head.

Trigga watched her for a second more, and then released his grip. One thing that he knew was that a bitch like Luxe told no lies in the face of danger. She was a stripper, and the mentality that came along with that was to always be out for self. The fact that she'd stuck to her story with his banger wedged deep into her gut let him know that she was telling the truth.

Without saying another word, he turned around and jumped into the whip, and took off towards the front doors of the hospital before Luxe could even catch her breath. Panting laboriously, she turned around and took a look behind her in time to see Trigga pull right up in front of the doors of the hospital, as if he owned the place, and jumped out. She rubbed her neck with her hand and slid back into the vehicle, determined more than ever to get the hell out of dodge before someone else found her.

The next person who happened upon her might not allow her to escape with her life.

CHAPTER TEN

"Don't look like things between you and baby bro going too well, hmm?" one of the detectives asked Mase as he walked down the road with his hands shoved in his pockets.

Pouting slightly from the fact that the detective's words were true, Mase trudged on at a quick pace, somewhat happy about the fact that he had police trailing him at the moment. As long as they were following him, he could find a semblance of comfort in the fact that Trigga would be nowhere around.

Mase still couldn't believe his brother would try to kill him. Sure, he'd planned on doing the same thing to him a few months back but since then, he'd realized that his brother was all he had in the world. To kill him would be to kill the only person in the world who had his back.

"We good," Mase replied, lifting a brow to peer at the detective from the side of his eye.

West was leaning out of the window as Burns drove, and on his face was a grin that bore a nearly exact resemblance to the Cheshire cat on *Alice in Wonderland*. He was finally feeling like he was about to happen on a break in the case that had been bothering him for more time than he cared to admit. Running his tongue along the bottom of his razor-sharp, coffee-stained teeth, he ignored his partner's long, heavy sigh behind him as he thought of a way to use Mase and the obvious rift between him and his brother to their advantage.

Burns, on the other hand, was totally and fully sick of anything dealing with Maurice, Mase, or Lloyd. After he'd arrested Maurice the very last time, expecting to get a fat bonus and a nice promotion courtesy of his eyewitness pinpointing him as the one who had murdered Kenyon St. Michaels and a few other men, the case fell through and he'd become the laughing stock of the entire precinct. But even that was preferable to being stuck working the streets with West again. His obsession with nailing Lloyd and now Maurice was suffocating and irked Burns to the core. He tried to play along as a good partner should, but he couldn't wait until West left this yuck mouth creature alone so that he could remind him that the Captain said anything concerning Maurice, aka Trigga, was off-limits.

"Well, what about Lloyd? You know anything about him?" West asked Mase as he continued walking down the long, dilapidated road. "You and Trigga good with him, too?"

Mase shot a look at the dope fiends and homeless people who were staggering along around him, making sure they were out of earshot of the questioning that he was being subjected to. The last thing he wanted was for anyone to think he was working with the pigs.

"Hell naw, we ain't good wit' no muthafuckin' Lloyd," Mase said gruffly. "Trigga hates that muthafucka, so I do too." The worst thing in his life that he'd ever done was to work with Lloyd and go against his brother. That was his deepest regret.

"Well, it seems like your brother's a little fed up with you. Maybe if you help us with Lloyd, it may change his mind about you?" West baited, and Mase's ears piqued at the suggestion.

Stopping in his tracks, he cast a hopeful glance in West's direction and that was the exact moment that West felt a twinge in his gut.

Got him, he thought to himself.

Coercing a witness was always merely a matter of finding their weakness. Everyone had one. As soon as you were able to key in to what it was they wanted, you could get what you wanted. It was obvious to West that Mase wanted the approval and affection of his brother. Easy.

"What you want me to do?" Mase asked finally, with his shoulders slumped over in a defeated manner. He didn't want to work with the police but at this point, he was desperate to do something to get back in Trigga's good graces.

"How about this, you tell us when you have made contact with Lloyd and we'll be in touch," West told him with a wink.

He slid his arm inside of the car and when he pushed it back outside of the window, it came with a card sticking out from two of his fingers. Mase grabbed it with a scowl as he looked down the road to make sure no one was watching, and stuffed it into his pocket.

"I'll do it. You just make sure none of this shit falls down on my brotha, a'ight?" Mase lifted one brow into the air as he waited for West's response. "Oh, and I'ma need you to write all this shit up in a contract or some shit to make sure I'm protected. I heard about what happened to Black's cousin after workin' wit' y'all muthafuckas."

He's not as stupid as I thought, West thought, trying to conceal his surprise.

"Deal. Keep in touch," West agreed.

The police scanner started sputtering a garbled sound, and Burns mashed the gas. The car sped off down the street, leaving Mase in its dust with a dumbfounded look on his face as he thought of what he'd just done. He'd thought he had hit rock bottom before, but a false floor gave way and dropped him onto a new low, welcoming him to the lowest of the lows. Now he was working with the police as a certified snitch.

Taking a precarious look around him, the street seemed to be busier than he'd noticed before and all eyes were on him, the man who had willingly made a deal with the devil right in the middle of the hood. He might as well have had a blinking red light on him that read 'snitch'. Gritting his teeth and surveying his surroundings, he dredged on down the road, hoping that no one would decide to fuck with him for turning pig.

Suddenly, the sound of a loud engine erupted in the air creating an immediate distraction away from where he wallowed in his misery, and all eyes turned towards a dark blue BMW as it sailed down the street right by him. As the car whipped through where he stood, he stared into the driver's side and a jolt of surprise surged through him when he realized that he recognized the face of the chick in the driver's seat. It was the fine ass bitch from the club.

The night of the ambush, Mase had been eyeing her sexy ass the entire night, and had even got a lap dance from her before Lloyd declared her to be his and took her attention the rest of the night. Mase turned around fully and watched as she sped down to the end of the street, and pulled over near a bus station. The taillights flashed as she hit the brakes to place the car in park, and then turn off the engine.

This might be my chance, Mase thought to himself as he ran his forefinger and thumb over his chin.

He ain't have shit to his name but the lil' bit of stolen cash in his pocket and clothes on his back, but she didn't know that. All she knew was that he was the nigga throwing up hundreds in the club all over her ass some nights back. Hopefully, that would be enough to convince her to give him a ride. Mase took off in a jog towards her, praying that luck was on his side.

"Aye!" he called out when he saw Luxe stepping out of the vehicle.

Startled, she nearly jumped five feet into the air before clutching onto the duffle bag over her shoulders and turning his way. Upon seeing him, her face went nearly white and she froze in place with her eyes wide like a deer caught in headlights. Her bottom lip started to tremble, which made Mase slow down into a brisk walk instead of a jog.

"Aye, you rememba me?" Mase asked with a toothy grin once he was only a couple feet away. "What da business is, shawty? Can a nigga get a ride? I got some stacks to give you for the favor."

Blinking furtively, a shadow passed through Luxe's eyes as she processed his words.

"A ride?" she repeated. Her eyes started to dart around them, as if she were searching for something. Or better yet, looking out for someone. Mase frowned to himself as he watched her. She was obviously in some sort of trouble, and he didn't know if he wanted to involve himself in it. He had enough shit happening of his own.

"Yeah, a ride. You a'ight?" he asked, her paranoia getting the best of him as well. He took a wary glance around them to make sure that he hadn't walked into no bullshit.

"I'm good. Here," she said, throwing something towards him. Instinctively, Mase caught it in his hands before realizing what it was. It was a set of keys, including a key fob for the BMW behind her.

"You can keep it," Luxe told him. Glancing down the street once more, she waved her hand at an approaching cab and jogged over towards it as it slowed down. Mase took a look at the keys in his hands, and then back at her as she jumped inside and closed the door behind her. He watched as she drove off in the cab without even bothering to take another look at him.

Must be my lucky day, Mase thought as he dangled the keys in his hand.

Whatever the hell she'd gotten herself into made her dumb as hell in his book, because nothing would make him give away a perfectly good new BMW.

Her loss, my muthafuckin' gain.

CHAPTER ELEVEN

"Keisha?" Trigga's voice cracked as he looked at the frail, emaciated person who lay in the hospital bed below his pain-stricken gaze.

There was no way this was Keisha. There was no way this could be the woman he loved.

She was so thin and malnourished that it seemed as if the weight of the blankets the hospital staffed had wrapped around her would crush right through her bones. Her eyes were closed, but they sunk into the hallow holes of her face like a skeleton. Her skin was dry and stretched to cover over her bone. She looked like nothing but a shell of herself; thin, wasted away, and lacking every bit of everything that made her the beautiful, upbeat, sassy, and sexy woman he'd been in love with, probably since the moment he'd seen her.

Biting his lip to stop the tears that had welled up in his eyes at the sight of her, he reached out with his hand to smooth down her hair atop of her head. Some of it had fallen out from the lack of nutrition she'd received, and the rest lay in dried up, tangled clumps. He swiped one finger under the top of the sheet that covered her, and pulled down to expose the rest of her small frame. He wanted to inspect every bit of her. He needed to see if she was going to be okay.

Sucking in a breath of anguish, he ran his hand over the bandages covering a large part of her thigh. They needed to be changed, which was obvious from the amount of blood that had seeped through since they'd been placed there. Trigga squeezed his eyes closed tightly and fought the urge to break down in tears. Kneeling down at her side, he dropped his head and rested it on the side of her bed as he held her small, delicate hand in his.

A man was at his weakest moment when he realized that he couldn't protect the ones he loved, and that was precisely where Trigga was. Nothing could bring him to his knees or produce tears in his otherwise cold and callous eyes like she could. In this moment, he felt like less of a man. He'd been unable to save the one he loved and bring her back unharmed. She was alive, but it was not because of any action of his. If it hadn't been for Luxe, she would be dead.

"Sir, are you family?" a voice crashed into his consciousness just as he'd stopped cursing himself for failing Keisha, and started planning out the suffering of the one who'd caused her pain. Lloyd's days were numbered as it was, and now more than ever Trigga was certain that his focus would be on decreasing that number as much as he could.

"Yes, I am. I'm her only family. Her fiancé," Trigga found himself saying before he realized it.

Creasing his brow to steady his gaze, he scrutinized the young, blond woman who appeared to be in her twenties who stood before him. She looked much too young to be a doctor, and much too upbeat to be the one to undoubtedly deliver to him bad news about Keisha's condition. From the looks of her, there could be nothing good to be said about her state. Trigga braced himself for bad news as he kept his eyes on the lightly tanned white female, with rosy cheeks and sparkling emerald green eyes.

With a look of care and concern tucked behind her professional disposition, she searched his curious stare for a moment longer before opening her mouth to speak.

"I'm a resident doctor here. You can call me Dr. Tinsley. Ms. O'Neal's friend gave the police a statement earlier about finding her in a house where people went to get high...she said that was how she was shot. She did have a considerable amount of drugs in her system. Do you know anything of this?"

Alarmed, Trigga's lips moved as he pulled away to glance at Keisha's body once more, as if she would feed him the words to say.

"Sh—she had drugs in her system?" Trigga repeated the information he'd received slowly as he tried to push away the feeling of guilt that began to settle in on him once more.

Anger seeped in once the guilt was removed, and he felt the icy feeling wash over him like a cool breeze in the middle of the sweltering sun. His hatred for Lloyd grew with each second. He couldn't wait to commence to hunting him down. How many more of Lloyd's men had to die for him to come out of hiding? He didn't know, but he would damn sure keep it going until they were all gone.

"She did. Right now the baby is fine, but—"

"Baby?!" Trigga yelled so loudly that the doctor nearly jumped straight up in the air. He stood up and stepped away from Keisha slowly as he looked down at her body, digesting the news.

"I'm so sorry! I wasn't supposed to—I—I'm sorry, I thought you knew..." Doctor Tinsley continued to speak, but Trigga's mind tuned out everything that she was saying. The only thing that kept cycling through his mind was that Keisha was pregnant...pregnant with his child, or so he hoped. She'd been away for a month while he was locked up, and an additional four and a half weeks that Trigga spent hitting up Lloyd's trap houses and hunting his men.

Two months she'd been gone. Depending on how far along she was...the baby could be Lloyd's. She'd been gone long enough for him to rape her and make her pregnant.

"How far along is she?" Trigga asked suddenly, interrupting the woman who was muttering something about HIPPA and privacy laws.

"I—I can't say. You're not technically married or related so I—I can't—"

"*How far along is she?!*" Trigga repeated with an even, coarse tone.

He wasn't shouting, but the intonation in his voice was just as threatening as if he were. Beads of sweat sprouted up at the doctor's hairline and she shot him a look of desperation, as if pleading with him not to force her to go against her training. Trigga stared back at her with an unwavering glare, as if to say 'fuck your training'. If she was waiting for him to let go of the issue, she'd be waiting a long time.

"She's about nine weeks...almost ten. I can't be exactly sure, but definitely over nine weeks," Dr. Tinsley answered him quietly with an anxious look stricken across her flushed red face.

Trigga felt a weight fall off of him with the surety that the baby Keisha was holding was not Lloyd's. That was one less issue on his list that needed to be dealt with.

"When can she go home?" Trigga asked in a low voice as he turned back towards her. He was about to look away when he saw something that caught his eye. A lone tear was traveling down the side of Keisha's face. Her eyes were closed, but she was awake.

"We would like to keep her a little longer, just because she's so malnourished. Also, we need to clean out her system, but she's fine otherwise. I would like to speak with her about substance abuse and getting her into a rehabilitation—"

"Save it. She won't be taking that shit ever again," Trigga cut in with his hand up in the air to signal the doctor to stop talking. "She'll be with me from now on, and she will be fine."

Dr. Tinsley eyed him for a minute before letting her guarded expression fall upon Keisha for a few seconds. Finally, she cleared her throat and shook away all traces of caution from her being as she prepared to say her final words.

"Okay, well, just a little longer until we can make sure she's well-nourished and she can be on her way," the woman chimed. "I'll also give her a prescription for some prenatal vitamins and a recommendation for an OB/GYN for the pregnancy."

Trigga nodded his head silently without looking at her. He was slightly bothered by the lack of care the doctor seemed to have for someone in Keisha's state, but he brushed it off. Doctors and hospitals were notoriously negligent when it came to the poor Blacks who needed services without the promise of payment from a large insurance company. In this case, Trigga was somewhat fortunate for it. He needed to get Keisha into his care at a private location, and he didn't need a nosy doctor to obstruct his plan.

As soon as the doctor exited the room, Trigga pulled up a chair so that he was sitting right next to Keisha's face, and stared right into it. Lifting a finger, he traced the outline of the dried tear that had fallen down the side of her face, and took a deep breath.

"I know you're up. We need to talk."

CHAPTER TWELVE

"WHAT IT DO, NIGGA?"

A malicious grin crossed Lloyd's face as he held an ice pack to the throbbing knot on his forehead. He grunted with annoyance at his situation as a sliver of ice cold liquid slid down his face from the melting ice pack, and fell into the cradle of skin under his bruised eye. Throwing the ice pack to the floor, he grabbed a half-smoked blunt from off the table next to him and prepared to light it, to calm his nerves that were frayed as a result of his fucked up day.

By the time he came to, he knew that Keisha and Luxe were long gone and even if he wanted to go after them, he ain't have shit in place to get them with. Trigga had done a great job of making sure every single one of his most trusted goons were dead, and he'd put a dent in their profits for the month by hitting each trap house and taking the money and dope. The bag of money and product that Luxe stole was all Lloyd had left without going into the city for more, and with Trigga murking all his niggas, he was on defense with no team to help him turn the tables. He needed help bad, and that's why he called on Austin.

"Aye, cuzzo, the fuck goin' on wit' you? Ain't heard from ya in a minute so I guess business been good," Austin said on the other line.

Something about his tone made Lloyd pause, as he contemplated hanging up the phone and waging war the way he did when he was nothing but a lil' nigga trying to come up in the hood. Him and Kenyon got it from the muscle without asking any nigga to help them. They were true to the heart jack boys and what they didn't have, they took it from the next nigga who had it. Lloyd had done it once, and he could do it again.

"Business ain't been all that good lately. You ain't heard?" Lloyd asked with his brow lifted with skepticism. He lit the blunt and pinched it between his fingers as he waited for Austin to respond.

He knew for a fact that Austin kept his ear to the streets on the daily. It didn't matter that he ran shit in Dallas; he always seemed to be on top of anything that went down in the streets of Atlanta that concerned Lloyd's EPG crew.

Austin was Lloyd's cousin on his mother's side. Like Lloyd, his mother also hailed from the Dominican Republic, but she'd married a ruthless Haitian drug lord and birthed Austin into the world. Austin was fair-skinned, but had a dark, evil countenance about him that intimidated everyone who met him. He had deep blue eyes that held a twinge of green and brown when he was at his happiest point, which meant that he was about to bring death to some poor, unfortunate soul.

Lloyd's mother and his were sisters, but they never got along and Lloyd's mother never liked Austin. Even on her death bed, she refused to see Austin, saying that he had the devil in his eyes. Lloyd often thought back to that day whenever his mind ventured off to the whereabouts or happenings of his cousin.

Lloyd watched with tears of anguish in his eyes as his mother, Hamida, struggled to take her last breaths with great effort and even greater pain. Holding her withered and weak hand firmly in his, he leaned over and kissed her on the forehead as she lay with her eyes closed, and a slight smile on her face as she reveled in her final moments spent with the person she loved the most in the world: her son.

She knew this moment was coming and she'd prepared him for this day. She'd taught him every single thing he needed to know in order to become the ruthless, powerful and supreme ruler like his father had been. And with his loyal and cunning cousin Kenyon by his side, Hamida could rest in peace knowing that her son would carry out the legacy of his father and live the life that was owed to him. His parents had lived a life of struggle, hunger, and pain, but Lloyd would ensure that no one in their line would ever struggle again. And with that thought, Hamida had peace.

A knock at the door put an end to the silence in the room that had, until that moment, only been accompanied by the occasional hum of the machines which kept Hamida comfortable in her final hours. Hamida's fingers tightened around Lloyd's fingers, and he gritted his teeth at being disturbed while he spent his last moments with his mother.

"Who's there?" Lloyd barked out gruffly, careful to not be too loud and disturb his mother.

"Aye, cuz, it's Austin. I just got in and I wanna see Aunty."

At the sound of Austin's voice, Hamida's eyes shot open and her fingers curled tightly around Lloyd's. Her chin dropped as her lips trembled, unable to sputter the words that she wanted to say. But her eyes held an expression of terror and warning as she looked off into the distance at something that only she could see.

Leaning in closer, a frown of trepidation and concern crossed Lloyd's face as he examined Hamida's sudden change of spirits. She was trying to tell him something, but he couldn't hear it.

"Mama, what is it?" Lloyd asked her as he leaned in closer, placing the rim of his ear nearly on the edge of her lips.

"Don't—don't let him come!"

Lloyd sat back and let his eyes wash over her as she repeated her words over and over again. He knew that Austin had never been her favorite person. When they were younger and Austin came to visit, she *rarely left them alone and she always watched Austin carefully as they played, with a cold, somewhat fearful look on her face.*

When Lloyd was older, he figured it was due to the racial tension between the Dominicans and the Haitians, which was also the reason why his Aunt Maria was thought of as the Black sheep of the family. Hamida marrying a Jamaican wasn't that much better, but she was their parents' favorite child so she'd never been ostracized as Maria had. But surely on her deathbed, she would put her hate for Austin's lineage aside and allow her nephew to pay his respects. Wouldn't she?

"Mama, da f—...dis is your nephew. He's fam!" *Lloyd tried to reason with his mother as he rubbed her shoulder and tried to calm her down. He turned around to look at Kenyon, who was sitting in a chair by the door with an equally bewildered expression on his face as he watched his aunt start flailing her arms, moving with strength that she hadn't possessed in the last couple weeks since her condition took a turn for the worst.*

The doorknob rattled as Austin prepared to enter. Hamida became even more animated and Lloyd flew to his feet with his face twisted with worry as he tried to figure out what was making her so upset. The door opened, and Austin stood at the entrance holding a bouquet of over a dozen roses, which partially covered his heavily tattooed face. He wore his customary sideways grin as he looked directly at his aunt, as if there was nothing amiss about the way she was staring at him, wide eyed with a look of absolute terror etched across her bluish-tinged, pale face.

"Hey, Aunty, you a'ight?" *Austin greeted nonchalantly as he entered the room.*

"Diablo!" *Hamida spat, raising one of her wrinkled fingers and pointing it straight at Austin.*

Lloyd teetered uneasily on the balls of his feet as he watched the exchange between the two of them. Hamida's health had declined drastically in the past few months, but the doctor hadn't said anything about the cancer spreading to her brain.

"Mama, no, that's Austin—"

"*DIABLO!*" *she yelled even louder.*

Stricken with disbelief and pain at his mother's condition, Lloyd turned to his cousins, first Kenyon then Austin, and threw his hands up helplessly.

"Ken, y'all get out of here. My bad, Austin," Lloyd said apologetically to his cousin as he ran his thumb over Hamida's hand to calm her. Her breathing was still elevated, but she had stopped fighting and was lying still in the bed, with her penetrating eyes focused directly on Austin.

With a blank face, Austin stood for a moment with his eyes on Hamida, returning her stern gaze before his face broke into a smile and he turned to Lloyd. Chuckling lightly, he shrugged and nodded to Lloyd.

"I understand, bro. Aye, let me just leave these, if that's a'ight wit' you," Austin said, lifting the vase of roses up. Lloyd nodded his head and moved to grab the vase from his cousin, but Austin took off walking towards Hamida's bedside. Hamida shrunk away from him as he walked over to the table next to her bed and dropped the vase on top.

"I love you, Aunty. May you rest in peace," he said quietly as Hamida glared at him with her thin lips twisted into a sneer. Lloyd watched on curiously, and kept his eyes on his cousin until he made his exit. Kenyon gave a pointed look at Lloyd before following behind him, out the door.

Although Hamida was supposed to die that night, per the physicians, she stayed alive for three additional days, until the moment she heard that Austin was on a plane headed back to Dallas. In her last breath, she asked Lloyd to be careful of his cousin.

Ever since then, Lloyd figured that it was Austin she'd been warning him about. But here he was calling Austin to help him in his time of need after his most trusted cousin, Kenyon, had betrayed him.

"I heard that you been hittin' hard times lately, courtesy of some New York nigga. And of course, somebody told me about that nigga Ken gettin' murked. My condolences, fam—"

"Man, fuck dat nigga," Lloyd chimed in. "Nigga turned on me over some dried up pussy. He was fuckin' around wit' Dior."

"Word?" Austin asked, sounding genuinely surprised.

I guess word of her thottin' ass ain't hit him yet, Lloyd thought to himself as he pulled from the blunt. He shook some of the ashes off onto the floor before he responded.

"Word. Bitch had me convinced that she was havin' my baby when all the while she was fuckin' that nigga. I tried to murk her and that ugly ass baby, but da bitch still alive."

"Damn, you killin' babies, my nigga?" Austin's laugh thundered through the phone in a way that made Lloyd frown.

Who da fuck laughs over a nigga killin' a muthafuckin' baby?

"Da fuck you laughin' 'bout dat shit fo'?"

"Wait, nigga, you *did* the shit and you tryna talk shit for me laughin'?"

With a deep crease settling across his forehead, Lloyd took the blunt from between his lips and adjusted in his seat. He talked while waving the blunt in the air, as if Austin was right in front of him to see his movement.

"Listen, I ain't wanna kill that bitch's baby. A nigga just snapped on some goon shit. Da bitch had me so muthafuckin' mad...I regretted dat shit as soon as I did it."

Silence invaded the space between them, then suddenly Austin exhaled heavily into the phone.

"Yeah, dats some sad shit," he said in a nonchalant manner, void of any real emotion. "Anyways, what you want nigga, because I know it's somethin'."

Now here it was, time to get to the reason for his call. Lloyd placed the blunt down on the table beside him, and put his feet squarely on the floor as he arranged the wording in his mind for what he wanted to say. Austin was his younger cousin and he didn't want him to think that he was being called to save a nigga. Truth was, Lloyd did need his help but his pride wouldn't let him recognize that fact or bow down to Austin's egotistical attitude that would soon reveal itself once Lloyd asked for his assistance.

"This nigga...Trigga, he the one been hittin' up my spots. He done murked all my top men and stole all my profits for the past couple weeks. I need you to come through and help me handle that nigga real quick. That's all," Lloyd told him quickly, as if it was no big favor that he was asking for.

In truth, it was. Both Lloyd and Austin knew that in order to help him get his operations back running and to toe-tag Trigga, Austin would have to leave his own operation in the hands of his most trusted members of his crew for a few weeks, to say the least. That was the amount of time it would take to get Lloyd's shit back in order. With all his leaders dead, ain't no telling what was going on in the streets of Atlanta; and with Lloyd being unheard of since his crew started dropping like flies, niggas probably were running wild in the streets.

"I got you, cuz. My shit squared away so it ain't nothin' for me to come bail you out real quick," Austin responded with a cool tone that made Lloyd's blood boil.

He swallowed down the urge to tell Austin to forget it and stay the fuck out his city, and simply nodded his head.

"A'ight," he muttered as he grabbed the keys to his old school Cadillac that he kept out back behind the house. It was the first whip he'd copped on his own, so he kept it as a tribute to that achievement. It would be his ride into town until he was able to get back on top of his shit. He didn't need to be in nothing too flashy that would bring attention to himself.

"I'll be on the next thang comin' in tomorrow. Call ya when I get in, lil' cuz," Austin added.

Instantly enraged, Lloyd cringed and stood up so fast that his knees bumped the coffee table in front of him, flipping it onto its side.

"Don't start wit' dat 'lil' cuz' shit, nigga. I don't play dat shit," Lloyd reminded him.

"You know I don't mean nothin' by that shit." Austin's words were accompanied by a dry laugh, but Lloyd didn't see shit funny.

That 'lil' cuz' shit was something Austin started saying to point towards the fact that he was a full two inches taller than Lloyd was. At 6'4, Lloyd was taller than the average man, but Austin never let go of an opportunity to remind him that he stood over him at 6'6.

Without responding, Lloyd hung up the phone and grabbed the keys up that had fallen from his hands when he stood up. Taking a second to peer out the window, he saw that the sun was making its descent to give way to his ally: the night sky. Pulling up the app on his phone, he clicked the button to track down the location of his BMW. Although he was sure that Luxe had long ago abandoned it, he wasn't in any position to leave a whip of his unaccounted for.

Peering down at the location that displayed on the screen, his face twisted up in astonishment as he recognized the address on the display. It was the address to a location he frequented often, *Pink Lips.*

Could it be that Luxe was still in possession of the car, and was stupid enough to go back to her place of employment with hopes that Lloyd would forgive her for her transgressions and welcome her back by his side?

Bitch must have believed all that bullshit I was tellin' her, Lloyd thought with a chuckle as he pulled on his shirt and walked hurriedly to the front door. *Pussy ain't that damn good.*

Placing a hoodie on his head to cover his identity, as well as the bulging knot that graced his head courtesy of Keisha, the bitch breathing on borrowed time that he should never have granted her, Lloyd stepped outside of his country home and stood on the front stoop as he thought over his plan.

The first nigga on his list to be dealt with, after bodying Luxe at the club, would be Trigga. With the help of Austin, that would be an easy feat. Next would be that bitch Keisha. With Trigga dead first, there would be no reason to keep her ass breathing because he wouldn't need the bait. Her death would come fast, just so he could get the shit over with.

CHAPTER THIRTEEN

"I just want to go hoooome," Keisha whined as Trigga watched her with a straight face.

He was trying his best to mask his anger at everything that she'd told him but the more he thought about it, the closer he got to failing miserably. Sighing, he bent forward and ran his hands over his face as he tried to quiet the unrest in his body that only grew with every moment that he spent next to Keisha's hospital bed, instead of out in the streets finding Lloyd and making him pay for what he'd done.

But he couldn't be two places at once.

To focus on Lloyd meant to leave Keisha, and to be with Keisha meant that Lloyd was able to walk freely in the streets. His mind was torn between two desires, which left him in a place of turmoil where he was content with having the woman he loved by his side. But he was infuriated with the reality that making sure she was breathing and out of harm's way meant that Lloyd was granted the same liberties.

Gritting his teeth together, Trigga stood up and tore his eyes away from Keisha's pleading face. He reached over her head and pressed the red button on the wall to call for a doctor. The machines in the room beeped intermittently as the weight of his reality weighed heavily on his mind.

Keisha lifted her eyes and, with a tender and gentle expression on her face, tried to deliver an unspoken message to him that relayed to him her needs. She needed to be somewhere safe, with only the two of them there. She was tired of the harsh life of crime and pain that she'd been pulled into. She needed Trigga to leave that all behind so they could move on with their lives and put the past behind them.

Even still, as he stared into her eyes, reflecting the same love for her that she felt for him, she knew that her wishes of a peaceful present and future were futile at the moment. Trigga would not stop until he'd had his revenge on Lloyd.

"How can I help you?" an older African-American woman asked, walking into the room.

She had on pink scrubs with cartoon characters throughout, as if she should have been working on the children's floor. Her annoyed and frazzled demeanor sharply contrasted with her joyous appearance as she lumbered into the room, dragging her feet as if she'd worked two full days.

"When can I leave?" Keisha asked suddenly, without waiting for Trigga to respond.

The woman's dark eyes traveled from Keisha's face to Trigga, who was staring at her expectantly as he awaited her response. With a sigh and her mouth pulled into a thin line, the woman walked over and grabbed Keisha's chart from outside the door, then began flipping through it with her brows pulled into a tight frown. She sucked her teeth as her eyes washed over a particular portion of the notes made by the doctor before she snapped the folder closed and, walked closer to where Keisha lay.

"Honey, you are dehydrated and from the looks of this, you haven't had a proper meal in weeks. You have a slight infection from where you were shot...although you claim that whatever is on your leg is not from a bullet," the woman looked at Keisha with deep-seated skepticism.

"You came in with an incredibly high amount of drugs in your system, and you will definitely suffer from withdrawals once they wear off. You have two fractured ribs that have been treated, your blood pressure is incredibly high and needs to be monitored...there are a host of other issues. But on top of everything, you are pregnant and your baby is in danger as long as you are in your current condition. So, to put it bluntly...you will be here for a few days at least," she finished as she snapped the folder closed and gave Keisha a look of concern.

Turning to Trigga, she said, "And you...if you care for her and your child, the best thing you can do for her is let us treat her. Letting her leave would put both of their lives at risk."

"But the doctor said—"

"Dr. Tinsley is a resident doctor," the nurse informed Keisha, cutting her off. "She's in training under the guidance of an attending physician here. Per the notes in your chart, that physician is not willing to sign off on your discharge until your health is in order."

With a look of desperation, Keisha turned to Trigga in hopes that he would speak up on her behalf to demand that she be allowed free to leave. When she saw the disheartened expression on his face, it erased the last ray of hope that she had of being released. There was no way Trigga was going to allow her to leave knowing that it would put her and their baby in danger.

"We will stay and follow every recommendation the doctor has," Trigga responded sincerely with a stern look.

The nurse's face lifted as she beamed at him with approval of his determination to take care of Keisha, in spite of her objections. Nodding her head once, she turned around and walked out of the room.

"I don't wanna stay," Keisha pled as soon as the door closed, announcing the nurse's exit.

Trigga let his eyes run over her face. With a sigh, he observed the beads of sweat sprouting up at her hairline. She was beginning to sweat, although it was so cold in the room it was a wonder their breaths didn't fog up around their face. The withdrawals were starting.

"You heard what she said, didn't you?" he asked her as he reached out and wiped the moisture off her forehead. Keisha nodded her head 'yes' as her eyes blinked heavily, as if she were exhausted.

"Okay, then you know there ain't no way I'm lettin' you leave," he told her.

"Are you goin' to stay wit' me?" she asked him, biting her bottom lip.

With a trembling hand, she reached up and started scratching hard at her chin. With her eyes squeezed closed, the scratching grew increasingly more forceful as if she were trying to break the skin. Trigga crinkled his nose as he watched her move from her neck to her arm, still digging into her flesh as she tried to satiate her discomfort.

"I'll..." Trigga started, pausing when Keisha looked at him with hopeful eyes. It crushed him to see her needing something from him that he knew, at the moment, he wouldn't be able to give her.

"I gotta go, but I promise I'll be right back," he told her, sliding his eyes to the side to avoid the downtrodden look he knew was in hers.

Grabbing his hand from by his side, Keisha fought for his attention as she struggled to deliver her plea.

"Don't leave! Please...let's just forget about it all. Forget Lloyd, forget Queen...forget it all! I just want you. Please," she begged.

By this time, her face was completely covered in sweat as she fought with desperation for Trigga to listen to her and take heed to her words. Her heart was beating a mile a minute, and she felt like her entire body was on fire. Her energy was waning and she felt like she wanted to go to sleep, but she was too uncomfortable to do so. She felt as if she were covered with ants, running rapidly under her flesh; the more she scratched at the skin above them, the more furiously they traipsed throughout her body.

But above all, there was the feeling of panic that flooded her consciousness. She couldn't bear to be alone again with only her thoughts to provide her with comfort. She'd spent so much time alone when Lloyd held her captive that the thought of Trigga leaving her scared her more than anything else ever had. Coupled with the fact that she knew what he wanted to leave to do, and the possibility that he may never return, Keisha was terrified almost beyond words.

"Just stay wit' me, please!" she uttered once again as Trigga stared at her with an unreadable expression on his face. When he shook his head 'no' and cast his eyes away, her heart broke.

"You don't love me!" Keisha spat out, delivering her hardest blow and hoping that it would hit as hard as intended. "If you did, you wouldn't do this! Look at me...look at what I've been through! This is because of you, it's all because of you! But I'm alive and if you loved me, you would leave this shit alone and be here for me and our child! You wouldn't be runnin' to follow the orders given to you from some fuckin' fake ass ghetto queen."

Until that point, Trigga had been holding back his words for fear that he would upset Keisha, who was already dealing with the beginning stages of drug withdrawal and had more to come; but to hear her speak to him in a way that doubted his love for her infuriated him, and he couldn't leave her accusations unchecked.

"The fuck you talkin' 'bout, Keesh?!" he barked back at her as he moved closer to her bedside and leaned in so close to her face that their noses were almost touching. "Who the fuck you think I'm doin' this shit for? This is beyond Queen! This is about the fact that a muthafucka messed wit' my woman...my child! I don't give a fuck about no other bitch right now but you!"

Backing away from her bedside, Trigga fell back and slowly pulled the hood on the back of his sweatshirt up and covered his head. His grey eyes were so dark that they looked more charcoal rather than their normally smoky grey as he spoke.

"You right tho'," he said finally. "This all happened to you because of me. And I'ma finish it. I ain't no soft ass nigga, Keesh. I been doin' this shit since I was seven years old. I don't expect you to understand all that, but the night you jumped yo' ass into my whip, you welcomed ya'self into my life. I'm a hood nigga, and I'll be damned if I let a muthafucka roam free after he chose to fuck wit' mine."

Tears of frustration and helplessness traveled down Keisha's cheeks as she listened to Trigga's words. As with everything that he said, they were spoken from the heart and she knew there was nothing that could be done to counter his determination. He was leaving, and that was that. The only thing she could do was pray that he would return.

Trigga walked forward and placed his hand on Keisha's stomach as he stared down at it, thinking of his child. There in that room, right in front of him, was everything that mattered in the world to him. In fact, this was his world: his baby and Keisha. Never before had he been so certain that anything was worth dying for before then, in that moment. He would bring Lloyd to an end, even if it killed him in the process.

"Do you love me?" Keisha asked him as she looked at him through tear-filled eyes.

Trigga paused for a second, and then licked his lips. A small smile graced the edge of his lips.

"Do I look like a lovin' ass nigga?" he inquired, lightening the tense mood around them.

Keisha made a snorting sound, the closest she could get to a giggle without causing herself more pain than she was already in.

"Yeah, actually you do," she responded.

Trigga leaned down and kissed her on the forehead first, then the lips. When he pulled up and looked into her face, her eyelids had grown heavier as she struggled to keep her eyes open. He knew she would be sleeping soon.

"I am," he whispered before turning around and walking away from her.

With every step, he had to fight a battle in his mind and ignored the warnings sounding off that told him he needed to stay and watch after her...to make sure that nothing happened to her. Shrugging them off, he walked out of the door into the busy hallway of the hospital and closed the door behind him.

The only way I can really protect her is to leave, he thought to himself as he continued on towards the elevators.

Although he knew this was true, he still couldn't rid himself of the prickly feeling traveling up his spine that normally signified that there was more pain, hurt, and agony left for him to experience.

CHAPTER FOURTEEN

"Mrs. Mitchell-Ev—"

"Ms. Mitchell," Dior corrected without looking towards the person who she heard walking into her room.

She continued to look out the window next to her bed, even when she could feel the person's presence next to her. She didn't want to turn to them because she knew it would encourage them to speak, and she couldn't bear any more bad news. She felt absolutely numb. To be told that she would possibly never walk again, that her child was missing, and the man she loved and expected to spend her life with was dead was traumatizing to her. The only way that she'd been able to deal with all of that was to pretend that she had no feelings whatsoever. She couldn't take feeling anything, because then all she would feel would be her pain.

"Ms. Mitchell...I think I have someone who you would like to see," the female voice said from behind her. Dior could hear the smile in her tone.

Still facing the window, Dior frowned to herself and could feel herself getting annoyed. Everyone in the hospital had to know about the woman who had been screaming and crying out in agony for the past few days because she was paralyzed and her child was gone. So why would anyone come into her room, actually, walk into her room happy about something? Didn't she know that nothing or no one could bring her joy?

"Listen, I—" Dior started, turning around with attitude all over her face as she prepared to tell the woman where she could shove her annoying ass, along with her happy-go-lucky attitude.

But she stopped short when she saw that the woman was holding a baby in her arms. Her baby. Immediately, Dior's mouth and eyes opened wide and tears came to her eyes.

"Oh my God! You found her!" Dior exclaimed.

She stared at her daughter, who looked absolutely perfect. After carefully inspecting every part of her that she could see, she let out a deep breath, satisfied that not a hair was harmed on her child's head. Then, as any mother would do, she tried to reach out to grab her baby so that she could hold her in her arms, smell her hair, and hold her close to her chest. But she couldn't. Fresh tears came to Dior's eyes as she remembered her predicament. She couldn't move. She couldn't even hold Karisma now that she had her back.

The nurse's expression changed as she looked at Dior, and it was obvious that she understood the sudden change in Dior's mood.

"Here," she offered. "I can scoot you down a bit and make a spot on your chest where she can lay and rest against your neck and face. You'll be able to feel her there."

Dior nodded slowly and tried to blink the tears away as the young, red-haired woman cradled Karisma in one arm and moved about the room, using one hand to get everything in order. When she was finally finished creating the spot on Dior's chest for Karisma to lay, she sat her down and pushed the light pink sheets she was swaddled in up around her to create a barrier, and sat in a chair near Dior just in case she was needed.

Dior bent her neck down and looked in her daughter's eyes. Karisma looked just as happy, cheerful, and innocent as the last time she'd seen her when she was giggling in her father's arms. Closing her eyes, she nestled her nose into her daughter's hair and took a deep breath. Her hair smelled like Johnson & Johnson baby shampoo. The fresh scent warmed Dior's heart. She hadn't thought she would ever smell that scent again. She thought her baby was gone forever.

"Where did they find her?" she finally asked the nurse as she kissed the top of Karisma's head.

"Someone left her at a fire station about a block away from the hospital. They brought her here and we ran some tests on her, which let us know exactly who her mother was. I'm so happy that she is okay. In light of everything you've been facing, you needed this," the woman said with a sincere smile on her face as she looked at Dior. She was pregnant herself, only by three months, so she barely showed. Every day that she tended to Dior made her think of her own unborn child, who she had yet to meet but loved dearly. She could only imagine what Dior must have been going through.

"There is one other thing," the woman added. Dior looked over at her and saw that she had an uneasy expression on her face.

Oh God...not any more bad news, she thought to herself.

"The detective who was here a few days ago...he wants to ask you more questions. Dr. Stephens tried to keep him away as much as possible, saying that you weren't in a state that you could speak to them, but he is pretty adamant about pressing forward with his case."

Dior sat silently for a while as she thought about all the things that had happened in the past few weeks. She was paralyzed, Kenyon was dead, but Karisma was unharmed. If she was honest about everything, she had to admit that her and Kenyon knew what they were dealing with when they decided to target Lloyd. The only innocent one was Karisma, and she was unharmed, but her and Kenyon knew death was a possible ending for them if they carried out their plans. Karma was definitely a bitch, because both of them got punished severely for their actions. Now the only one left to get what he deserved was Lloyd and if she could help, she was all in.

"No, it's okay. I'm fine. I'll speak to him," Dior said. She turned back to Karisma and kissed her again on her head. The girl giggled, reached up, and grabbed at Dior's chin, which made her and the nurse smile.

"I have my baby back, so I'll do whatever I have to do to make sure she's never hurt again."

"Ms. Mitchell, you look like you're doing a lot better today!"

Blinking away the memory from months ago when Karisma was finally returned to her, Dior turned around and gave a tight smile to the young, attractive, almond-colored woman who was standing in the doorway. She eyed her up and down quickly before grabbing the list of duties she'd scribbled down and held them out for her to grab.

"Thank you, Janae," Dior stated as she waited for her to walk over and grab the piece of paper from her fingertips. "There's not much that I need you to do today. My mother has been helping me as much as she can, but I've been trying to get her not to since she has issues with her back. Anyway, here you are."

Twirling one of her braids around her forefinger, Janae read the list quickly to herself and then tucked it into her pants pocket before smiling once more at Dior. She was only about eighteen years old, and already worked as hard as a woman with a family of five to feed, although she only had one son.

Janae came from an impoverished background with an alcoholic mother and an absentee father. At thirteen, she became pregnant with her son, who was born as a result of puppy love. Once she told her boyfriend that she was pregnant, his mother moved him across the country to stay with his father and left her to be a single mother, struggling towards finishing her schooling to obtain her diploma. Currently, Janae was in a program for single mothers like her which would lead to her obtaining her nursing degree.

Something about her struggle resonated with Dior when she was first looking for someone to help her around the house with the baby, all while she tried to come to terms with the idea that she was paralyzed, and would be a single mother to Karisma with no one around to help her. She hired her immediately after learning of her story, even though she hadn't yet been released from the hospital.

Soon after hiring Janae, Dior's mother came to the hospital, to her utter surprise. She told her that the Dior's doctors had called her since she was still listed as her emergency contact, and she'd convinced her father to let her come back home as long as Lloyd was no longer in the picture. In the matter of a few months, Dior's life had drastically changed from being the pampered, top label-bearing wife of a hood king, to the wheelchair-bound, penniless, single mother everyone now saw her as. Although her situation had changed, Karisma's presence and love was the perfect addition to her every day.

Dior's cell phone started to vibrate against the specially made changing table across the room, creating a light rumbling sound that made Karisma stir slightly in her crib. Dior wheeled over to the table, which was made at the perfect height for her, and grabbed the iPhone. Checking the caller ID, she sighed to herself and mentally prepared herself to answer the call.

It was her doctor. Dior prayed, the same as she did every time he called, that this time he would be delivering good news.

"Hi Dr. Stephens," Dior said with a melancholy tone as she glanced at Karisma to make sure that she wasn't disturbing her sleep. The beautiful little girl continued to sleep with her thumb secured between her soft lips as she sucked heavily, pulling herself back into a deep sleep.

"Hello Dior, how is everything going today?" Dr. Stephens asked in his normal carefree and comforting tone.

"I'm good...considering," Dior responded. She glanced at the mirror that sat on top of Karisma's bamboo-colored dresser and stared at her reflection. She could barely recognize herself. No matter how much time had passed, she still wasn't used to seeing herself in this way.

"That's good to hear, for the most part," Dr. Stephens replied curtly. "Listen...I wanted to check with you again on this, because from what we're seeing, the feeling in your body should be returning to you. Are you sure you don't feel anything at all?"

Dior shook her head sadly before responding, "No...nothing. I don't understand why...am I doing something wrong?"

"No! It isn't you, I promise," he assured her. "Sometimes these things just take time. What I need you to do is to just keep doing everything you're doing. Keep tending to Karisma. One day, hopefully sooner than later, you will feel something and then each day, you'll feel more and more. Just...make sure if you feel anything at all that you give me a call, okay?"

"I promise I will let you know as soon as I feel anything," Dior told him. Hearing a rustling sound behind her, she turned and noticed that Karisma was wide awake and staring right at her, with a hint of a smile across her chocolate face. Dior smiled at her daughter, then tucked the phone so that it was held securely by her chin as she wheeled over to her.

"Thank you. Have a good one!"

"I will. And thank you." Dior hung up the phone and dropped it in the crib as she lowered the side so that she could pull Karisma into her arms.

A sliver of fluorescent sunlight spilled in through the room, and shined on Karisma's bright face as she giggled in Dior's arms. Her laughter was everything that was right in the world, although there was so much that was wrong.

Dior leaned over and placed her on the floor in front of her toy chest. Like a prisoner who'd just served twenty-five years and was now set free, Karisma took off in a mad dash on her hands and knees towards the chest, and wobbled to a seated position as she grabbed at one of her favorite toys. As soon as the rattle was secure in her pudgy fingers, she shook it for a few seconds before popping it directly into her mouth.

Laughing softly as she watched the sight, Dior admired her daughter once more before she reached out for her cell phone. Even though she was reminded of Lloyd every time she glanced at her, it did nothing to dim her love for her child. Karisma was every bit of her father, even down to her stubborn and authoritative personality. It was her way or none at all, a trait she'd definitely received by way of Lloyd.

"Hello?" Dior spoke into the receiver of her phone when she felt the line pick up. She glanced towards the entrance of the room to make sure that no one was standing near and able to listen to her call.

"Aye, what's gud, ma?" the deep voice responded on the other line.

"Just checking in with you. You know you're my only connection to the outside world," Dior chuckled, pulling a long tendril of her dark black hair behind her ear.

She bit softly on her pinky fingernail as she smiled into the phone. For the last few weeks since Kenyon's death, she'd been speaking to an old friend who had been helping her get over losing him. Never before had she felt anything romantic for him, but there was something about a nigga being there in your time of need that always made a chick grow weak in the knees. Every now and then, she felt herself longing for him to send a texted response or something, but she tried to shake the feeling off. It didn't go away though.

"Yea, you tell me dat shit like you need me or s'umthin'. You got dat package I sent you?"

"I got it," Dior answered with a full smile.

She glanced over at Karisma once more as she hoisted herself up so that she was standing on her two feet as she reached into the chest. She was only nearly four months old and was already pulling up. Her advancement in that area almost seemed as if it were a gift from God, making sure that in Dior's weakness, Karisma was strong and had abilities that most children didn't develop until later on.

"Don't spend it all in one place," he laughed as Dior rolled her eyes.

"I couldn't even if I tried! Anyways, you heard anything about Lloyd?"

"You know I have. Nigga in hiding or some shit because some dude named Trigga been hittin' up all his trap houses and straight murkin' his crew. One nigga done single-handedly destroyed damn near all of EPG. Dat shit is funny as hell to me. How in da fuck dat shit happen?"

"He trying to take over?" Dior asked. She frowned and looked towards the ceiling as she racked her brain to think on where she had heard of the name Trigga. It sounded remotely familiar to her for some reason.

"Naw, don't seem like it. But you kno' I'ma find out more 'bout dat cat."

"When you do, tell me. I gotta make sure me and Karisma are safe."

"I got'chu," he replied. "But for now, you stay where you are. It ain't safe for you to come into the city. I wish you woulda listened to a nigga and moved out here."

"Naw, I couldn't do that," Dior said sadly, shaking her head. "My parents wouldn't have me go anywhere away from them once they found out what was goin' on. But they are about an hour outside of the city, so I'm good."

"I woulda moved they asses, too!" he piped up, making Dior almost fall over with laughter.

Suddenly, a loud slamming sound sounded off in Dior's ears and Karisma's cries of anguish filled the air. Turning sharply in her seat, Dior's mouth dropped when she saw that Karisma had fallen head-first into the toy chest with her tiny feet dangling in the air, waving back and forth ferociously as she tried with all her might to get out.

Throwing the phone to the floor, Dior jumped to her feet and ran over to the chest, yanking Karisma from the chest as fast as she could. As she turned her over, she examined every bit of her body to make sure that she was okay as Karisma continued to cry out to the top of her lungs, showcasing every bit of her gums.

"MS. MITCHELL!" Janae yelled out. Her voice was followed by loud thumps as she ran through the hall towards the room.

Panicked, Dior slid down to the floor, making sure not to cause any more harm to Karisma, and pulled her wheelchair down with her to set the scene for her lie.

"OH MY GOD!" Janae shrieked when she entered the room and saw Dior sprawled out on the floor with the overturned wheelchair lying over her ankles. "What happened?!"

Dior winced in mock pain as she held Karisma out to Janae and breathed laboriously.

"She fell in the toy chest...I tried to get to her but my chair..." Dior gritted her teeth and twisted her face in agony.

"Oh my God!" Janae repeated.

She placed Karisma in the crib, and then pulled the wheelchair off of Dior. Hoisting her up over her shoulders, she helped Dior rise from the floor and held her breath as she mustered up the strength to usher her back into her wheelchair.

"Are you okay?" Janae asked as she bent down to look Dior right in her face.

Her eyes traveled over Dior's body quickly as she tried to look for any sign of injury. Dior nodded her head quickly, and let out a forced laugh to assure Janae that all was well.

"I'm good now. I'm sorry...so stupid of me but she was in danger and I—I—I couldn't help her!" With a trembling lip, Dior broke out into tears and placed her hands over her face as Janae rubbed gently across her back, and made a shushing sound to calm her.

"It's okay, don't cry," Janae told her as she ran her hand back and forth over her back. "That's what I'm here for. You have me and soon you'll be better. Don't worry."

Wiping the tears from her eyes, Dior smiled gratefully up into Janae's eyes and sniffed. She took a deep breath and brushed away her hair from her face.

"You're right. One day, I'll be able to walk again. I'm okay."

With a smile of encouragement, Janae delivered two pats to Dior's back and stood up to walk out of the room. As Dior watched her walk away, she breathed a sigh of relief that she'd been able to hold on to her secret a while longer.

CHAPTER FIFTEEN

"I GOT HIS FUCK ASS," LLOYD SNEERED WITH MALICE.

He had blood in his eyes. As he watched Mase ahead of him, his first thought was to roll right up and pop him—one to the cranium—and keep it moving. It took everything in his power not to. Never in his life could he ever remember a time a nigga had straight up played him the way Mase had, by claiming Trigga was dead and that he had murked him himself. Lloyd fell for the lame's game—hook, line and sinker.

And not just that, Lloyd had reason to believe Mase could have been behind the reason Luxe escaped with Keisha again. Keisha had robbed him for the second time, but it was all starting to make sense. Maybe dumbass Mase was the mastermind! Then on second thought, Lloyd knew it couldn't make sense because Mase was as close to mentally retarded as they come. Or was it all an act?

Just goes to show you, you can never underestimate a nigga, not even a dumb ass nigga like Mase, Lloyd thought as he crept into the parking lot.

It took everything in his power to fight the urge to splatter his brains on the concrete pavement.

MASE WAS POSTED up outside of *Pink Lips* with the widest grin plastered on his hideous face. He donned a pair of Gucci shades he had found in the glove compartment of Lloyd's car to hide the large, hideous shiner on his eye. His entire appearance with the expensive car and name brand shades seemed to have rejuvenated him and changed his swag. He felt like a rock star, even with the disastrous and crooked bucked teeth in his mouth. He just reveled in the attention of the money hungry hoes around him.

Mase was sitting on top of Lloyd's nearly new, dark blue BMW that was most likely the reason for all the attention he was getting, because from his clothes and disheveled appearance, he ain't have shit else poppin'.

Looks could be deceiving, and Mase was the best example of that.

Lloyd had crept into the parking lot of the club unnoticed, which was no surprise to him. Usually, he made sure that anything he rode in had just the right amount of flashiness to pull the attention of anyone in a three-mile radius, but this time he was whipping around in the Caddie so he could be low-key. From the looks of things, his plan was working.

Turning the engine off, Lloyd grabbed his banger from the passenger seat next to him and opened up the door slowly. As soon as he stepped one foot outside the car, he stifled a groan as pain ricocheted throughout his body from when Keisha struck him with the car. He also sported a golf ball-size knot on his forehead that was so big, it was hard to conceal with his red A-Town fitted cap.

The old Caddie door screeched a complaint as he shut the door and grimaced in pain, causing him to take several deep breaths. Yes he was hurting, but it would be nothing in comparison to what he intended to do to Mase, he thought as he took off walking with a serious limp. Mase was only about thirty yards away when Lloyd startled a flock of pigeons, causing them to fly overhead to their sanctuary in the sky, as if they sensed the deadly confrontation about to erupt. The birds' abrupt flight created a sinister shadow over his face as he kept his eyes focused on Mase, his target.

As Lloyd neared, getting closer, he was only ten yards or so away with his hand on the trigger. Mase was ahead of him with his back turned, licking his lips as he ran his fat finger down the front of an ebony stripper's body. He swiped his hand behind her body and gripped her fat ass that stuck out deliciously from beyond her tiny, gold-sequined, coochie-cutter shorts.

The chick giggled as she sauntered closure between Mase's open legs as he sat on the hood of the car, stuntin' like it was his. Her booty jiggled effortlessly, like the pro she was, with each movement as if tempting him. The whole while, danger lurked as Lloyd crept up from behind. All Mase had to do was turn around, but his attention was focused on the bodacious big booty chick standing in front of him doing a sensuous dick tease. She playfully stroked her long, pink manicured fingernails, gyrating a figure eight up, down, and across his pants zipper, causing Mase to get an erection. A large pre-cum stain was visible on the front of his pants. The chick had him, and she knew it. The other three girls standing around gave each other identical looks that acknowledged the fact that the ebony chick had won out, and they had been defeated, before all turning to walk inside the club and prepare for a night of work.

Mase's eyes focused on what he was certain was a pussy lip between her bowed, thick legs. He licked his lips as he then stared at her hard nipples, the size of Christmas light bulbs, on the prettiest set of delicious double D's he had ever looked at. The entire time, her lady parts continued to jiggle with each practiced movement as she played with his zipper.

Lloyd had closed the distance. He had the perfect opportunity to approach Mase without being noticed, and slump him without resistance. He eased his hand onto his banger in his pants but instead, Lloyd had something better in mind, something more sinister. If only he could bridle his urge not to kill him in broad daylight and not catch a case because of a bunch of bitches watching.

Lloyd thought for a second about extracting information from him, like where was Keisha and Luxe at with all his muthafuckin' money and dope? And, most importantly, how was his dumb ass able to rock him to sleep with that lie about he had murked his twin brother Trigga, when the whole while Trigga had masterfully been on some serious gangsta shit wreaking havoc on his trap houses?

Lloyd eased right up to Mase, bobbing slightly and inconspicuously, making sure that Mase could feel the hard, cold steel of the .9mm pressed against his ribs.

"Fuck nigga, I got yo' bitch ass. You was tryna run but I'ma wet yo' bitch ass up," Lloyd said with grit in his voice and vengeful, red bloodshot eyes.

Mase had been so engrossed with the fact that he was about to possibly get a shot of ass from a bad ass stripper bitch without spending a dime that he didn't even know what was happening until it had happened. As soon as he turned and saw Lloyd, his jaw dropped and his body did some type of jerky motion like he wanted to take off running, but his legs refused to oblige. His lips just began to move silently without words. To any unsuspecting person, it looked like he was about to go into shock, or was about to have an epileptic seizure. But the reality was he was about to get shot.

"And bitch ass nigga, how you get my car?!" Lloyd yelled. He was so angry, a large vein protruded from the middle of his forehead as he reached up and snatched the Gucci glasses off Mase's face, and the large shiner had grown so big it had turned deep purple. Mase's eye was completely closed.

"Damn nigga, what the fuck happened to your face? You need to learn how duck or some shit," the big booty chick said with a frown, like she smelled something as she clutched her bosom, taking an apprehensive step back. She then added with a frown. "...and this ain't YOUR car?" Her voice came out in a high-pitched angry tone, like she had just realized she had spent her time finessing his ugly ass and to find out he was both ugly and broke. He had just committed the cardinal sin, to be a fake baller at a stripper's club.

She then scrolled her eyes over to Lloyd; he had on a Rolex watch and was dressed nice. Right then, a light bulb went off in her head. She recognized who he was instantly as much as him and his boys frequented the club. She gave him her full attention and smiled as she pushed her double D breasts up in his face like pussy on a platter.

"So this your whip, Black?" she cajoled while giving Lloyd a sexy once over like he could get it, and placed a hand on her curvy slim waist.

Lloyd must have looked like a mass murderer from the way he was locked in on Mase, with his hand concealed in his pocket and fiery blood red eyes.

It didn't take long for her to figure out something was wrong, terribly wrong. She abruptly turned and strutted off with a brisk pace, her hips rotating seductively with each step, making her booty bounce from side to side with each urgent stride.

"M-m-m- lemme talk, let me explain."

Lloyd pressed his lips tight and flashed him the chrome-plated tool that sat securely in his pants' pocket.

"Get yo' bitch ass in the trunk, fuck nigga. You wanna play games, I'ma show you how to play the game...gon' see can you swim in the ocean, hogtied with a three-hundred-pound backpack strapped on your punk ass," Lloyd said barely above a whisper. His voice was like dry ice dragged across sandpaper.

"The trunk??" Mase quipped wide eyed; his eyebrows shot up nearly to his hairline as he continued and gestured with his hands. "Come on man, don't do this. I can expla—"

WHAM!

Lloyd struck him upside the head so hard that Mase did a full 360 turn as the blow dazed him and opened up a deep gash. Mase began to do the two-step like he was listening to one of his grandmother's old melodies in his head; he wobbled on his legs as if he was drunk.

A group of women just happened to be walking by on their way to work at the club; some of them were dressed in leggings, or tight-fitting blue jeans.

One of the women exhorted, horrified with her hand over her mouth, "Ohhh shit girl, he just knocked a patch of hair out that dude's head to the white meat."

Another female chimed in, "Somebody get Cash or call the cops or somethin', he gon' kill 'em!" They scurried by and rushed inside the club.

Lloyd could not help but to overhear the conversation, even though it felt like his mind was in a fugue. The only thing that mattered was killing Mase, but since Mase was semi-unconscious and leaking blood, Lloyd abandoned the idea of getting Mase in the trunk. He needed to just get him in the car and get out of there.

He quickly walked over and opened the passenger door as he dragged Mase along like he was his hostage, droplets of blood staining the worn concrete red. Mase almost tripped and fell on his face as Lloyd shoved him.

"So you set me up, huh?"

WHAM!

Lloyd struck him again, that time with the butt of the banger on the side of Mase's head.

"I s—s—swear, I didn't know this was yours! The bitch that gave it to me worked here! Sh—sh—she said I could have it!" Mase stuttered as he stood next to the driver's seat with his hands in the air, and blood streaming down his face and neck. "I saw her over near the Greyhound station...I'on kno' what's going on! I'm innocent!"

"No nigga, you guilty, and you tried a nigga like a sucka! Now get your bitch ass in the car or I'ma push your wig back right here. Try me nigga," Lloyd said, prepared to do serious bodily harm and possibly catch a body in broad daylight.

Mase feigned being more hurt then he actually was. He knew if he got in the car, the next stop would be at his gravesite. To get in would be suicide.

Mase placed his foot on the door's step, resisting to get in. They began to tussle. Lloyd was going to bust on him right there in front of the club.

"Man lemme explain, pah-leas," Mase pleaded for his life with tears in his voice.

"Fuck dat shit. Nigga, I'ma blow yo' fuckin' brains out. From what I heard, yo' brotha ain't dead! What kind of games you playin'? You think this a joke nigga? Now you ridin' around in my mutha-fuckin' shit. What, you was part of them bitches that set me up nigga, you think this a game?"

Lloyd was livid. He reached over and grabbed Mase by his dirty shirt and shoved the barrow of the banger into his mouth, nearly breaking his front teeth as he cocked it.

"Pussy ass nigga, you set me up. Get your bitch ass in the car!" Lloyd said like a craved maniac as people began to rush by gawking at them. Truth be told, this was nothing new; every week or two, there was a shooting or a fight outside the club, but not normally in broad daylight.

"No! Man, pah-leas!"

Mase wailed and broke down, and began sobbing pitifully as the words came out gurgled with the gun jammed in his mouth. A trickle of blood ran down Mase's chin and his body went rigid, stiff as a board. He prepared for the inevitable and began to flail his arms, yelling for help. Lloyd was set on murking him and the situation was getting worse.

Just as Lloyd was about to squeeze the trigger and catch a case with an audience of strippers that were streaming out the club of watching, Cash, the club's owner, a short rotund of a man with hound dog eyes, rushed through the crowd and up to the vehicle as the two men tussled. The short trek of rushing nearly fifteen feet had him winded when he began to speak, with a stub of a cigar smoldering in his mouth, his brow creased with perspiration and a slight wheezing sound coming from his lungs.

"Come on Black, man, you gon' kill 'em. Don't do it man. Let him go!" Cash's cherub cheeks were flushed beet red as he huffed and occasionally glanced over his shoulder. The truth was, he didn't really care about Lloyd, or Mase for that matter. His problem was for the past few months, the city ordinance was already in the process of trying to shut his place down due to all the crime and violence the neighborhood citizens blamed on the strip club.

"Okay man," Lloyd suddenly said capriciously and pulled the gun out of Mase's mouth. A glint of relief flashed on Mase's face as he stood straight up and wiped his bloody face with the back of his shirt sleeve and wobbled slightly, muttering an apology through his bleeding mouth.

"Now gone head and leave before the cops come giving me trouble agai—"

WHAM!

Before Cash could get the words fully out his mouth, Lloyd reach over and slapped Mase square in the face with the .9mm. The morbid sound was like meaty flesh and gristle bone being pounded with a hammer.

A stifled ripple of hushed voices rose from the female spectators gathered in the doorway of the club as they looked on in horror.

Just as Mase was about to keel over, landing on his face on the concrete pavement, Lloyd caught him and shoved him in the car. He ran around the other side of the vehicle and hopped in. The tires screeched as he burnt rubber driving off.

A FUTURE SONG blared in the next room in a muffled sound as Mase was awakened by the feel of scorching, agonizing heat. The pain was unbearable. Startled, he glanced down at his chest to the sound of frying meat, like bacon on a stove. He could smell the rancid scent of his flesh burning as he began to wail, howling an almost animalistic unhuman sound. As he began to thrust and struggle against his restraints, at first he hoped it was a nightmare. *No, this can't be real.* But the pain was unbearable as he realized he was tied to a chair. Somebody was standing behind him holding the chair still as Lloyd pressed an old electric clothes iron to his bare chest, causing smoke and vapors to rise to the ceiling.

"GGGGGod, pleasssseee, noooooo!" Mase wailed, struggling against his restraints as his legs lashed, kicking and thrashing like he was being electrocuted by a million volts. There was a gag in his mouth, a dirty sock. The huge figure standing behind him slammed his meaty fist into the back of his head.

"Stop all dat muthafuckin' cryin,' bitch nigga."

A thick, baritone voice rumbled like thunder in the confines of the small room. Dirty clothes, trash, and used drug paraphernalia littered the floor, along with a malodorous smell that was nearly unbearable. A worn sheet covered the window.

With a menacing scowl, lips pressed tight across his teeth, Lloyd pulled the hot iron off Mase's flesh, taking a way a large piece of skin with it, and leaving a pink and white indent shaped like a hot iron. Mase's rib cage was nearly exposed.

"Fuck nigga, didn't I tell you I was going to get your bitch ass!!" Lloyd snarled with the burning iron still sizzling, smoldering in his hand with Mase's flesh on it.

Crazy Mike was one of Lloyd's East Point Gangstas, overzealous and loyal, eager to get his position back in the operation. He was just coming home from prison, muscle bound like a black hulk. At 6'8, over three-hundred pounds and severely cockeyed, he was all brute force with no patience. He left the street ten years ago and recently returned home. He was a man and a terror in the hood. His loyalty was cemented in the cemetery with all the tombstones from all the men he had personally put in the dirt because of his allegiance to Lloyd.

"You want me to choke his ass out again Black, or just pop one of his eyeballs out with this knife and snap his neck?" Crazy Mike asked with a confident shrug as he held the large, carved deer hunting knife, with its serrated edges gleaming in the dim light in the dingy, smoke-filled room of the crack house that also served as a trap house in East Point.

"Naw'll, I have something special for this nigga, big homie," Lloyd said while never taking his eyes of Mase.

"So you set me up two times to get robbed by this bitch Keisha, and you lied about killing your brother to give him enough time to learn about my trap houses so y'all could rob them," Lloyd said as if he was heavy with contempt. The entire time, Mase wiggled his head frantically trying to speak, but there was a gag in his mouth.

"This is for taking my shit and lying and conspiring with your brother," Lloyd hissed with a vengeance, and turned the heat volume up on the old, cast steel iron, causing it to glow pink.

He then lunged forward with all his might and pressed the hot iron on Mase's face, causing a sizzling sound as smoke billowed, rising from his face like steam. Mase howled out again. When Lloyd pulled the iron off his face, a large portion of his skin peeled off with it, so grotesquely scarred you could see his cheekbone. In one quick motion, he took a step back, removing his banger and firing simulta-neously, hitting Mase in the chest and causing his body to jerk. He then nodded to Crazy Mike.

"Do him!"

Wasting no time and happy to oblige his boss man, Crazy Mike slammed the twelve-inch hunting knife into Mase's chest, rupturing organs. Mase late out a long, protracted breath with a deep sigh.

"Die muthafucka, die! Fuck nigga, tell Lucifer I said hi." Satis-fied, Lloyd kicked the chair over, causing Mase to fall over backwards.

"Where you want me to dump his body at?" Crazy Mike asked as he untied Mase by cutting the ropes that held him with a bloody knife.

"Oh, we gon' do something special. I'm finna make this nigga Trigga feel my gangsta. We gon' dump his brother's body right where he can find it, then next I'm coming at his bitch. This is what we gon' do..."

As they both plotted and conspired, neither one of them paid much attention to Mase. His finger twitched slightly as he laid in a puddle of blood face down.

CHAPTER SIXTEEN

TISH FLICKED THROUGH THE TELEVISION CHANNELS UNTIL SHE landed on VH1. Her eyes rested on the screen just as she saw Princess grab a handful of Teairra Marí's hair and yank it so hard it was a wonder that it didn't rip away from her scalp. *Love & Hip Hop: Hollywood* was ratchet television at its finest, and it was the only thing that could take Tish's mind off what was going on around her long enough for her to calm her nerves, if even only for a short hour.

"Bitch! You ain't nothin' but a fake ass, wannabe me with your fat, busted ass!" Princess crooned as she reared back and hauled her fist into the air, struggling against security to meet her target.

Pulling her knees up to her chest, Tish wrapped her arms around her legs as she happily watched the women tussling on the screen over a man who didn't seem to be any good for either one of them. The emotions of a woman when it came to a man she'd shared her heart with couldn't be explained. Tisha knew this all too well and had seen it first-hand countless times, more recently when it came to Keisha and Trigga.

The enormous weight of guilt that she felt from calling the police on Trigga would haunt her forever, even though she did it to help

Keisha. What she'd done to save her actually put her right in harm's way, and now she wasn't even sure that Keisha was alive. She couldn't blame anyone but herself. Had she not provided to the police what they needed in order to arrest Trigga, he might possibly have been able to save Keisha before she became subject to whatever twisted form of torture Lloyd had come up with specifically for Keisha before she met her blessed end.

Tish's first order of business once she had recovered was to find a new apartment and a new job. With Lloyd free, she feared that one day he would come to finish what he thought he'd already dealt with the day he shot her in her last apartment. There wasn't a doubt in her mind that if he knew she was still alive, he would come back to kill the only witness left of the crime he'd committed.

The sound of the wind rustling the branches on the tree that stood right outside of her living room window caused her to jump slightly in her seat. The swooshing of the branches came to a halt just as Tish's heartbeat returned to its normal pace, but nearly stopped when she heard the sound of footsteps approaching. As an instant reflex, she reached out and grabbed the small pink container of pepper spray that was on the table in front of her, gripping it tightly in her hand as if her life depended on it.

The blaring noise of the catty shrieks from the females on the screen, a new set engaged in a new fight, drowned out the sounds from outside as Tish struggled to decide on whether or not she should be alarmed. With her other hand, she grabbed the remote and clicked the button to mute the sound.

The reality was that she was suffering from PTSD: Post-Traumatic Stress Disorder. Ever since she barely survived her altercation with Lloyd, she spent every second of every day worried about her safety. When she was home, she made sure that every single light was turned on at all times so that she would never walk into a dark room. Subconsciously, she had convinced herself that every shadow could be the cause of her demise, because Lloyd could be there. She was scared beyond her wits. More than anything she wanted to move, but her meager savings could barely meet her day-to-day needs, much less assist her in moving to another city.

Bam! Bam! Bam!

Knocking at the door.

She felt the sensation of something tickling the back of her eyeballs before her eyes filled up with tears of fear. Covering her mouth, she willed herself to not make a sound, less she alerted the person at the door of her presence within the apartment. No one knew where she lived; her rent was paid, as well as every other bill. There was no telling for how long she'd be able to keep up with them, but for the time being, there was no reason for anyone to be knocking on her door in regards to anything concerning payment.

Tish stood up slowly, holding the pepper spray in her hand as if it was a trusted weapon used for murder, and crept over to the door. With her eyes focused on the peephole, she moved steadily, hoping that she was successful in her attempts to not make a sound as she shook violently with each step. Once she got to the door, she stood up on her tip-toes and peered out the peephole.

There was nothing.

"What?" she muttered softly as she frowned and searched around the minuscule circumference, eagerly looking for the person who'd knocked on the door.

Her stomach flipped in her chest as she searched around. There was no one.

Then suddenly, just when she was about to back away from the door and convince herself that the knocking was done in error, a face appeared. Tish gasped loudly as she looked at the urbane, ruggish person in front of her. His cool gray eyes and thick, furrowed brows were pulled in a sinister manner as if he were pissed off to the highest degree, as was the norm with him regardless to his actual emotional state.

Tish clamped her hand down over her mouth, but she knew it was too late when Trigga turned towards her with his eyes focused on the other side of the peephole. He'd heard her.

"Tish, open up...I need your help with Keisha," he said as Tish continued to watch him.

Trigga lifted one brow up and surveyed the area around him. With the sunset came the crisp, frigidly cold air but he wasn't bothered, although he only wore a simple, short-sleeved black tee and jeans. His hatred and anger provided him warmth. The wind whipped behind him, slightly lifting his shirt up to expose his banger tucked in at his back. He adjusted his clothing and scanned the area once more to make sure the few people scattered about, engaged in various activities, hadn't noticed.

A woman sauntered by slowly, wearing a short, tight yellow dress with UGG boots and her piercing brown eyes focused on Trigga, with a seductive smirk on her pecan-colored face. Her long weave was pushed all the way to one side, and cascaded in long ringlets over her shoulder. The only reason for Trigga bothering to inspect her for longer than half a second was for the fact that she was walking towards him, and he wanted to make sure that she would continue her slow trot right on by him without stopping to strike up a conversation. After getting caught up with NeTasha, he was done with everybody if it wasn't Keisha.

The woman licked her lips and opened her mouth as if she was prepared to say something, but Trigga turned away sharply and positioned his back to her, hoping it was signal enough that he didn't want to be fucked with. She took the hint, blew out a sharp breath, then sucked her teeth before walking away.

"It's open," Tish's voice said from the other side of the door.

He grabbed the handle and turned slowly with his brow creased more so than usual. He knew that Tish had been through some shit and that she was probably still on edge about it, but he was getting a vibe from her that he wasn't sure that he liked.

"What up, Tee?" Trigga asked once he'd opened the door. His words were cheerful and light, although his tone was not.

He hadn't planned on walking in, so he stood with his feet firmly planted on the mat outside the door, although Tish didn't even bother to move to let him in anyways. She grabbed the door-knob suddenly and used the door as a shield while sticking her head out.

"Wh—what's goin' on with Keisha?" Tish asked, not answering his question.

Trigga didn't mind it. It was just a formality anyways since she seemed to be on edge about something. He wasn't the best in his line of work because he'd ignored details, and he was picking up on a lot of cues from Tish that told him she was extremely uncomfortable, and that fact made him extremely uncomfortable as well.

All of a sudden, Trigga started having second thoughts about what he was there to ask her to do. He ran his eyes over her face and noted the glassy, wet look of her eyes, and the light perspiration that covered her entire face. He lowered his eyes and watched the rise and fall of her chest in sharp, brusque uneven movements, as if she were trying to calm down her breathing. Lastly, he noted the way the edges of her lips pulled to the side ever so often, as if she wanted to cry. Her bottom lip started trembling as she watched him observe her. She sucked it in to her mouth to try to hide it, but Trigga had already caught it.

"She's in da hospital. I just need someone to be there wit' her while I...handle some shit."

He didn't have to explain to Tish what 'shit' he was referring to. She knew all too well what it was that Trigga did, and why he'd earned his nickname.

"She's alive?" Tish asked, her hopeful tone quavered as she spoke.

Pulling his lips tight while he watched her reaction, Trigga nodded his head curtly, feeling somewhat more trusting at the fact that Tish seemed joyous that Keisha was well.

"Thank GOD!" Tish cried out as she broke out into tears. "I've been so scared that—I thought she was gone and it was my fault! Oh God, thank You!"

"Why would it be your fault?"

Tish's eyes nearly dried instantly as she contemplated possible responses to Trigga's questions that would not implicate her in any wrongdoing.

"I just...b—b—because I couldn't call the police to help her," she blurted out as soon as a worthwhile response came to her.

"Fuck da police. Ain't shit they can do for her that I can't," Trigga mumbled angrily. "Room 614. Same hospital from before."

Reaching down into his pocket, Trigga pulled out a few bands of the money that he'd taken from Lloyd's trap houses and pushed a strap of hundreds in Tish's hand.

"Get some girly shit before you go so that she won't be in there worrying and shit. Keep tha change," he told her. He shrugged when he said 'girly shit' and hoped that Tish knew what he meant.

Turning around, Trigga walked away and jumped in his whip. He was gone in the blink of an eye, as Tish stood there standing at the door with a dumbfounded look on her face. As was customary with Trigga, he hadn't given her much of a choice when it came to what he'd needed her to do. His request was said more like a command, because that was exactly what it was.

Squeezing the bills in her hand, she closed the door and locked it behind her. As happy as she was about Keisha being alive after blaming herself for her death, the idea of going to the hospital to sit by her bedside didn't excite her in the least. Once again, she was being thrown into a situation that could lead to Lloyd finding her ass and killing her for something that she didn't even have anything to do with.

Staring down at the band of hundreds, Tish toyed with the idea of just getting lost and using the money to relocate. If she packed a few things in her car and skipped town, who would find her?

Trigga would.

The chilling realization that she would only be putting herself further in harm's way if she tried to leave came to her as clearly as words spoken aloud. No matter where she went, there was one thing that she knew about Trigga although she hadn't known him all that long: if he wanted to find her, he wouldn't stop until he did.

After all, he'd just left her apartment...an apartment he shouldn't have even known she had. Tish hadn't even bothered asking Trigga how he'd found out about her new place, because there wasn't a point. The fact was that he did, and if he had then Lloyd could too. At this time in her life, she needed more allies than enemies so with a heavy sigh, she grabbed her keys and got ready to go to the hospital, with her pepper spray tucked into her back pocket.

A foolish attempt at safety when she was involved in a battle where niggas toted pistols, shotguns, and AKs.

CHAPTER SEVENTEEN

THE VIVID, GLEAMING SUN PROVIDED THE PICTURE-PERFECT backdrop to align with plans filled with malicious intent. Austin sucked in the pungent odor of smog-filled air as he stood outside the luxury rental that he'd secured specially for this trip. Lloyd had been blowing up his phone ever since he'd landed at Hartsfield-Jackson two hours ago, but he had been sending call after call to voicemail. One thing that his cousin didn't yet understand, though he would before long, was that Austin was a muthafuckin' boss nigga, and that meant there wasn't a nigga breathing who could rush him when it came to what he had in mind to do.

Right now, he wanted to eat and he had a taste for some Gladys Knight Chicken and Waffles. As he stared at the entrance of the building, he had a feeling that he was being watched but didn't pay it any attention. He was dressed like money and had just stepped out of a Maybach; everybody had their eyes on a nigga.

"WELL, IF IT AIN'T MUTHAFUCKIN' AUSTIN!"

Cutting his eyes towards the voice, Austin stared from over the top of his exclusive, custom-made Ray-Ban shades at the man walking towards him with his fist outstretched to dap him up.

"What it do, nigga? You good?" Austin asked with a smirk on his face.

Standing in front of him was O.G. Banks, one of Lloyd's crew members. He wasn't high up on the totem pole, but he always seemed to know what was going on and was happy to run his mouth about it. Atlanta was just about as much of Austin's city as it was Lloyd's. Although Lloyd and Kenyon ran it, everybody who was anybody in the trapping game knew Austin.

His reputation stretched out all across the south because of how he'd single-handedly been able to put every major city in Texas on lock. Dallas was where he laid his head at night, but the entire state bowed to him. The stories of how he operated with no mercy sent a chill down anybody's spine. He had the most creative and terrifying ways of encouraging niggas to follow his lead, and those who crossed him were used as examples of how ruthless and crazy he was. He reigned in Dallas under the law of terror, which provided him the utmost respect from even the most fearless nigga on the streets. Even his enemies had to respect his gangsta. He was *that* nigga.

O.G. shook his head sadly, making his long dreadlocks shake from left to right as he prepared to speak. He looked bad as hell; his clothes were wrinkled and his jeans had a stain in them. His sneakers were dirty and covered with grime. Even though he was nothing but a low level corner boy, he usually stayed on top of his shit when it came to his appearance.

"Hell naw, ain't shit good right now, my nigga. Niggas ain't eatin' because some New York nigga been hittin' up our spots, stealin' tha dope and shit. And muthafuckin' Black ain't nowhere to be found. Only reason we kno' dat nigga ain't dead is because Truth still been gettin' orders and shit from him." O.G.'s face twisted up as he spoke, becoming increasingly agitated with each word.

"Damn, that nigga ain't been takin' care of his peoples...that's some bullshit," Austin replied, giving the best expression he could muster up to make it seem as if he was truly concerned.

"Yeah, and I kno' dats yo' cuz and shit, but dat ain't how EPG do shit, naw' mean?"

"You right."

Austin reached down in his pocket and grabbed a stack of hundreds. He peeled ten of them off and handed them over to O.G., who was staring at him with wide eyes as if he'd never seen so much money before. He probably hadn't. Lloyd didn't compensate his corner boys as well as Austin did his team. He was flashy and stingy as hell, but the only niggas who were really making money were his top leaders. He didn't understand that you could build a loyal team by making sure that every single person in your operation was making more money than they'd ever make by double crossing you.

Austin never had to worry about anyone backstabbing him, because they thought of him as their god. Lloyd's niggas hadn't seen him in three weeks, and they were already talking shit and dressed like scrubs. Austin's team would die before they opened up their mouth to say a word against him, and they made enough money to last for over a year even if they never made another dollar.

"Here, this should be enough for ya until I get this shit together," Austin said as he handed out the bills to O.G.

"Damn nigga, dat's what's up!" O.G. exclaimed as he grabbed the bills and stuck them in his pocket. "And did I hear dat right? You comin' to get shit in order?"

Austin nodded his head as he rubbed his hands together. His eyes shot over to a fine ass female who was walking into the restaurant. She had on dark red jeans that looked like they had to be painted on her body. Her bodacious hips swayed from right to left as she walked sexily while staring down at the cell phone in her hands. There was a cool breeze in the air so she wore a sweater, but it was short and showed off her flat, toned belly. Austin licked his lips as he let his eyes wash over her appearance. There was something so natural and regal about her; she even wore her hair in a natural, curly afro, which was so sexy to him. A brown-skinned chick with natural hair was his weakness, especially if it came with a banging ass coke-bottle figure.

"Yeah, I'ma get everything right and when I do, you ain't gotta worry about not eatin' ever again as long as I can count on you to have my back, feel me?" Austin asked with one brow lifted as he scrutinized O.G. to make sure he caught his drift.

"Bet. You know I always got 'cho back, nigga. You that muthafuckin' nigga and I'm down wit' da fam," O.G. responded. He held his fist out to dap Austin up and then started walking in the opposite direction down the street.

Austin licked his lips once more and rubbed his hands together as he walked to the door, his mind focused on the chick he'd seen walk in there only seconds before. He had a bitch back home who he kept around because she was a certified freak, and did whatever he asked. She was his down ass bitch and never hesitated to do what he wanted, whether it was to deep-throat his dick or bust on a nigga who had tried him. But more pussy never hurt anyone. Since he planned on spending a lot of time in Atlanta, it would be worth his while to have a chick here to spend some time with when he wanted company.

As soon as Austin walked inside of the building, just about every eye turned towards him. The attention didn't bother him because he was used to it. The hostess walked from behind a table and stood in front of him. She was an older lady, probably in her 40's, with almond-colored skin and bright brown eyes. Her hair was in long twists that were pulled into a loose ponytail. On her face was a tight smile, which told him that she was less than pleased to see him walk in.

Austin was used to chicks giving him that reaction as well. The teardrop tattoos down the side of his face often made people immediately pass judgment on his lifestyle, but once he started speaking he could woo any person who stood before him. He was able to read people well, and he worked that to his advantage every time.

"Table for one?" the woman asked him. Her eyes focused in on his tats briefly before they traveled back to his face. She sucked in a breath and tensed up; the normal person wouldn't have noticed, but Austin's trained eye caught it.

"Yes, ma'am," Austin replied with a soft smile. "And I don't mean to be difficult because it looks like you're the only one up in here workin', but can you sit me back there near the wall? You can take this for the trouble." He held out a fifty-dollar bill.

The woman's face softened and she shook her head from side-to-side. "I can't take that, sir. This is my job, but you are so kind." She grabbed a menu and smiled back at him.

It was Austin's turn to shake his head this time. "I can't take no for an answer. I know how it is workin' and shit on Mondays. A queen as beautiful as you shouldn't even be in here servin' niggas like me."

He laughed softly, and the woman joined in. He watched as her eyes explored him once again, and she nervously fixed her hair. And just like that, he knew he had her. Reaching out, he tucked the bill into her pants' pocket and winked at her, which made her blush.

"Thank you," she replied breathlessly, as if she had run a mile just that quickly. "Right this way."

Chuckling to himself at his propensity to win the affection of any woman who crossed his path, Austin followed her to a table in the back near the chick he'd seen walk in earlier. He couldn't help but notice the hostess had an extra twist in her step, making her booty jiggle freely in her loose-fitting pants as she walked. When they had arrived at his table, she turned around slowly, looked him up and down, and laid his menu down on the table.

"Here you are. My name is Diane. If you need anything, let me know," she told him, making sure to lick her lips and pause before saying the word 'anything'.

The chick at the table across from them snorted and rolled her eyes, which earned a frown from Diane and a smile from Austin.

"Thank you," Austin replied, patting Diane on her arm to pull her attention back to him. "I'll keep that in mind."

Instantly, Diane forgot all about snapping on the other woman and smiled deeply at Austin, who winked again and sat down. When she walked away, he grabbed the menu and stared at it, although he already knew what he wanted.

"It's just that easy for you, huh?" the chick asked suddenly.

Austin tried to fight back the smile that threatened to grace his face, but he wasn't smiling at what she was saying; he found it interesting that flirting with one woman had helped him to attract the attention of the one he'd actually had his eyes on. Sometimes his skills even surprised himself.

"I'on kno' what you mean, shawty," he lied, still looking at the menu.

"Oh, you don't?" the chick asked; he could hear the smile in her voice. "I find that hard to believe."

Dropping the menu, Austin picked up a toothpick he'd grabbed from the front and placed it between his thick lips, moist from having just licked them. When he turned towards the woman across from him, she had her chin rested in her hand and was staring pointedly at him. He stared at her for a few minutes intensely without saying anything, letting his eyes do the work. She returned his stare, looking right into his blue eyes as if he didn't intimidate her at all, but when he broke their gaze to let his eyes travel over her body, she blushed and adjusted nervously in her seat.

Without saying anything, Austin exhaled heavily and stood up from his seat. He walked over and sat right in front of her, which made her jump slightly when he sat down. Her eyes rose slowly and she looked into his, a smile teasing the edges of her lips when she saw the grin on his, but she fought to suppress it.

"What are you doing?!" she asked him, looking around to see if anyone was watching them. A few people shot curious looks in their direction, which seemed to bother her, but it did nothing to stir Austin in the least.

"Don't act like you ain't feelin' a nigga," Austin told her, which made her blush again. She had a proper air about her; it was even in the way that she spoke and pronounced her words. He could tell she was a college chick, which only intrigued him even more.

"And you just know that right off?" she asked him with a teasing tone as she pursed her lips, like she was about to tell him he was wrong.

"Yes," Austin confirmed as though it were fact. "I kno' it is. Now stop askin' me all that silly shit so we can enjoy our first date. So what's yo' name, shawty?"

She laughed heartily with wide eyes at him mentioning them being on their first date.

"So this is a date?"

Austin gave her a blank look, as if to say "Didn't I already tell yo' ass that?" She caught it without him even saying a word and shook her head as a sexy smile graced her pure, unblemished ebony face. She was like a Nubian queen, and he knew right away that she had to be his. She seemed innocent, like the type of chick he normally didn't see in his circles.

"Okay, well in that case, I guess I'll tell you my name," she giggled.

She leaned down, placing her weight on both of her elbows, making the collar of her sweater fall in a way that gave Austin a glimpse of her perky, round breasts. Austin took a glance when she looked away, and had to fight away the image of him sucking all over the chocolate morsel at the tip of each bosom. He could tell that she didn't even know that her sweater was betraying her by showing him something that she'd probably wanted to keep hidden for the time being.

That turned him on. He liked the idea of feeling special, as if he was getting a look at something that was meant to be hidden.

"I'm NeTasha, but you can call me Tasha. Everyone else does," she added. She ran her hand over the top of her afro, which was so long it cradled her thin, toned shoulders. It was obvious she either worked out or was an athlete of some type.

"Well, I don't wanna call you what everybody calls you because I ain't everybody."

"So what you gon' call me?" NeTasha asked him with a raised brow.

His rugged attitude, so commanding, aggressive and strong, was pulling at her in a way that she didn't want it to. After her run-in with Jamal...Trigga...Maurice, whatever the hell his name was, she was still hurt by the way that he'd treated her after taking something so sacred to her, something that she'd been saving for the one: her virginity. She could tell by looking at the tats on the face and arms of the guy in front of her, that he was a bad boy. That much was obvious. He had a vibe that came with him too that said he wasn't one who could be fucked with.

It reminded her of what she felt when she first saw Trigga. He felt like the exact definition of a man. He was a hood nigga of the roughest type, but he had a way of making you feel like he was a king trapped in a hustler's body. Every man around them, whether they knew it or not, bowed to them when they entered the room.

"I'ma call you 'mine' because that's what you are from this moment forward. Ya dig it?" he teased, licking his lips once more, which almost hypnotized her. "And you can call me Austin."

Diane returned to their table with a frown on her face as she looked back and forth between NeTasha and Austin, obviously annoyed by the fact that he was now engaged in a conversation with the female she'd almost told off only a few minutes before.

"Oh, so you like to pick your own seats, I see," Diane scoffed as she held up a pad to take their order. "What y'all drinkin'?"

Austin pulled off his black fitted cap and ran his hand over his low-cut Caesar as he chuckled to himself. NeTasha watched him with a curious look on her face, as she ignored the daggers that Diane was shooting at her profile.

"I'll take a Root Beer," Austin told her before turning to NeTasha for her to voice her choice.

"Do you have cream soda?" she asked, grabbing the menu to research her answer for herself.

"No, we don't. We got Coke products and tea, so whatchu want?" Diane replied with an aggressive tone that made NeTasha snatch her neck up from the menu in front of her.

"Aye, that rude shit ain't necessary." Austin gave Diane an icy look that made her freeze in place.

It was such a sharp difference from how he'd been when he walked into the restaurant and first laid eyes on her. The look on his face now reminded her that he didn't have those teardrops on his eyes for no reason. He may have been able to throw on the charm, but he was a certified thug.

Diane watched as the color in his eyes seemed to shift right in that exact moment, going from a dark blue to a bluish color tinged with a little brown, like something she'd only seen happen with reptiles. It felt like icy fingers were traveling up her spine as he held her gaze in a way that made her unable to look away. Her brain shouted out warnings for her to hurry and get him whatever he needed so he could get the hell up out of her place. He was dangerous, able to go back and forth between charming and deadly like a chameleon.

"Uh...I'll take a sweet tea for now. No lemon," NeTasha cut in, providing the perfect distraction for Austin to finally tear his eyes away from Diane's. He could tell that she understood what he was trying to convey. He wasn't going to stand for somebody disrespecting his chick, and that's exactly what NeTasha was.

"Right away," Diane murmured as she scurried away.

An awkward silence hung in the air as NeTasha stared down at her menu, although she wasn't reading anything on it. She was turned on, but also a little put off at the way that Austin had looked at Diane. She didn't know much about him, but it seemed odd that he could go from being so charming and alluring to cold and menacing in a matter of seconds. She didn't know whether to be afraid or grateful for the way he'd shut down Diane's disrespectful attitude.

"Aye," Austin called for her attention.

When she looked up, his smile and soft expression had returned to his face, which made her relax a bit.

"Figure out what you wanna eat so we can get outta here. We got a lot on the schedule to do today," he told her, as if she had no other choice but to cancel whatever she had planned and chill with him.

"I got class and—" she started, but stopped short when Austin lifted up his hand and cut her off.

"No, I got class," he told her. He leaned over and looked deeply into her eyes, which made her heart start pounding in her chest. "I wanna learn everything about you...every single thing. And you gon' be my sexy ass teacher that I got a crush on, a'ight?"

Despite the warnings sounding off in her mind, NeTasha nodded her head and giggled as Austin smiled at her, showing off his beautiful and perfect teeth. He was sexy and his thuggish nature was making her weak in the knees. He had her in his grasp at that very moment. Once again, she'd fallen for a thug.

CHAPTER EIGHTEEN

TRIGGA STOOD OUTSIDE THE DOOR OF KEISHA'S ROOM, WATCHING as her and Tish laughed while they talked about something that had both of them so engrossed in their conversation, they didn't even know he'd been standing there for the last five minutes watching. Tish was painting Keisha's toenails while Keisha eagerly watched her face, listening to every word that came out of her mouth.

Trigga took the opportunity to admire his woman. She didn't look like her normal self, but she was every bit of perfect to him. Her weight was coming back, although she hadn't been there long. Her tan coloring was returning to normal, making her appear less pale. Though still weak, her strength was slowly returning. In a few more days, she would be the woman he'd fallen in love with again.

Watching her made him contemplate the 'm' word, a word that he'd never thought of before in any serious way because he knew with his lifestyle, it could never be. But knowing that Keisha was carrying his child made him wonder if it were possible to one day leave this life he'd made for himself alone and make her his wife. Could marriage one day happen for him?

I gotta get rid of these muthafuckas first, Trigga thought, thinking about Lloyd and Mase.

The last few hours hadn't been a waste, although he hadn't yet caught up with Lloyd. He called Queen to brief her on everything that happened so far. She was disappointed that Lloyd hadn't been taken care of yet, but the fact that Trigga could tell her that all of his top men were dead brought joy to her tone. It also bought him more time.

Trigga had also gathered some information that he thought might prove itself useful at some point. He wasn't sure, but he kept it in mind in case he needed to play a wild card to draw Lloyd out if his other methods didn't work.

"She's getting better," a voice said from beside Trigga.

He had been so deep in his thoughts that he didn't even realize someone was walking up on him until they were right beside him. That could have been a tragic mistake, but he was always off his shit when he was around Keisha.

He slid his hand to where his banger was as he turned toward the presence next to him. It was the nurse from earlier. Trigga relaxed and dropped his hand to his side. After casting one final look in the room, he moved away from the window and beckoned for the nurse to follow him.

"Earlier she was sweatin' and shit...she a'ight?" he asked.

The woman shifted her weight from foot-to-foot and crossed her arms in front of her chest before answering. Waiting for her to respond, Trigga glanced at her nametag and felt a strange feeling pass through his body. Her name was Tasha, which made him think back to the chick he'd fucked who happened to be Keisha's classmate. She was also a virgin, which he hadn't known at the time, and that fact left him with deep-seated regret at how he'd dissed her immediately when it came to Keisha.

"She's goin' through withdrawals, but it shouldn't last too long. She seems to be tryin' to fight it off for herself, which is good. I can tell she doesn't want to use the drugs, which helps her get through the withdrawals. She's fightin' the urge off on her own, but it is hard on her."

Relieved and also impressed by Keisha's mental strength, Trigga nodded his head at the good news. Keisha had struggled with drugs in the past so he knew this was especially hard on her, but she was stronger than he'd thought. He had underestimated how much of a bad ass his chick she was.

"And the baby?"

A look passed through the nurse's eyes and she looked uncomfortable all of a sudden, which made Trigga's heart begin to pound loudly in his chest.

"Did it...is it..." Trigga's voice trailed off. He was unable to speak the words to the question he was dreading to ask.

"The baby is alive," the nurse assured him with her hands raised in the air to calm his spirits. She could see that he was swiftly approaching a state of panic at the idea of anything happening to his seed.

"We need to...an obstetrician has been assigned to her, and will be speaking with her soon about the baby. I'm not at liberty to share anything else beyond that," the woman replied.

Before Trigga could ask another question, she patted him on the shoulder and walked away quickly. He started to walk off behind her, but the door to Keisha's room slammed open and Tish ran out, with her eyes wide open in panic and terror, in a mad dash towards the nurse's counter in the center of the hall.

"SOMEBODY PLEASE HELP! I don't know what's happening!" she yelled out to anyone who would listen.

Time seemed to come to a dramatic halt as Trigga's thoughts echoed in his mind. The loudest of them all commanded him with urgency and it was the one he listened to as he took off, ripping through the hall back towards Keisha's room. When he burst inside, he saw her thrashing back and forth while grinding her teeth with her face twisted in pain.

"Keesh!" Trigga yelled out as he stood by her side.

He grabbed her hands and held them tightly in his. The pungent stench of vomit filled the air as he held her and lowered himself so that his face was near hers as she writhed in pain. Her beautiful, thin face was covered with sweat, and her eyes were pulled tightly closed. The red nail polish that Tish had been using had stained the sheets and the nearly empty bottle lay on the floor, ridding itself of the remainder of its contents.

Keisha's eyes tore open and she gave a pleading look at Trigga as she grunted in painful agony. Her body was fighting her to satiate it with the drug she craved, but she wouldn't allow herself to succumb to its desires.

"You're okay, baby. You can fight this," Trigga whispered against her hairline as he held her hands and laid his head on the top of her head to calm her. She was feverish. Her skin was boiling against his.

"When you get out of this, we're going to leave and go far away from here. I'll let you pick the place. I'ma buy you a big ass crib, might even grab you one of those lil' ass rat dogs you be talkin' 'bout..."

Trigga started talking, pulling things out of his mind that he knew she wanted, and hoped that it would help pull her through. These were also things he knew he wanted, but present circumstances left him uncertain of whether they'd ever be able to get any of them.

The sound of the door opening made his ears twitch, but he didn't move and didn't stop talking. Keisha needed him, and he was determined to be there for her.

"After my son makes his exit, we gonna try for a lil' girl because I know you want a daughter, no matter how much you kno' dat shit gonna give a nigga a heart attack. But my daughter gonna be a gangsta just like her mama...strong as shit and able to fight anything. And whateva my shorty can't handle for herself, her big bro gon' step in to assist."

"Wait!"

He turned slightly to the door and saw that the nurse, Tasha, was standing there with her hands out to stop the medical crew behind her from walking further into the room. They all continued to watch as Trigga held Keisha and gently rocked her while he spoke into her ear about how their life would be as soon as she was able to get herself together and get out of there.

Keisha's movements became less and less as he held on to her and she listened to his words. Her grunts stopped and were replaced by low moans as her breathing began to return to normal. Trigga hadn't even realized until that moment that he had tears in his eyes, as he thought out the life that he wanted for the two of them and their child. It was so different from their current reality, but he knew in his heart of hearts that he wouldn't rest until he could get it for her.

"Trigga," Keisha's soft voice said finally once she was able to catch her breath.

He looked down at her and saw that her eyes were open and clear. He leaned over and kissed her lightly on her lips.

"Okay, it looks like everything's all good in here," the nurse said from behind them. Trigga didn't turn around to watch them, but he heard feet shuffling as they walked away.

"I'm goin' to give y'all some privacy," Tish's voice chimed from behind him. He nodded his head, still focused on Keisha.

"You good?" he asked her after he heard the door close behind Tish.

In spite of the sweat all over her face, Keisha shivered before speaking so he adjusted the comforter over her thin frame.

"I am now," she told him. "It's happening less and less."

Unsure of what to say, Trigga pulled out a small box of something he'd bought to give to Keisha when he came back. Her eyes lit up when she saw the small, red rectangular box that he held in his hands.

"I dunno if you allowed to have dis, but I know it's yo' favorite," he told her as he pulled the top of the box and pushed the chocolates in front of her face.

The smile that spread across her face warmed his heart as she reached in and grabbed one, inspected it, and then put it back in the box. She grabbed another one, looked at it, then put it back. She did it two more times before Trigga pulled the box away and gave her a playful frown.

"Man, nigga, why you fingerprintin' all my shit?!" he asked her, which made her laugh. He held the box back out for her to grab another one, which she decided to keep. She closed her eyes in a dreamy way as she chewed on the chocolate.

"That's the one I was lookin' for," she said in between chews. "You neva know how much you miss sumthin' until you ain't had it in a while."

"You ain't neva lied," Trigga replied, thinking about something else that he hadn't had in a while. Something more of the caramel variety.

Keisha was laying up in the hospital bed and he respected the fact that she needed to get better, but he also couldn't ignore the fact that he hadn't tasted or felt her in over a month. Being close to her set his skin on fire with desire, regardless to what she looked like or what was going on. He couldn't wait until the moment that she was doing well enough for him to dive back in her warmth once more.

Making the decision to settle for the only thing he could get at the moment, Trigga leaned over and kissed her once more, but stopped when he noticed her pulling back a little as if she didn't want to kiss him. Backing away, he gave her a confused look.

"The hell that's about?"

Keisha stirred nervously under his scrutiny. Her eyes danced around nervously, and then finally a shameful look crossed her face.

"I stink...and I just threw up," she told him finally with her eyes down.

She made a movement to cloak herself with the blankets on the bed, as if that would hide the smell. It didn't. Trigga's keen sense of smell picked up on every odor in the room, he just didn't give a fuck.

His feelings for her didn't change just because she was going through something and wasn't as put together as she would have liked to be.

"A'ight," Trigga replied.

Sitting the chocolates down on the table next to her, he rolled up the sleeves on his black hoodie and then rubbed his hands together. Keisha lifted one brow and watched him, waiting to see what he was up to. When he ripped the blankets from off her body, she tried to grabbed them away from him but he was too quick. She tried to pull her knees up to hide her appearance but the reproachful look on Trigga's face stopped her.

"Don't you ever hide from yo' nigga, Keesh."

She nodded her head.

"Can you walk or do I need to carry you?" he asked, point blank.

Keisha frowned slightly and looked around the room. "I can walk but—where we goin'?"

"You're gonna take a shower. I'm gonna help you," he said matter-of-factly.

Feelings of admiration and horror fought against each other as she mulled over his words. There was nothing quite as romantic as hearing the man she loved tell her that he was going to bathe her, but she paused at the idea of Trigga seeing her without her clothes on. He'd seen some of the evidence of what she'd been through the past few weeks but he hadn't seen it all, and she wasn't sure she wanted him to. The sight of it all might disgust him. The first time she'd peered into a mirror after leaving Lloyd, it had disgusted her. She didn't want him to feel the same thing she'd felt.

"Let's go," he told her, leaving her with no other choice.

Keisha nodded begrudgingly, her eyes filling with fresh tears that she fought to keep from falling. Trigga noted them and had a guess at why she was getting emotional, but he tried to play it off like he didn't notice. He knew this had to be hard for her, harder for her than it was for him, but he had to be her protector in all ways...not just protecting her physically, but he had to protect her emotions as well. He made it his goal to show her that he didn't give a shit what had happened to her; she was the most beautiful woman on Earth to him.

"Put your weight on me," he said as he helped her move from the bed.

Fighting away her tears, Keisha obeyed silently and put all of her trust in him as he led her to the small shower in her room.

If he truly loves me, this will tell it, she thought to herself.

CHAPTER NINETEEN

THE SOAPY LATHER WASHED OVER EVERY BIT OF KEISHA'S BODY as Trigga inspected every part of her before he ran the washcloth over. Each scar, some fairly fresh and others covered by dark scabs, locked into Trigga's memory. He made a mental note to make Lloyd pay for each one. Every affliction residing on her body that had been placed there at his hands would be accounted for, and Trigga would make sure that what Lloyd received was far worse than anything he'd done to Keisha.

Biting his lips, he stared at her boney hips and thighs. He remembered when they made love, she would wrap her thick thighs around his waist and pull him deeper into her. Those same thighs looked like if he pressed against them, they would shatter under his weight. She spun around and turned her back to him so that he could apply soap to her back. Her spine stuck out against her flesh in a way that it never had before. She'd gained a few pounds, but she was a far cry from how she'd been the last time he'd seen her.

Unknowingly, Trigga had paused when his eyes rested on the bones that poked out through her back. Noting his delay, Keisha turned around and glanced at him to see if everything was okay. He caught her glimpse and saw the hurt in her eyes when she'd seen how he had been staring at her body. Before he could say anything to soothe her mind, she'd already turned back around. Crossing her arms in front of her, she grabbed onto her shoulders and bent herself in a way that made it seem as if she were trying to shield herself from him.

"Keesh..." he started. He stood up from where he was sitting on the toilet next to the shower and ran his hand down her waist, but she didn't relax or react to his touch.

Dropping the soapy cloth to the floor, Trigga pulled off his hoodie and his shirt, then kicked off his sweatpants. He tossed it behind him and came up behind Keisha, trailing light kisses at the nape of her neck and then over her shoulders. He grabbed her around her waist and pulled her back against him as the water beat over the both of them. She relaxed and fell against his chest as he snaked his hand around and fully circled her entire waist. Pushing her hair to the other side, he stared at the exposed side of her neck, then lowered his head and started sucking lightly.

When she moaned, he began to suck a little harder as he felt his manhood rise. He'd already been hard from the sight of her naked body, but he'd been able to control himself thus far. Even when he made her part her thighs so that he could run the washcloth through her sweet folds, he bit his lip and fought the urge to dip a finger inside her tight, wet treasure box, but the erotic moaning sound that provided evidence of the ecstasy she was feeling was beginning to be too much for him to ignore. He could feel his control growing weaker by the second.

"Shit," he muttered against her neck when he felt her press back against his manhood that was growing harder and harder through his dark blue boxers.

He knew that he was treading on dangerous ground and quickly approaching the point of no return. Keisha had been through hell, and she was slowly recovering from everything that she'd endured. He didn't want to hurt her.

"We gotta stop," he said softly when he felt her hand cover his. It was his last attempt to stop the inevitable and even when he said it, he knew that it was a waste to even utter the words. Neither one of them were ready to put a stop to anything that was happening.

Trigga allowed Keisha to guide his hands as he dropped his hand and commenced to sucking on her neck so hard that there wasn't a doubt in his mind that he would leave a passion mark. Then his hand finally found the destination that Keisha had planned for it, and he smiled to himself. Baring his teeth, he bit lightly on Keisha's neck as he stuck one finger inside of her. She sucked in a breath and started to move her hips slightly when he started to stir around inside of her.

"Mmmmmm," she moaned, and let her head fall back against his shoulders.

Her legs went weak and Trigga turned her so that she was facing him, with the wall behind her to provide her with a foundation to lean on. She placed her hands on the railing that was cemented into the wall and gripped it firmly, as she squeezed her eyes closed and enjoyed the feeling of every sensation Trigga was providing to her.

Every part of her that Lloyd hurt, Trigga brought pleasure to. The warm water beat down on them as he kissed every part of her body, making her feel like the most beautiful woman in the world. Her tears of ecstasy and love mixed with the pounding droplets of water that ran down her face as she lost herself in the love that she felt.

Suddenly, she felt Trigga gently push her thighs apart, and she pointed her knees in opposite directions to allow him access to whatever he wanted. With her eyes firmly closed, she almost yelped out in shock and surprise when she felt his soft, wet tongue flick over the top of her box. She felt a sting of shame at the fact that she hadn't shaved in weeks since Lloyd had taken her, but that all went away when Trigga's mouth kissed her second set of lips with as much passion as he kissed the ones above.

He made love to her gingerly and lovingly, using only his fingers and tongue. It was like nothing Keisha could ever have imagined. He brought her to the precipice of pleasure over and over again with his skillful movements of his tongue, until she found herself murmuring words that she couldn't understand.

"I love you," he said when he finally gave her clitoris a break from his sweet assault.

Blinking her eyes open and closed with lethargy, Keisha struggled to get her breathing together enough to profess her love to him, but before she could respond, she felt Trigga move his hands and spread her ass cheeks. Her eyes shot wide open when she felt the sensation of his tongue flicking back and forth across both orifices below in rhythmic sequence.

"Oh...God...I—I—I—I looooooove yooooou!" Keisha managed to get out through clenched teeth as he brought her to a magnificent orgasm that sent chills up her spine.

Every nerve ending inside her shot off what felt like electric tremors throughout her body as her knees shook violently, while Trigga continued to lick and suck as if he were on death row and enjoying his very last meal.

Trigga pulled away just in time to catch her when she crumbled into him, her trembling legs too weak to continue to support her weight. Holding her with one hand, he grabbed the washcloth with the other and cleaned her up quickly before wrapping her up in a dry towel and carrying her to the bed.

Once he laid her down, he dried her and dressed her quickly as her eyes fluttered drowsily. This was what he had been fighting to avoid. He already knew she was weak and exhausted, but what he'd done only made it worse. Now she couldn't even open her eyes, but he couldn't help himself and to tell the truth, if he'd had another chance he would do the same shit over again.

Backing away, he stared at her for a second longer as he continued to breathe in the sweet scent of her that still lingered on his lips. He grabbed the towel and patted himself dry, and walked into the bathroom to grab his clothes. Once he placed them on, he checked his watch. As much as he wanted to spend the night with Keisha, he couldn't. He had stayed with her the night before, against his better judgment, but he had moves to make.

Trigga walked over to her and kissed her on her forehead, which made her stir lightly when she felt his touch.

"Don't go," she pleaded with her eyes closed. Her fingers reached out and searched until they landed on his shirt. She walked her fingers over him until she was able to find his hand, and folded her fingers into his.

"Don't," she repeated.

Biting down hard, he grinded his teeth together and shook his head as he watched her angelic face twist up with desperation as she repeated her request. This shit was becoming too hard. Every time he had to leave her, it became harder and harder, but that was even more of a reason to hurry up and do what he had to do.

"Keesh, I'll be back in the morning. I gotta—"

"Don't go, please," she repeated, and it was just enough to push through Trigga's wall of resistance. He wasn't going anywhere any time soon.

Pussy-whipped ass nigga, he chided himself in his mind. *Her ass gotchu weak as shit.*

He saw a motion by the door and tore his eyes away from Keisha's face to investigate. It was Tish, waiting for Trigga to give her a signal on what she should do.

"You stayin'?" she mouthed to him when she'd caught his attention.

He shot a look at Keisha, and then nodded his head. Tish put her hand to her head and saluted him, which was her way of telling him she was leaving and would be back later on.

Sighing heavily, Trigga folded both of his massive hands over Keisha's tiny one and sat down in the chair behind him. Leaning down, he bent his head down and placed his forehead gently on her leg as he listened to her breathe.

Music to his ears.

"Thank you," Keisha said finally.

Trigga lifted his head and looked at her. Her eyes were open and she was staring at him graciously.

"Anything to make you happy, Keesh," he told her sincerely.

She nodded happily and looked away at nothing in particular.

"They tell you anything about our baby?" Trigga asked suddenly, thinking back to what the nurse had said earlier.

Keisha looked at him and shook her head softly.

"Okay, they said they assigned a doctor to you for the baby. Whatever they tell you, I wanna hear it," he told her in a way that seemed more like a demand than a request. Normal "Trigga" shit.

Keisha nodded her head in agreement and tried to hide the feeling that was rising up in her. Thankfully, Trigga looked away which was a blessing. He could read her like his favorite book, and she needed to be able to keep this one thing to herself. The obstetrician had already been there to speak to her earlier when Tish was in the room with her. The doctor told her that there was a mark on the baby's heart when they did an ultrasound, and though it could be nothing, based on her history and current medical state, they had to run a few more tests to make sure that everything was okay with the baby's development.

In her heart of hearts, Keisha knew everything would not be fine. That just wasn't how life was for her. If God had taught her anything, he'd taught her that everything bad that could happen would happen to her. The only piece of happiness He'd ever given her was Trigga, and even then, with every day it seemed like He got closer and closer to taking him away. Every day that Trigga went into the streets searching for Lloyd so that he could avenge her, he played Russian roulette with his life and their future.

"You good?" Trigga asked her finally. Keisha looked at him and tried to bring a smile to her face.

"Yes." Trigga seemed satisfied with her response and squeezed her hand a little tighter before dropping his head back down on the bed.

No, it's not okay, she thought to herself. *Nothing is and probably will never be.*

CHAPTER TWENTY

FIVE DAYS LATER...

"I DON'T UNDERSTAND WHY WE GOTTA COME TO THIS HOT ASS muthafuckin' place! All these muthafuckin' flies and shit! Damn, I hate the fuckin' south!"

Gunplay shook his head from side to side as he watched LeTavia swat at a bug that only her eyes could see, in her normal dramatic fashion. They were standing inside of the Hartfield-Jackson airport, which was air conditioned, and there wasn't an insect in sight. They had only been off the plane a total of five minutes and she was already fussing and complaining.

If dis bitch ever quit her day job, she could make it in show bizness wit' her actin' ass, Gunplay thought to himself.

"Tavi, stop all that waving and shit! You know I got shit on me and you callin' attention to a nigga! What, you tryna get me locked up or some shit?" Gunplay scowled as he watched her fuss with the collar of her shirt, like she was going to die from a heatstroke.

"De'Shaun, don't you start dat shit wit' me!" LeTavia began as she shot him an annoyed look while using his government name. "I'm 'posed to be in the city enjoying myself, but you got me in hot ass Atlanta sweatin' out my brand new damn weave and shit!"

"Man, chill," Gunplay warned her with a frown as they passed by some police officers who shot them curious glances as LeTavia continued to mess with her clothes and curse under her breath.

"All the shit I do for you, and you still wanna talk shit just cuz I ask you to do this one thing for me?" Gunplay's question was greeted by an eye roll, but LeTavia didn't say anything else. "Trigga is my nigga, and if he say he need sumthin' then that's what it is."

"Well, why the hell what he need gotta involve me babysittin' his chick while y'all run the streets? You act like I ain't got shit to do!" LeTavia stormed off towards baggage claim, her sour attitude growing a mile a minute.

"You ain't!" Gunplay retorted. He grabbed LeTavia by the arm and turned her so she was facing him. "Tavi, why you always gotta fight a nigga?"

LeTavia looked at Gunplay right in his eyes that were narrowed at hers. He had a frown etched on his handsome, angular face as he waited for her to respond. LeTavia blew out a heavy breath and shot him an apologetic look.

"I'm sorry," she apologized with her arms folded over her small, round bosoms as she stood with her hip kicked out to the side. "I was just about to go get Zu and Thena."

Gunplay smiled as he watched her try her hardest not to pout. She knew she was in the wrong, and no matter how much mouth she had, she'd never been the type of chick not to admit it when she was. Along with her curvaceous, but thin figure, almond-shaped eyes and smooth chestnut brown skin, her fiery attitude was part of what he loved about her—especially since he was the only nigga skilled enough to curve that mouth of hers.

Gunplay had been at the gun range doing what he did best when he got a call from Trigga asking him to come to Atlanta. Truth was, as soon as Trigga asked, Gunplay was ready to hop on the next plane, but Trigga explained a little bit of what was going on anyways. When he mentioned what was going on with his chick, Gunplay was nearly at a loss for words.

For one, he was surprised as hell to even hear that Trigga had a chick. He wasn't a virgin by a long shot, but any bitch Gunplay had ever seen Trigga with wasn't around long enough for him to even learn her first name. She probably was barely around long enough for Trigga to learn it; he never was interested in getting to know a female on that level because he was gone before sunrise.

My nigga finally got one, Gunplay had thought when he listened to Trigga talk about Keisha.

Then he promised to bring LeTavia along for the ride, so she could keep Keisha company while he helped Trigga settle some street shit he needed help with since his idiot ass twin had betrayed him.

"Why you still lookin' at me like that?" LeTavia said with her arms outstretched. "I said I was sorry!"

"I don't do no muthafuckin' 'sorrys'. You betta get yo' shit together," Gunplay said in a rough tone that he knew she liked. True to his thinking, LeTavia bit down on her lip to try to hide the smile that was creeping up on her face, and swiveled around slowly to commence her stroll towards the baggage claim.

"Got damn," Gunplay muttered to himself as he watched her walk away with an extra pep in her step. "Shawty got a *fat* ass."

"IT'S BEAUTIFUL IN HERE," Keisha exclaimed as she stepped through the doors of the most beautiful home that she'd ever seen.

It wasn't a mansion, but it definitely wasn't small either. It had to be no less than 4,000 square feet total, and was fully decorated with top of the line furniture that had to be handpicked by an interior decorator. There were beautiful bay windows that let in so much natural sunlight that Keisha had to squint when she looked at them. She walked throughout the entire house, marveling over each room that she walked into, while Trigga followed her looking less than impressed. She knew what was on his mind, and she also knew that as soon as he got to the point where he felt satisfied that she was secure, comfortable and safe, he would hit the streets again.

True to his word, as soon as Keisha was released from the hospital, he drove her to a place that he'd picked out especially for her; a place she could call home for the meantime, and it had security that was probably duplicative of what was being used at Fort Knox. Trigga had a security camera system that connected to an app on his phone so he could see all entrances at all time. Not a damn thing could happen without him knowing it, and just in case something popped off and he was held up, he had an extra layer of protection for Keisha that would be arriving any minute now.

Keisha walked into the master bedroom and admired the huge California King bed that lay in the middle of the room in all its majestic splendor. Everything about every piece of furniture in the house was over the top. Trigga walked around looking at each item like it wasn't a big deal, but Keisha hadn't seen a single item yet that hadn't nearly taken her breath away.

When she opened the doors to the walk-in closet, she saw that she'd unknowingly saved the best for last. The entire closet was stocked with clothes; expensive, high-end and brand new attire from the looks of it. Keisha tugged at the tag on a few of the items. Just her size.

"The house and everything in it is yours...for now. I'm paying by the week because we ain't gonna be in the A for too much longer," Trigga said as he walked up behind her.

Keisha flinched at being reminded that he'd neglected to stand true to one promise he'd made her...the most important one, at that. He'd said that they would leave all this street shit behind them and go, but Trigga knew when he said it that there was no way he was going to stand behind that bullshit. He knew Keisha knew it too, so he theorized that it didn't count as something he lied to her about.

Pulling her towards him, Trigga wrapped his hand around her and rubbed over her belly, then kissed her on her neck softly. An uneasy feeling crept into Keisha's consciousness and made her feel queasy. She reached down and grabbed his hand from her belly and held it in hers as she tried to mask the feelings she felt. She still hadn't received the results of the tests they'd run at the hospital concerning the baby, and Keisha still hadn't mentioned anything to Trigga about it. He had enough weighing on him as it was, and it was bad enough that she had to deal with worrying until she heard good news from the doctor. She didn't want him to have to put up with it too.

The heat coming from Trigga's body, along with the tenderness of his touch, calmed her as the bright light shining in through the wall of windows that completely covered one side of the room, grew dim. Although it was only a couple hours into the afternoon, clouds were moving in and bringing with them some cool air and dark skies.

Suddenly, Trigga's cell phone chimed and the sound pulled them from their moment of brief reverie as they enjoyed the feel of each other's body. With a sigh, Trigga pulled it out and pressed a few buttons. About a minute later, the doorbell chimed.

Anxiety building, Keisha turned to Trigga with her eyes searching for any reason to be alarmed, but she didn't see any in his.

"Who knows we are here?" she asked him as he started to walk out of the room to answer the door.

"Somebody I'd like for you to meet," he replied, beckoning with his head for her to follow him.

Hesitant about meeting someone new just yet, Keisha hung back for a minute while Trigga walked to answer the door. When it opened, she heard the heavy bass tone of a male voice, followed by the light, airy chiming of a female's. It was the woman's voice that piqued her curiosity, and she started to slowly walk out of the room and down the hall so she could have a peek at what was going on at the front of her new home.

When Keisha turned the corner, the first thing her eyes settled on was the sight of two large Dobermans that sat calmly on the floor with their sight scrutinizing her every movement. It was obvious they were very well-trained and they didn't move a muscle as they sat, appearing to be harmless but from their stance, it was obvious that they were trained to attack on command. If the correct word was uttered, Keisha knew they could get vicious in a heartbeat.

"These two here are Zeus and Athena," a male voice said suddenly, drawing Keisha's attention away from the dogs, one of which had already decided Keisha was no longer worthy of attention and had started licking its paw.

Keisha looked up and saw a man about the same height as Trigga standing next to him and looking at her. He had no tattoos on his face, but every other part of his body seemed to be covered with various skillful artwork. His thick, medium-length dreads stopped about an inch past his shoulders. He looked like the brown-skinned version of Alexander Masson, and even had the goatee to match. He had a muscular build, like Trigga, but was bulkier whereas Trigga was lean. Trigga had the build of a basketball player, while this man was built like a running back with broad, wide shoulders.

He was easy on the eyes, but Keisha looked away almost as quickly as she'd focused on him. Never had Trigga ever caught her gawking at another man, and he wasn't about to catch her doing it now. Her eyes fell to his side, and Keisha took a moment to admire his companion, a woman with a lean build that held subtle curves. She didn't have much when it came to ass or breasts, but she had a decent portion.

What she did have was something that Keisha often envied, and that was long, toned and blemish-free legs that she obviously had no issue with showing off. Her shorts stopped right below the crook of her ass, and she paired them with strappy high heels that made her legs appear even longer. She was still shorter than the man next to her, but she stood well over Keisha. Her face was blank and overall unreadable, but her eyes flickered with interest as she examined Keisha.

"Keesh, this is who I wanted you to meet," Trigga spoke up as he stepped up and held his hand out to Keisha. "This is my nigga, Gunplay, and his girl, Tavi."

"Gunplay?" Keisha repeated, thinking about how ironic it was that Trigga would have a friend named Gunplay. "Y'all choose your names together?"

"Hell naw," Gunplay laughed as he looked at Trigga. "But this nigga stay biting my style."

Trigga chuckled at Gunplay's joke, and then his face went serious. "We 'bout to go handle some business real quick. Keesh, you and Tavi can do whatever it is chicks do. We'll be back."

"Y'all leavin' them here?" Keisha asked, pointing at the dogs while hoping the answer would be 'yes'. They looked harmless at the moment, but she didn't want them snapping on her as soon as Gunplay left.

"Yes, Athena will be inside and Zeus will be out. Tavi knows the commands and if any muthafucka tries to creep his ass up in here, he's gonna wish he hadn't," Trigga replied.

"Zeus...Athena, *Komm!*" Gunplay said in what Keisha assumed was German.

Both dogs stood up at the exact same time and walked directly in front of where Gunplay stood, with their eyes focused on him as they waited for the next command. He made a motion with his hand as he walked over to Keisha. The dogs followed him.

"Hold your hand out," Gunplay told her with a smirk on his face that she didn't appreciate. Just because he thought his dogs were harmless didn't mean she was crazy enough to think the same.

Keisha darted her eyes at Trigga, who was watching her with furrowed brows. He bent his head and gave her a slight nod that told her to go along with Gunplay's request. Taking a deep breath, Keisha leaned over and held out her hand. Each dog teetered over slowly and took a few sniffs.

"They have to catch your scent so they know you're not an enemy," LeTavia said, her first time speaking since Keisha had walked in the room. Keisha gave her a skeptical look. It didn't matter how many times they sniffed her hand, she knew that if LeTavia said the right word, they would chew her up into dog meat.

"Alright. *Braver Hund!*" Gunplay said, meaning 'good dog'. "*Platz!*"

Both dogs immediately dropped down to their bellies, into full relax mode.

"Okay, we'll be back soon." Trigga walked over and gave her a kiss as Gunplay did the same with LeTavia. "Y'all...do shit. Fun shit, I mean," Trigga said with an awkward look on his face. He had no idea what females did when niggas weren't around.

Keisha nodded her head and watched him and Gunplay walk away, talking back and forth calmly as if they were headed to a basketball game, rather than into the most dangerous parts of the hood looking for Lloyd. When they walked out of the door, LeTavia turned to her with a look on her face that said she wanted to be there about as much as Keisha wanted her there: not at all.

This should be interesting, Keisha thought to herself as she turned on her heels and headed back to her bedroom.

"You can make yourself at home," she said right before closing the door behind her.

TWENTY-ONE

"So what's the word?" Gunplay asked Trigga as soon as they had walked out of the house and out of earshot of Keisha and LeTavia.

"Word is, Black got dis nigga from Dallas up here helpin' him get his shit in order and buy him a few mo' days 'fore I put a hot one in his ass," Trigga grumbled as he got in the driver's side of the new whip he'd copped right before picking Keisha up from the hospital. He wanted to make sure he didn't attract unwanted attention with her in the car.

"A nigga from Dallas, huh?" Gunplay asked thoughtfully while stroking his low-cut beard. He sat down in the car and then turned to Trigga. "He wouldn't happen to go by the name Austin, would he?"

Frowning, Trigga shot Gunplay a look out of the corner of his eyes and nodded his head.

"How the hell you know that? You heard 'bout dis cat before?"

"Not too much," Gunplay lied. "But I know he supposed to crazy as fuck, but he just ain't ran up on some real niggaz like us," Gunplay said with his chin raised in confidence.

Trigga grunted as he pulled out of the gates that surrounded the house and shot off down the road at top speed. He wasn't worried about being pulled over; he was sure every cop in a thirty-mile radius of Atlanta had probably gotten word that he wasn't to be fucked with unless they called for backup.

"I can promise you any shit you done heard 'bout him ain't shit compared to what I'ma do when I find they asses," Trigga said with his mind heavy into his thoughts.

Gunplay smirked with a sinister sneer while nodding his head. He knew that Trigga wasn't talking nothing but the muthafuckin' truth. He'd first met Trigga years ago before Trigga even started working with Queen. Back then, he and Gunplay wasn't nothing but bad ass teenagers who weren't afraid of shit and earned respect behind the barrel of a gun, but even though their roads ventured into opposite directions with Gunplay heavily involved in the dope game and Trigga a hired killer, they kept in touch and often called on each other to assist when they ran into some bullshit.

"The fuck goin' on wit' Mase?" Gunplay asked, speaking of Trigga's twin brother.

He had a scowl on his face that he reserved specifically for when he spoke of rats and snakes. Gunplay had never trusted Mase from the first time he laid eyes on him. First off, he was a bitch. Secondly, he was a leech who owed his entire existence to another nigga, which couldn't be respected even if it was his own brother. You can't put your trust in a nigga who couldn't survive on his own two feet unless he was standing on the next nigga's back.

"Fuck him. I'm focused on Black at the moment but as soon as that muthafucka out the way, Mase's razor mouthed ass is next," Trigga said with the immediate threat of death looming.

He then slowed down to a creep as they started to drive through the slums of the ghetto. Despondent vagabonds staggered on the sidewalks so severely cracked that there was more dirt and rubble than anything else. A woman staggered across the street right in front of them with her bulging belly jiggling in front of her, so big that it wasn't clear whether she was pregnant or just fat. She was wearing clothes that looked like they were made for a chick more than half her size, but she strutted to the other side of the road with the confidence of Beyoncé, with her raggedy flip-flops barely covering the filthy, black soles of her feet.

"Shit, dis how they livin' in the A, huh?" Gunplay scrunched up his nose as he glared at the backside of the chick. She was built like a linebacker at the top with a tiny ass square booty and knock-knees.

"Naw'll, dat's how DAT bitch is livin'. Pull yo' piece out," Trigga told him as he reached behind him and pulled out a brand spanking new AR-15 with a hundred round drum from the back seat under a blanket. Trigga had come to bring the pain in the worst way.

Gunplay immediately reached back and grabbed his desert eagle, his mind already set to go when Trigga said the word but when he turned to wait for him, his eyes nearly bugged out his skull when he saw the AR-15, with the big ass drum of ammunition attached.

"Daaaaamn, nigga! You got me totin' this lil' ass shit and you holdin' that big boy joint."

Trigga almost laughed, but his mind was on mayhem and murder at the moment, and it didn't take long for Gunplay to catch his drift.

Trigga eased on the brakes in front of a two-story apartment building that had four doors on the outside, one of which had a solid gold doorknob.

"You just never know with these nigga, they stay strapped; every time I rush one of Lloyd's spots, them niggaz got big guns so I got them shits too. Na'mean?" Trigga said, the entire while his eyes were locked on the building as if he was strategically measuring the layout, in and out. Gunplay gave him a subtle nod.

"Let's go, we on some 'take no hostage shit', niggaz gon' tell us what we want to know, and we shooting first and asking questions later."

"True dat my nigga," was all Gunplay said, enthused as he held his banger at his side looking at the window.

Balmy, cerulean clouds covered the bright sun with a hint of rain, causing a momentary amber-colored overcast. Trigga hopped out the whip with the AR-15 at his side and walked briskly with purpose, like a man on a mission. Gunplay followed suit, placing the silencer on his piece. Both of them cocked their weapons and lifted them in the air, taking aim.

"Mike Dee is the nigga," Trigga uttered as they took the old dilapidated stairs two at a time.

It was a two-story home. Across the street, little black girls were jumping rope as several boys frolicked in a grassless front yard, playing football. An ice cream truck passed playing some type of musical jingle that sent the children racing to the truck before it could stop fully.

Gunplay nodded his head 'yes', fully understanding what Trigga intended to do to Mike Dee if they found him. The only reason you went after Mike Dee was to get information. He was a known snitch, ready to offer up any information he had whenever it served his purpose.

Trigga stood back and took one final look around the area as Gunplay eased the weapon out his pocket, and aimed it at the front door lock. The entire time the children played, Trigga and Gunplay moved as stealthily as possible.

"You ready?" Gunplay asked and took a noticeably deep breath like he was inhaling high octane fuel, nerves on edge.

The one hazard about a house invasion was it truly was like walking into a danger zone. The occupants could be waiting on you. You never know what to expect. Truth be told, both of them could be walking into a trap.

"Let's go!" Trigga said just as the ice cream truck pulled off.

Prrrsh!

The sound of the silencer on the gun was like a metallic snap of a finger. The only problem was the door lock busted out with a loud cling as it was propelled with force to the other side of the door.

The two of them wasted no time and rushed inside the house. This was to the point of the unknown and no return.

"Hey, what da fuck you doin'?" a frantic voiced asked as loud music played in the background.

K-BOOM! K-BOOM!

Trigga let loose with the drum, shooting everything in sight. Not even Gunplay was prepared for the sudden barrage of bullets. As he returned fire, several bullets whistled past his head. It was as if the people inside were waiting on them.

BOOM! BOOM! BLOCKA! BLACKA!

A fusillade of shots rang out.

Trigga wasn't even wearing a bulletproof vest or, for that matter, any armor that stopped bullets as he boldly rushed forward letting loose with his superior weapon, blasting through walls and furniture, causing bodies to drop. A woman and her child cried in the carnage. The three gunmen that had foolishly positioned themselves behind a couch were now open targets. Trigga had blown the entire place to smithereens, including the three men he discovered when he moved the couch back. Their bodies were lapped over each other, like distorted rag dolls in a pile.

A luminous light bulb dangled solitarily from the ceiling as he moved the couch with him for cover, while Gunplay's gun stayed leveled. They were making sure everyone was dead.

One of the men was a guy in his early 20's, the top of his head was partially blown off, gorily resembling a watermelon that had exploded, spewing blood. The other guy lay on the floor on top of him with his eyes closed, in his right hand—a .9 mm. A blunt and scattered money littered the floor by his right leg, and a gaping hole was in his neck. The other guy, a big man, was lying on his back with a perpetual stare; eyes wide open like he was looking out into space. All he had on was a pair of boxer underwear and a wife beater t-shirt.

His penis hung out the boxers. There was a hole in his chest the size of a softball, staining his white t-shirt red.

"Fuck man, that big ass shotgun ain't no joke," Gunplay said as he stood in the rubble with paint chips and wall plaster on his face and beard, latent gun smoke billowing around them. He wrinkled his face as his ears rang from the deafening blast.

Then they both heard it again; a woman and child were crying. The sound was coming from the adjoining room. The kitchen. Broken glass and debris cracked under their feet as they both gingerly walked towards the noise.

As soon as they entered the kitchen, they spotted the woman and child in the corner, face down, huddled on the other side of the makeshift island kitchen counter. The woman was using her body to protect the crying child, a little girl, about three-years-old.

"Bitch, shut up!" a husky man's voice threatened in a hushed tone, causing both Trigga and Gunplay to look around puzzled. There wasn't a man in sight.

"Don't look this way, we are not going to harm you," Trigga said softly.

"Okay, just don't hurt me and my child," the woman said with some type of accent as she hung her head, shielding her eyes. The baby began to cry harder.

Trigga stepped closer as Gunplay walked over cautiously. With his gun leveled, hesitantly, he opened the pantry door. It cracked with a loud noise as he aimed his gun inside.

"Empty," Gunplay mouthed. There was a sheen of perspiration mixed with some type of paint smeared on his forehead as he looked around befuddled.

"We looking for Mike Dee. I heard a dude's voice in here. Tell us where he is and we will let you go," Trigga said.

For some reason, he was whispering. The woman began to cry harder. She wagged her head, "Sir, I dunno."

It was then that Trigga recognized the accent. She was Spanish.

"Man, this bitch lying!" Gunplay ranted angrily. He marched

over and placed the gun to the child's head and cocked it, one in the chamber.

"We ain't got all day to be playing hide and seek, where dat muthafucka at?!"

It looked like Gunplay was on the brink of losing it, and with good reason. They heard a man's voice and, at that very moment, the guy could be preparing to open up on them with a weapon.

"He... he... he... over dere," she said in broken English, pointing to the cabinets under the sink.

Both Trigga and Gunplay exchanged quizzical expressions. There was no way in hell a person could fit inside that little ass cabinet under the sink.

Doubtfully, Trigga walked over and opened the cabinet and sure as shit, there was Mike Dee's fat ass balled up under the sink like a human Pretzel, with sweat dripping off his body like he had just come from a swim in Like Michigan.

"Nigga, get yo' fat ass from under there!" Trigga accosted him and squatted down. He struck him hard with the butt of the shotgun, opening up a deep gash that gushed blood like a faucet.

Together, they dragged Mike Dee from under the sink as the woman and child wailed hysterically, then they pistol-whipped him unmercifully as the woman continued to scream at the top of her lungs along with the baby's crying.

"Where da fuck is Black?"

The man's mouth opened as if he was about to speak, but the only thing that came spilling out was blood; then he bobbed his head as he struggled to breathe, panting and moaning.

"I dunno..."

"Oh, you know and you gon' tell me something," Trigga threatened.

Then he reached back and struck him with the butt of the shotgun again, causing Mike Dee to cry out in pain once more. Word on the street was that he was a snitch. If that was the case, why wasn't he snitching now?

"Man, I swear to God, I dunno nuthin' man!" the man crooned with his eyes bloody from the bloody gash on his forehead.

"Fuck dat!" Gunplay spat out of the blue, and walked over and shot him in the shoulder.

BLOCKA!

The shot echoed throughout the room.

"Nigga, talk. The next shot is to your dome, fuck nigga."

Mike Dee's body jerked and thrashed, like he had been hit by lightning as he writhed in agony on the kitchen floor, clasping the wound with his hand as it bled like a bud of crimson, red-colored roses.

Then suddenly, in the distance, they all heard it at the same time: police sirens blared.

Both Trigga and Gunplay stared at each other in disbelief. The damn woman and child were still crying, working both of their nerves. Aggravated, Gunplay rushed over to the kitchen window and peered out. The sound got louder.

"Fuck!" Trigga scuffed and looked toward the front door, as if expecting it to come crashing open any minute with irate, angry cops.

The baby and woman continued to wail behind them.

"Bitch, you and that goddamn baby better shut the fuck up!" Gunplay shouted from the window as he pulled the curtain back and aimed the banger at the lady.

Silence.

She began to rock the baby rhythmically back and forth with her hand over her mouth.

The sound of the sirens grew faint as it passed by. Both Trigga and Gunplay released deep sighs, but the drama wasn't over yet.

Trigga was running out of time, and he knew Mike Dee may have had some answers to questions he needed to know.

"Again, where is Black? Hurry up and tell me or I'ma have my dude here to shoot you in the other arm."

As the blood dripped from the wounds, Mike Dee looked around frantically, like he was on the fringe of delirium.

"Man...me and Black fell out...He don't fuck w—w—wit' me no mo'..." Mike Dee said and winced in pain.

"Why you and him fell out?" Trigga asked, then stole a glance at the door.

"Dior had me following him...she had me spying...I use'ta work for her too."

"Doing what?" Trigga asked, his brow furrowed with concern.

"I think she was setting him up...this was around the time ... the time..." Mike Dee stopped and looked down at the blood forming a river in front of him. It was obvious by the amount of blood that he had been hit in a main artery. He was bleeding out on the floor.

"Man, I need to go to the hospital...bad!" Mike Dee said in a high-pitched tone, and clamped his hand tighter over the wound.

"I'll take your fuck ass to the cemetery and drop you off if you don't tell me what I want to know. It was around what time? Finish the statement."

"... it was round the time your brother Mase was setting you up."

"Wait...you fuckin' know me?!" Trigga screeched. The guy nodded his head and groaned.

"Black showed a picture of you to the whole crew...he has a bounty out on your head, two bricks of cocaine and a hundred stacks." The big man winced in pain as his eyes started to roll to the back of his head.

Gunplay whistled out loud and said, "That's a lot...this nigga wants you bad."

Trigga ignored Gunplay's warning and focused on Mike Dee, who was starting to black out.

"Nigga, so you must have saw Black, when?"

"Last...I—I—I saw him w—wa—was at...Cash told 'em..." the man sputtered a few more times and spat out more blood. Time was winding down. Trigga shook him once more.

"Cash what?"

"C—C—Cash kicked him out. Da club...h—he was at da club. He said he had somebody that was real close to you that was going to set you up. The last person...you...would suspect..." the man said, then his body went limp.

"FUCK!" Trigga cursed, and suddenly went berserk and began to kick him viciously in his leg, then chest, and in the gunshot wound.

"Talk! Nigga wake your ass up." Trigga kicked him again, not realizing Mike Dee was dead.

"I think the nigga dead. Let's bounce my nigga, before the law come, yo," Gunplay persuaded and walked over, taking Trigga's arm gently. He was concerned for his friend. It was the first time he had actually saw him about to lose it.

Trigga pulled away and muttered, "Somebody close to me was going to set me up."

He had to be talking about Mase, Trigga thought.

Standing up, he walked past Gunplay and straight out of the door. They'd burst in, fucked up some shit, murked some niggas...but for the most part, it didn't seem to him that he knew shit that he didn't know when he came in.

As the door thundered closed behind Trigga once Gunplay made his exit, something occurred to him as they ducked back into the whip and took off down the street.

*Cash kicked him out...*Trigga thought to himself.

It wasn't much, but he'd been known to make something out of nothing many times before.

CHAPTER TWENTY-ONE

TRIGGA AND GUNPLAY RODE IN SILENCE TO THEIR NEXT destination, each of them enveloped in their own thoughts of war and revenge. The sun cast a shadow over Trigga's face, creating an eerie glow on his stoic expression. His mind swirled with thoughts of his responsibility as a man to a woman he loved, and the future father to a child that he already adored. He placed his hand in his pocket and fingered something he'd been holding there for quite some time, as he thought about Keisha. He had some big decisions to make when it came to her. He just had to make sure he could be the man she needed him to be before he did.

The light in front of him flashed from red to green, so he took his foot off the brake and mashed the gas. Looking out the window at the sight around him, all he could do was laugh to himself as a memory came to his mind. It was the worst day, which turned out to be the best day: the day he met Keisha. Here he was driving down the same road they'd been on that same day. The day he almost lost his life... the day he unknowingly lost his brother as a life-long ally. Ironically, the same day Mase made a decision to double-cross him, Trigga lost the one person who had been with him from birth, but he found the woman who would be by his side for life.

Life was a bitch of the cruelest type, but she could be sweet even when she wanted to.

"Dis a strip club? You feelin' like you need to let off a lil bit of steam 'fore you get home, my nigga?" Gunplay asked with a smirk as he looked outside.

One thing was for sure; Gunplay loved the hell out of LeTavia's crazy ass, but it didn't stop him from appreciating bad bitches from time to time. He wasn't no Mase; he knew how to push pussy off the brain when it came to handling business, but he wasn't one to turn down an offer for a chick to suck his dick from time to time.

"Naw," was all Trigga said. He felt like he'd done too much talking already for the day. He wasn't about that shit. He let his gun speak for him.

Just like it was about to do now.

Rat-tat-a-tat-a-tat!

"YEEEEOOOOOOOOOWWWWWW!" Cash cried out to the top of his lungs.

He fell forward and dropped like a sack of bricks, right into a concoction he'd made on the floor of his own blood and piss. Gunplay couldn't help himself and he nearly doubled over in laughter as he watched the fat man scramble to grab onto his injured thigh, while making a swiping motion that looked like he was trying to swim in a sea of his own urine.

It was pitiful.

Gunplay reached out and kicked Cash in the back of the head, making the man yelp out once again in pain.

"Shut da fuck up, you bitch ass, greasy, fuck ass muthafucka!" Gunplay barked at Cash as he whimpered on the tile floor like a sniveling mountain of lard.

Trigga made a snorting sound and lifted one brow at Gunplay, who had his face twisted up in disgust as he watched Cash writhe on the floor while blood leaked from his leg.

"You still got a way wit' words, nigga," Trigga commended Gunplay as he walked over and stepped down on Cash's leg and pushed hard. His crimson red lifeline gushed out from the hole in his leg, and completely covered his fat fingers which were clamped down so tightly on the leg that his knuckles were pale.

"Aaaaarrrrrgggh—" he yelled out in pain as his eyes darted back and forth and rolled around in his head.

Suddenly, they focused in on the barrel of the gun in Gunplay's hand, and Cash froze in place with his mouth wide open and his thick, swollen tongue dangling out the side.

Gunplay curled his lip up and spat through his teeth, "Eitha shut da fuck up or I'll dot ya ass up one mo' time. What it is, nigga?"

The parts of Cash's terror-filled eyes that were supposed to be white, but were yellow instead, glazed over with pain and under-standing as his brain marinated on Gunplay's every word. The last thing he wanted was for the menacing, devilish man in front of him to shoot him again.

"Da fuck you think I am? A muthafuckin' joke?" Trigga asked as he bent down and looked him square in the face.

Aghast, Cash's eyes grew even wider with horror as he stared at the malicious expression on Trigga's face. Never in his life had he seen a pair of eyes so calculating and so cold. Trigga's icy glare was like what poor souls saw right before death ushered them home to their final resting place in the fieriest hot parts of hell.

Dis muthafucka iz crazy! Cash screamed in his head as he cowered under Trigga's glare.

Never did he think he would fear any man to the point that he would double-cross Black, the most feared gangster in the area, but here he was about to turn bitch and tell any and everything he ever thought he knew about Black; whatever it is that Trigga wanted to know.

"No! I don't think—"

"Dat's da muthafuckin' problem!" Trigga laughed, but the sound of his dry cackling didn't have anything joyous about it. It was the laughter that came from the cruelest of beings when he had finally set a trap for his prey.

"You don't *think* I'm a joke. I need you to *know* I ain't no fuckin' joke."

And with that, Trigga pulled out the sawed-off Mossberg shotgun that he had in his pants, and with Cash pinned down by his knee, he pumped it one time and pressed the tip of it into Cash's neck. Cash's mouth opened to let out a wail of sheer pain-filled agony, but the barrel of the shotgun was pressed so deeply against his Adam's apple that he couldn't even manage to allow a single sound to escape through his lips.

"I'm confused, so I'ma let you help me work dis shit out in my mind," Trigga started as he pressed harder into Cash's throat, who made a smacking sound with his lips as he fought to take a breath through his open mouth. "Nah, I told yo' punk ass to let me kno' if Black came through here and you gave me your word that you would. But I just found out he was here some days ago. I ain't get no mutha-fuckin' call from you, so that can't be true, could it?"

Cash struggled to speak against the pressure being placed on his esophagus, but he couldn't get a thing out and Trigga wasn't letting up. Suddenly, there was a knock at the door and Trigga shot a look at Gunplay, who put his hand on the gun at his waist.

"Who da fuck is it?!" Gunplay yelled out roughly through the door. "We in da middle of discussin' business shit!"

Shaking his head from side-to-side, Trigga gave Gunplay a reproachful look which was met by a shrug.

"It's Cinnamon! And I'm jess here tuh collect my muthafuckin' check! Cash, I know you in dere and you ain't finna cheat me out my muthafuckin' money! You know I been on dat stage every single night dis week workin' my ass off after that Luxe bitch left, and I want dat bonus you owe me!"

Trigga's ears piqued at the mention of Luxe's name. He hadn't heard of or seen her since the day he'd run into her in the parking lot of the hospital. Seemed like she'd made a clean getaway.

The knocking turned into banging as the stripper chick pounded on the door so hard that it seemed like she was going to knock it straight down to the ground. Cash couldn't even answer her if he wanted to, being that Trigga's gun was still shifting shit around in his throat.

"I ain't doin' shit tonight until I get my muthafuckin' money, and I want every red gotdamn cent—"

Suddenly, Gunplay opened the door, cutting her off completely. He reached in his pocket and threw a decent-sized knot of money at her, making it rain over her head. The brown-skinned beauty's face lit up like Christmas lights, and she started snatching the money straight out of the air.

"Bitch, be gone!" Gunplay said as he slammed the door in her face and turned back to Trigga and Cash, who was still lying on the floor with his mouth gaped open like a goldfish out of water.

"I ain't got time for dis shit," Trigga muttered. In one swift motion, he flipped the gun and before Cash could even take in a deep breath, he aimed the gun at one of his hands and pulled the trigger.

Ka-Boom!

Three of Cash's fingers flew off his hand, leaving a blood trail of pieces of bone and shattered tile in its place.

"You betta tell me some shit I wanna fuckin' kno'," Trigga gritted.

"And it looks like you betta start flappin' yo' muthafuckin fat ass lips fast because my nigga still left you wit' seven chunky ass fingers for tha takin'," Gunplay added, leaning over as he eyed each one of the trembling fingers that Cash had left. Cash tucked his remaining fingers underneath his palms in a feeble effort to hide them safely from the reach of Trigga's gun.

Trigga snorted out a chuckle. He hadn't been planning to take away any additional fingers anyways. If Cash didn't speak, he was taking off the whole hand.

"I—I—I don't know why he came! He left wit' dat nigga wit' da jacked up 'teefises'!" Cash drawled out his version of the word 'teeth'.

Trigga looked at Gunplay, and they both exchanged a look that let each other know they knew exactly who the 'nigga wit' da jacked up teefises' was.

Mase.

"Where dey go?" Trigga asked with a crooked brow as he tried to hold back his anger at Mase still double-crossing him and fucking around with Lloyd.

Shoulda shot dat nigga right in front of the fuckin' 5-oh like I wanted!

"I—I—I don't kno'! I just told dey asses dey had to leave!" Cash continued to ramble on. "The dumb one left da car he was drivin'. It belonged to Black cuz I seent him drivin' it and it had his name on da back."

"Where da car at now? It's still out there?" Trigga asked him, the wheels turning in his head.

"No! No, some light-skinned muthafucka came and got it, said he was takin' it out to Black's crib a lil ways south of here in da boon-docks." Cash cringed suddenly, and his body started jolting slightly as if he were about to go into shock.

Whap!

Trigga slapped the shit out of him, pulling his ass back to his dire reality that his muddled mind had been trying to escape. The walls of his office, his safe haven in the middle of his life's only successful venture, was sprayed with his blood and the two big ass athletic muthafuckas that stood in there with him didn't look like they were even entertaining the idea of letting him out alive. Cash's mind was near its breaking point. The pain was forcing it to shut down so he could retreat from the agony he felt.

"Who came and got it? What's his name?" Trigga asked as he watched Cash's eyes flutter weakly. His entire body started to go limp as his fat arms fell with a loud, echoing thud onto the floor.

Desperate for an answer, Trigga took the shotgun and pressed the barrel against one of Cash's eyelids.

"WHO da fuck took Black's whip to his crib?!" Trigga repeated as Gunplay shook his head sadly, and started counting the rounds in his gun.

I HATE when these muthafuckas die too fuckin' fast, he thought with a sigh.

"Au—Austin, Black's cousin. He's...there," Cash sputtered weakly.

He lifted up his index finger on his good hand and pointed out behind Trigga's back through the office door that led to the club, down the hall from Cash's office.

Trigga gaped at Cash. "Dat muthafucka is in the club?!"

As soon as Cash shook his head 'yes', Trigga had seen all he needed to see. Jumping up, he ran to the door, snatched it open and took off down the hall. He heard a gunshot ring out in Cash's office which let him know that Gunplay was handling business, and would soon be right behind him.

If Austin was still in the club, he'd better be having a good ass time because he was living the last moments of his life.

CHAPTER TWENTY-TWO

THE HEAVY SCENT OF SMOKE, PERFUMED-SATURATED PUSSY AND liquor permeated through the air as Austin bobbed his head softly to the beat in the V.I.P. section that had been custom-modified by Cash to fit his personal preferences. NeTasha sat next to him dressed in a soft blue dress that hugged every sumptuous curve on her beautiful body. It had a plunging neckline to show off nearly every bit of her firm breasts and peek-a-boo cleavage, saving only her nubile nipples for Austin's eyes. Her neck was laced with diamond necklaces, and in her ears were enormous teardrop diamond studs.

When Austin said that she was his, he meant it and made it his business every day to show her that she wasn't no basic bitch anymore, because he wasn't a basic nigga. In less than a week, he had elevated her to boss bitch status and every pair of eyes in the club knew the deal when they saw her sitting next to him, like an exclusive prize that was only for him to open when the time was right.

Every nigga in the club was trying to low-key glance at NeTasha without Austin noticing, but he did anyways. As long as muthafuckas didn't look too long, they could keep their eyes in their skulls. He could not blame them for wanting to look. She was drop dead beautiful but she was also his, so they knew better than to forget that.

Austin intended to fuck her later on that night for the first time and find out was she really a virgin. Normally he didn't wait that long when he was craving the pussy, but since she said she was a virgin, he was determined to take it easy until he was ready to find out first hand, because nowadays chicks be running more game than Nintendo. But there was something about her that was different; she had actually piqued his curiosity. In addition, she was the first chick that he even contemplated making it official with; he decided to play it different with her and wait a few days. He was working to charm her because it felt good to him to make her happy, and not just because he wanted something from her. She was different; she never asked him for money or expressive things. She just wanted to spend quality time with him. She once called him an enigma on her mind; when he looked at her perplexed, she went on to explain that she found him fascinating, like the allure of good girls falling for a thug.

As the music pulsated and they shared a good time swaying to the rhythm of the music, NeTasha was standing with her audacious hour glass hips and ass pressed up against Austin, as he drummed his fingers on her hips and occasionally palmed her round ass.

Just then, a guy bounced by with drink in hand. He momentarily stopped and ogled NeTasha's backside as she moved, bending down to get her drink off the table.

"Damn, shawty got a fat ass," he droned.

Austin damn near choked on his drink as he looked at the guy who had blatantly disrespected him. Suddenly, he pushed off from where he was. He was on him in a flash.

"Aye, my nigga, fuck wrong wit' yo' muthafuckin' eyeballs?" Austin gritted as he pushed up on the guy.

"Fuck wrong with you, nigga? These my eyes, that's a bad bitch, soooo I'ma look. These my muthafuckin' eyes," the guy shot back. He was dressed casual in a beige button-down shirt and black slacks. He was light-skinned with a mane of curly black hair cut into a Mohawk, a pretty boy to the ladies.

NeTasha stepped in between the two of them in an attempt to defuse the situation.

"Austin, it's okay. He just—" NeTasha started, grabbing his arm. She didn't want to cause a scene in the club, and definitely didn't want to be the reason why Austin got into trouble.

To say Austin was a thug was an understatement. In the few days she'd been with him, he showed her that his ass was nothing less than a full-fledged goon. Everything about him just seemed to intrigue her more, but what made her fear him at times was also what was so damn sexy about him. He didn't play by anyone's rules but his own, which he showed her the first day in the restaurant. He was rugged, commanding, and expected everyone to follow his demands without a second thought, which was normal because it seemed to be what he was used to. But he had a dark side to him that made her hesitant every time he called or said he was coming by.

However, NeTasha learned already that ignoring his calls meant that he would show up at her front door. After she watched him pistol whip the spit out of a guy that he said 'forgot who the fuck he was', she knew then that he was wild. He went straight from beating the man senseless to jumping back in the car, which he'd left turned on in the middle of the road when he first saw the man on the sidewalk, and drove her to Ruth's Chris where they had reservations.

NeTasha remembered feeling like she was in an alternate universe as she watched him pull out her chair, pour wine for them both, and adorn her neck with a brand new diamond necklace while at dinner, as if he hadn't just almost killed someone before her eyes. He was the perfect mixture of heaven and hell, though it seemed like there was more hell than heaven most times.

"Please," NeTasha begged once more for Austin to stop when he pulled away from her so forcefully that she teetered sideways and had to catch herself from falling off the velvet, cushioned bench they were sitting on.

"Fuck dat!" Austin spat. He lifted up his shirt to show off the handle of his gold-plated and diamond encrusted pistol that he had nicknamed 'Diablo' for obvious reasons.

"I—I—she just looks like somebody I seen before!" The guy suddenly got a change of heart and began to frantically explain, as his eyes grew wide with fear after he caught a glimpse of Austin's banger and the black, deathly stare in his eyes.

Instead of defusing his anger, the guy's lame excuse seemed to only infuriate Austin even more because he had turned coward. His face went white, which was curiously odd being that others with his complexion grew red in their rage. NeTasha felt the tremors of trepidation shoot up her spine.

She looked over and saw Austin's expression; his face was tight, like the calm before the storm. It was as sweet as the kiss of death, giving false hope that the worst of the worst was over.

But it wasn't.

The guy continued to babble almost inaudibly as he casually looked over his shoulder like he was thinking about running, but the club was packed and judging by the two drinks he had in his hands, he was with a date.

"... so if I'd have known that was your lady, I promise I would have never—"

Before he could finish the statement, Austin grabbed the guy by his neck, causing both drinks to fly in the air in the V.I.P. section; his gun came crashing down so hard on the man's skull that it dropped him instantly to the floor in a bloody mess. Screams and gasps filled the air as the bass of a song by Future continued to thump through the speakers. A scantily clad redbone chick with flaming orange hair and huge double D breasts had been standing next to the guy. Frantic stricken, she dropped down to her knees and wailed loudly for someone to call 9-1-1, while Austin watched with emotionless eyes. Then something occurred to him and he glanced next to where the unconscious guy had been standing, next to a dark-skinned man dressed in baby blue and white clothing.

"Dis yo' homeboy, nigga?" Austin asked, pointing his bloody gun down at where the guy was still lying unconscious as the female continued to crone and babble for assistance that everyone was afraid to give.

The man put his hands in the air and stepped back a few paces. "I know him, but dis ain't my beef," he responded with a gesture, throwing up both his hands like he didn't want any drama.

"Come here," Austin commanded fiercely, making NeTasha's heart thump even harder than it had. This was the part of him that strangely both excited her and filled her with riveting terror; she was enchanted by his raw thug appeal, and petrified by his gangsta.

Warning signs were going off in her mind as she watched with the anxious feeling boiling in her stomach that told her she needed to leave and get as far away from Austin as she could, and never come back. He was a loose cannon; violent and powerful, ferocious in his vengeance, and no one ever had the courage to control him. He was what happened when you gave someone with no empathy an enormous amount of power. There was no stopping him or holding him back.

And yet, like a dark moonlight to the stars, she enjoyed the glow of being near him.

The man in the baby blue outfit walked slowly towards Austin, while looking around at the crowd that had gathered as if he were calling out for someone to help him. No one moved or said a word to help him, but everyone shot various looks of pity or curiosity his way as some people rushed by and others just gawked. This was nothing unusual in the club. What was interesting to NeTasha was that a large part of the group of people were looking at Austin with awe inspiring fascination, and it was all because of his hubris; it exuded he was an authentic hood nigga, and with just one look it was easy to tell he would bust his gun with the quickness.

A few chicks licked their lips and panted softly as they watched, as if the entire scene was turning them on. The reality was chicks loved a new nigga like a novelty in the city; even though it was obvious he had a woman, that's what side bitches were for.

On the other hand, the men were looking at Austin with larceny in their eyes and the once festive atmosphere was turning tension-filled. A new nigga in a new city, with females galore jocking for his attention, was always a recipe for violence. All it took was for Austin to show any sign of weakness and he would be a casualty in the club, jumped on and rat packed, beat down by at least twenty dudes; but at that moment, Austin had the fear of God in them based on the strength of what he had just done—knocked their homie out cold and was bold enough to just stand there aloof like he was waiting on the next nigga get out of line.

After inconspicuously inspecting his weapon for a few seconds, Austin nodded his head in satisfaction that it was like new, and stuck it back in his waist. He whirled around on his feet and turned to NeTasha. His expression would have been blank, except she could read the sinister twinkle in his eyes. This was all part of his façade; a hood nigga on foreign territory staking his claim on a city he wanted to own. He reached and grabbed her slim waist and pulled her close to him again, and they resumed vibing to the music. Together, they swayed; she could feel his erection against her leg. For some reason, this excited her too.

Covertly, she leaned forward and whispered into his ear, allowing her long hair to splay over his face, lubricious lips on his earlobe.

"You didn't have to do that," she said in a breathy tone, lisping with sexual desire.

He responded by palming her ass and keeping his eyes on alert, just in case one of the dude's homies felt like he wanted to get some revenge for the home team.

"No, he didn't have to disrespect a nigga like that," Austin responded to her as if nothing out of the ordinary had occurred, and watched in his peripheral as several as the unconscious man's friends lifted him off the floor, including the chick with the flaming red hair and large breasts. She cast a glance at Austin with an evil eye as they toted her friend out the club.

"Wet Dreams" by J. Cole reverberated through the speakers, and Austin started rapping the words while moving back and forth in front of NeTasha. By then, his manhood was rock hard and she could see it getting harder against his leg as he began rapping the song to her.

It started off so innocent
She had a vibe and a nigga started diggin' it
I was a youngin' straight crushin' tryna play this shit cool
But a nigga couldn't wait to get to school
Cause when I seen 'em thighs on her and them hips on her and them
lips on her
Got me daydreaming, man what
I'm thinkin' how she rides on it, if she sits on it, if she licks on it
Make it hard for me to stand up

THE FEARFUL FEELINGS she had just felt about him immediately faded as she watched him swing back and forward with a sexy ass smirk on his face, and the print of his big dick rising up against his thigh. Again, she found herself mesmerized to the point of nearly being in a hypnotic spell. Austin was everything her parents told her to stay away from.

This was how it always was. Austin was crazy as hell, but also sexy as hell. He went from zero to a hunnid in a muthafuckin' minute, but just as quickly he would cruise right back on down to zero.

The music died down and Austin sat down next to her, wrapping his arm around her neck to pull her in closer to him so he could catch the scent of her Jasmine-scented perfume. NeTasha fell in line automatically, nestling up close to him and falling in love with each additional minute while he squeezed her ass and sucked on the nape of her neck simultaneously.

"Baby, you scare me when you act like that," she revealed to him in a soft tone, only meant to reach his ears over the loud thundering of the bass in the club.

"What you mean?" Austin asked, half-listening as he looked off across the room. O.G. was scurrying through the crowd, headed his way, with a look on his face that said he had some important information that he needed to give him.

"When you...do all that crazy shit in front of me. I don't like to see it," NeTasha said with a pout that made her look even sexier. Once again, Austin was reminded of her innocence and just how bad he wanted to fuck the shit out her young, fine, big booty ass.

He then smiled mischievously, but was careful to check his surroundings. He grabbed her hand and placed it on his lap, where his dick was hard and long, and nine inches of meat, thick as her arm.

She pulled her hand away like she had just touched a snake. Her heart beat faster in her chest. It was an exhilarating feeling. This was all part of his charm; the excitement, the danger, his wanton lust for her body, and now his big ole dick. She found herself shivering at the thought of him inside of her.

Austin pulled away slightly to look her in her face as he thought about what she was telling him. It was the first time a woman he'd been with had ever said that. Usually, the bitches he had around got off on seeing that type of shit. Something about the way she said she didn't like it made her even more attractive to him. She was a delicate flower that needed to be protected, and he would do what she wanted because he wanted her.

She hesitantly lifted her soft fingers up to his lips; he kissed them and gave her a promise. "You won't have to see that side of me ever again...if I can avoid it, but there is a side of you I want to see."

Squeezing her thighs together, NeTasha gushed and her eyes

grew heavy as she became overwhelmed with passion. If she could give up the pussy to him right that second in the middle of the club, she would; but she had told him that she was a virgin so she knew that she had to be a little coyer and demurring in her approach when it came to sex.

I'm pretty much a virgin, she thought to herself as she watched Austin's eyes slide up and down over her body. He licked his lips slowly and she almost lost her breath. She could tell he wanted it, but he was holding back out of respect for her. That only made her want to give it to him even more.

"AUSTIN!" O.G. panted, jumping up onto the V.I.P. platform and interrupting their moment.

"What?!" Austin snapped through his clenched teeth.

"Man, you won't believe who I jess saw!" he panted, dropping down and placing his hands on his knees so he could catch his breath.

Austin turned his attention to him and made a gesture with his hands that told O.G. to 'hurry the hell up'.

"Dat New York nigga! I saw 'im! Trigga or whateva his name is! He in dere talkin' to Cash right now! I saw 'im and sum dreadlock nigga walk in dere wit' bangers in dey hands! We can dead dat nigga right now!"

Austin clenched his teeth tightly and grabbed his gun out from his waist, then something occurred to him and he turned sharply towards NeTasha.

SHIT! he cursed in his head, thinking of the problem he'd just made. *If I'd known that muthafucka was in here, I wouldn't have said shit!*

NeTasha's heart was no longer in her chest. Instead, it was lodged in her throat, which was the reason she'd stopped breathing as soon as she heard O.G. say the name 'Trigga'. This was the first time she'd heard anything about Trigga since the day in front of the court-house when her and Keisha had come to blows about him. Now, in a matter of seconds, she learned that not only was he in the same club she was in, but he obviously had some beef with Austin. She began to hyperventilate, taking large gulfs of air; it felt like she couldn't breathe.

And just that quickly, NeTasha found herself in the heart of trouble that she knew could end her life. If Austin ever found out about her past with Trigga, he would fuck her up far worse than anything he'd done to any of the men she'd watched him punish. She had to get out of there as soon as possible and find a way to break up with Austin for good. Shit had just gotten a tad too fuckin' real.

"We gotta go," NeTasha said, and reached for his stripe. Suddenly, he began to act all jittery and paranoid. He lightly pushed her, causing her to stand. She ran the palms of her sweaty hand down her dress as she took a moment to gather her thoughts. She stood straight up, her eyes scanning the club and praying that she wouldn't see Trigga anywhere in sight.

"FUCK!" Austin cursed, which made NeTasha jump.

Then he got a bright idea. O.G. would become a casualty in the process, but Austin didn't care. It was the duty of the pawns to die in order to protect the throne. Besides, from everything he had heard about Trigga, the guy moved like an army. The word on the street was to have a crew of niggas and be ready to die when fucking with Trigga. Austin wasn't soft by a long shot, but he wasn't a fool neither. He knew to never engage an enemy in battle when you were not prepared for war. Austin wasn't prepared for war, simply because he was prepared to put his dick inside NeTasha's tight virgin pussy. 'Fight later, fuck now' was Austin's motto.

"I gotta get her outta here," Austin said suddenly. He grabbed NeTasha's hand in his and pulled her close. "You got yo' heat on you?"

O.G. nodded as his eyes continued to scroll toward the exit of the door, as if he was expecting somebody.

"A'ight, I need you to murk dat Trigga nigga for me. Then meet me out at Black's crib down south. I'ma give you da address to put in yo' phone. Ready?"

O.G.'s eyes bucked wide with his eyebrows forming a tight busy line across his face. He suddenly began sweating profusely, along with his doubtful countenance.

"I—I—I don't kno' if I can—"

"Sure you can!" Austin said in a way that made NeTasha shift her feet, as if she was ready to start walking without him.

"Besides," Austin added as he stole a glance at the entrance door, then displayed a fake smile that began to fade with the threat of murder from his face, "if you don't get at this nigga Trigga, you got me to answer to, ya feel me?" Austin said, grabbing his arm pulling him closer.

If ever a street nigga looked like he didn't know whether to shit his pants, cry, or piss himself all at one time, it was O.G. Without saying another word of protest, he lifted his hand and gave his iPhone to Austin, who quickly keyed in the location to where he was going. He handed it back and shot Austin a smile.

"Yo O.G., earn your stripes and do what you need to do, and then come see me. I'll make sure I hit you off wit' some stacks for ya troubles," he added.

A pleading look covered NeTasha's face, but she was more concerned with saving her own ass than O.G.'s. She felt bad for him, but he had picked this life. The only crime she'd committed was fucking the wrong nigga before being associated with the crazy ass one she was with now.

"Please, let's go," NeTasha begged once more.

Austin shot O.C. one last look before making a dismissive motion with his finger, and then turning to NeTasha. He nodded his head and held her hand a little tighter, hoping it would calm her nerves.

As they walked out the back entrance of the club, NeTasha still didn't let herself relax. It wasn't until they were safely inside of Austin's ride and cruising down the streets towards her home that she began to breathe more easily.

I can't deal with this shit, she thought to herself as her eyes filled with tears. She looked out the window, hoping that she could hide the tears in her eyes from Austin, who seemed focused on whatever was rolling around his twisted mind.

I have to break it off with him, she resolved.

But even as she said it, she knew Austin would never allow it as an option.

CHAPTER TWENTY-THREE

"So how you met Trigga?" LeTavia asked Keisha just as she pushed a forkful of chicken fried rice in her mouth before sipping on her cherry Coke.

Biting her lip, Keisha pushed her food around on her plate before answering. It was obvious that LeTavia wasn't the least bit worried as her man cruised the streets with the cruelest intentions of revenge and murder on his mind, but it bothered Keisha almost to the point that she didn't even want to eat.

"At a strip club," she said to her, exhaling a sharp breath. She dropped her fork and it fell onto her plate with a loud clang.

"Whaaaaaaaat?" LeTavia said with a smirk on your face. "Never in a million years did I think Trigga would fall for a stripper! Shit..." she looked around behind her, "...y'all got a stripper pole in here? I could use a few moves to lay on De'Shaun when he ain't actin' right."

Keisha felt a flutter in her chest at her calling Gunplay by his government name as she realized with shame that it had never occurred to her to ever call Trigga by his. That simple fact reminded her of how strange and unique their relationship really was. They were pushed into circumstances brought on by his street life so often that she hadn't even really identified with 'Maurice'. All she knew was Trigga.

Keisha wrinkled up her nose as she looked at LeTavia. "I wasn't a stripper. I was a bartender."

"Ohhhh...." LeTavia said, as if it all meant the same in her book. However, she did seem slightly disappointed at not being able to learn any stripper tricks.

Keisha pulled her phone out of her pocket and shot Tish a text. She still couldn't understand why Trigga wouldn't allow her to come over, but even more bizarre to her was the way that Tish was acting. Every response was all weird and shit, like she was talking to a stranger rather than someone who was pretty much like a best friend.

"Well, you wanna order a movie OnDemand or somethin'?" LeTavia asked after she'd devoured her entire plate of food.

"Listen, I kno' you the type of chick who think it's cool and shit that yo' nigga out there in this streets, but I'm not that kinda bitch and I don't feel like playin' the small talk game wit' you just because they expect us to play nice," Keisha shot off at LeTavia before standing up with her plate in her hands. She walked to the kitchen and raked all of her food into the trash before throwing the dish into the sink.

If the walls could talk, they would have told Keisha to watch her mouth, but their silence allowed for her to walk past LeTavia, ignorant of the fact that she was about to get snatched up.

"Bitch! I don't know who da fuck you think—" LeTavia stopped herself and squeezed her eyes closed, while biting her lip to stop herself from snapping.

Lawd, jeeeeezus, help me not to snatch this bitch! Her strippin' ass musta forgot dat hoes still gettin' pimp slapped for bein' disrespectful these days!

When LeTavia opened her eyes after counting to ten four times in a row, Keisha was gone, and it probably was a good thing because when she opened her eyes, she only got mad again.

Tavi, what you gonna do is stop from chokin' this bitch because De'Shaun wouldn't appreciate it. Then you gonna wait til' he get back and cuss his ass out for makin' you deal wit' her lil' rude ass!

LeTavia stood up and started walking towards the living room to watch a little television, hoping it would ease her mind; but then suddenly, she shrugged and headed to the master bedroom. She wasn't one to bite her tongue, and she wasn't going to start today.

Keisha's door was closed, so LeTavia said a quick prayer that it wasn't locked because otherwise, she was prepared to knock that muthafucka down so she could say what she had to say. When she twisted the knob and pushed the door open, her eyes fell on Keisha's shocked face as she stood at the foot of the bed with her top off. Her face twisted in anger and she covered her bare breasts to shield them from LeTavia's sight.

"You ain't got shit I ain't seen," LeTavia informed her, rolling her eyes. "Now listen, what you did back there was mad disrespectful but, I'ma let you have that because you pregnant and shit. What I'm not gonna let you do is judge me! You...don't...know...shit...about...me!" she clapped after each word, as if to accentuate her statement.

"You think I want De'Shaun out there fighting a battle that ain't got shit to do wit' him? Hell no! I bitched the whole way here about stupid shit because I didn't want him to come! Focusing on other things is what helps to pass the time until he comes back. YOU could stand to try it out sometimes rather than hold on to that stank ass attitude because no matter how much you may WISH that he'll stay out the streets, he won't! It's in him and it has been for as long as I can remember, and even before then!"

By the time LeTavia finished, Keisha's eyes were filled with tears because she knew that every bit of what LeTavia was saying was absolutely right. As long as she was with Trigga, she had to be comfortable with his life. He didn't seem like the type to ever get a desk job or anything else. He had built his skills based on his environment and circumstances and that's how he made a living.

"Ah, shit," LeTavia said when she stopped ranting enough to really focus on Keisha. "I done made a pregnant lady cry."

Though the tears had yet to fall, the mention of the baby made them cascade down Keisha's face, flushed red from anxiety, shame, and frustration.

"The baby..." she started. Her voice trailed off as she fought the words she wanted to say. She needed to tell someone what was going on, because the pressure of it all was too much for her to bear. Tish would have been her first choice, but she wasn't available and Keisha didn't want to tell Trigga just yet.

"Oh my God!" LeTavia gasped, putting her hand to her chest. She waltzed over and stood right in front of Keisha's face, with her brows furrowed in sympathy. "Did the baby...did you have a—is it okay?"

Keisha shook her head. "The baby is alive but—it's not okay. It has a hole in its heart and my doctor confirmed it for me today when I gave her a call. A congenital heart defect..."

LeTavia grabbed Keisha and hugged her tightly as she cradled her in her arms. She was at a loss for words, and didn't know how else to comfort her. There wasn't much that could be done anyways to comfort a mother grieving for the child that she was carrying without being able to do a thing about it.

"You can't worry about this right now...listen!" LeTavia pulled away and made Keisha look her in the eyes. "You and I will go to the doctor tomorrow to check on the baby, and speak to the doctor about what can be done. I'm guessing you haven't told Trigga?"

Wiping away her tears, Keisha shook her head 'no'.

"I figured. Let's get all the answers before you do." LeTavia reached over and grabbed the tank top from off the bed that Keisha had been about to put on, and helped her with it. Then she grabbed her by the hand and gave her a tender look before she said with all sincerity, "Look...that's 'bout as much of the female shit I kno' how to do, and now I feel awkward. I would offer you a blunt or a shot to calm your nerves, but that ain't gonna help. How about we watch some TV or somethin'?"

Keisha laughed at LeTavia's suggestion and nodded her head. Relieved, LeTavia turned around and walked out of the room, emerged in her own thoughts of her own set of secrets she'd been reminded about, of which she'd never told Gunplay.

CHAPTER TWENTY-FOUR

"Say da word Trigga, so I can go ahead and murk dis monkey ass nigga!" Gunplay spat as he shot a look of disgust at O.G.

As soon as they had walked down the hall from Cash's office and stormed into the club, they were greeted with a few poorly aimed shots, one which nearly caught Gunplay in the shoulder. When they turned to their side, they saw O.G.'s skinny ass looking like he'd seen a ghost. In his hand was a small Glock pistol. His body was shaking so violently as he held it that it was obvious why he had missed.

Trigga and Gunplay had pounced on him immediately, just before pandemonium erupted within the rather large building as naked strippers, niggas, and bitches went running out after hearing gunshots. They barely had to rough him up before he started trying to speak on everything he thought they would want to know. Less than ten minutes of work, and he gave them the address to where Austin had gone to with his bitch.

"Wait," Trigga said, holding up his hand. "So you don't kno' shit 'bout where Black is tho'?"

O.G. shook his head so fast that sweat flew off his forehead. "Naw! I ain't been fuckin' wit' Black too much since Austin been handlin' shit. I heard he was tryna find his baby moms or some shit. He ain't been 'round—"

Pow!

A bullet to the skull silenced O.G. instantly.

"Nigga..." Trigga was about to say something, but instead he just looked at Gunplay and placed his gun back at his waist.

A smirk graced his face, and he shrugged.

"I heard sirens," was the only excuse he gave, but it still was a pretty good one.

"A'ight, let's get to our next destination. Hopefully that nigga still there."

EERILY, a crescent moon shimmered high in the sky, illuminating a constellation of stars that looked like celestial holes cut in the canvas of the night as nocturnal sounds churned. Otherwise, it was quiet, but it wasn't quiet enough. For some reason, the hair on the back of Trigga's neck stood up as him and Gunplay crept slowly around the perimeter of Lloyd's ranch property, which was a rural, rustic area that lay in the middle of the woods.

Trigga stepped over a cinder block lying next to an old truck tire as they walked closer to the property. The entire time, his gut feeling was telling him to turn back, something was terribly wrong. Instead, he didn't listen; he didn't follow his gut instincts, something that had never led him wrong.

Checking each window as they tried to locate which room Austin may have been in, their only guidance was a single light on in the entire house that shinned lurid in the night. It gave the place a spooky, haunting appearance. None of the other room had lights, but that didn't alarm them. O.G. mentioned that Austin had left with his chick. He was probably diving deep off in some pussy, not even aware that he was about to be murdered and the chick too, if she was still with him.

"Trigga, dis look like da master bedroom right here," Gunplay gestured as he whispered pointing. He was standing next to a window, close enough to peer inside the room without being seen.

Trigga nodded his head and checked his weapon quickly. For some reason, his hands were shaking. Something was unnerving him, something he could not put his finger on.

The sound of crickets and the distant hoot of an owl filled the country air, as Trigga and Gunplay stood beside the window to where Austin was probably peacefully cuddled up with his female friend. Trigga's heart began to pound in his chest as his heartbeat quickened, and his breathing became labored. He was about to open the window, even though something in the back of his mind was telling him not to do it. He happened to glance over at Gunplay and he too looked spooked, like he didn't want to be there.

On the other side of them was woods and a lot of rustic, rural area, chopped up trees and verdure rubbish. An abandoned truck tire and wild weeds were only a few yards away in pitch blackness.

Beckoning, gesturing with his head, Trigga signaled for Gunplay to get ready. He lifted the window. It opened with a loud screech that echoed, resonating throughout the night and causing both of them to freeze.

Silence lulled.

Then Trigga thought he saw something, a shadow race across the window. If somebody was inside waiting on them, they would be sitting ducks.

His heart beat faster as he held the window.

Gunplay lifted his banger and took aim; his eyes were buck wide. They were both on alert.

And that's when they heard it.

"Tr—Tr—Triggaaaa," a ghastly voice groaned from somewhere behind them.

Without hesitating a single second, both of them pirouetted on their heels and took aim towards the sound. Trigga pulled his cell phone, which had nearly slipped from his sweaty hand. He needed to use it as a flashlight to find out what was going on, as Gunplay watched with his finger ready to pull the trigger if he sensed the smallest bit of danger.

The gnawing sensation crept deeper in Trigga's gut as he saw what looked like a mutated hand with fingertips buried under the grease, partially covered in dried blood, so old that it appeared blackish in appearance. Moving the light steadily up until he was able to see more of the body, he froze in place when the light finally focused on the full upper torso of the body lying only a few yards away.

Trigga's heart leapt in his chest, causing his legs to wobble as he and dropped his gun, startled, starting in utter dismay at the horrible sight beyond him. Gunplay stumbled forward a few paces to get a better look, and then his mouth dropped wide open with surprise.

"OH SHIT!" they said unison.

Then Gunplay bent over and began to vomit.

CHAPTER TWENTY-FIVE

"SHIT! I can't see a damn thing out here!" Burns whispered as they crept slowly down the road towards the house they had seen Trigga's car turn into.

The last thing in the world he wanted to do was to be trailing Trigga down what he knew would be a dead-end road for his career. However, West was still optimistic that if they continued to stick to it, one day they would stumble upon something that would be the key to success for their careers. So naturally, when they were on the way to investigate a call concerning gunshots at the notorious strip club *Pink Lips*, which was also the normal hangout spot for EPG gang members, and saw Trigga and some gangster-looking companion swerving out of the parking lot, he demanded they follow.

"There's no way this can just be a coincidence! We get a call about shots being fired...then we just HAPPEN to see him leaving the scene of the crime? I'm telling you that we're on to one this time!" West said with his hands moving about as he became more animated the more he thought things through.

As always, Burns couldn't say 'no' when he saw his partner, who was pretty much his best friend, in a position where he wanted something so badly, so he went along with it. Now, they were walking through grass so high that it went above their knees as they trekked down the deserted road towards the entrance to the property that they hoped was Ground Zero to much of Black's drug operations. West knew if he was right about what he was thinking, it could be the biggest bust of their careers.

"Just a little further..." West said with a smile as they continued to move forward as quietly as they could.

Burns was ferociously swatting at mosquitoes from behind him with a disgusted and annoyed expression on his face, which was only slightly illuminated by the dim moonlight.

"Hurry up!" West growled through his teeth. "We're almost there! Pull out your guns."

"I'm tryin'!" Burns snapped, halfway thinking that he wanted to turn around and go back the way they had come.

"There's some foliage up ahead that we can use for cover. Let's go!" West egged him on.

Burns shot him a wary look through the night. "Shouldn't we call for back up?" he asked, turning behind him to look down the desolate and deserted road.

"Only when we are sure about what is out here. I don't want to be embarrassed again."

Burns nodded his head with certainty as he agreed. "You can say that again!"

He stopped suddenly when he saw West turn around and push his forefinger up to his bubble lips, "Shhhh!" He motioned over in the distance where they saw Trigga and his companion standing.

Suddenly, they both pulled out weapons. The one with the dreadlocks aimed his at something that Trigga was shining a light on in the grass.

"Got him! Let's go!" West called to Burns as he began high-stepping briskly through the grass with his gun pointing at the two men, who were so engrossed in what they were doing they didn't even notice him coming.

"FREEZE! Put your hands in the air!"

TRIGGA HEARD the sound of someone approaching him and Gunplay, but his eyes were focused on something that stirred him inside in a way that he could not quite explain.

"Is dat Mase?" Gunplay asked with a frown, and a noticeable tremor in his voice. The words seemed to resonate in the fugue of Trigga's mind as time lingered. In the distance, there was the sound of footfalls nearing.

Just as Trigga shined the cell phone light on what looked like his brother's body...

"FREEZE! Put your hands in the air!"

Gunplay turned sharply, his eyes connecting with the figure of two pale white, country looking Bama boys who were approaching them with weapons pointed. Ignoring everything around him, Trigga walked steadily forward, his feet crushing the grass and leaves below them, which made a cackling sound with each step.

"DROP YOUR WEAPON! AND I SAID 'FREEZE'!" West yelled out, growing increasingly annoyed by the fact that Trigga didn't seem to be listening to a word that he was saying.

He thinks he's above the law and that's his problem, West scowled as his face twisted up when he looked at Trigga.

"Fuck, shit!" Gunplay spat, momentarily resisting the urge of an all-out gun battle with cops as he glanced over at Trigga; he seemed to be out of it, his mind was in a trace, eyes misty like they were teary. Gunplay couldn't be sure. Time stalled a beat.

"Drop your fucking guns!" the cop shouted this time, followed by the all too familiar sound echoed of a gun being cocked, one in the chamber. There was no doubt in Gunplay's mind that the cops would shoot him in the back, as police did on a regular basis in the hood.

Gunplay dropped his banger, glanced over at Trigga, and saw his stoic expression like he wasn't all there, mind distant.

Taken aback, West gawked at the boldness of the man ahead of him and prepared himself to fire away when suddenly, Trigga moved in the middle of them, blocking his aim. But Trigga wasn't focused on him; his eyes were still on the body that lay in the grass, covered with dirt, blood, and the kind of odor that you could smell a mile away.

West leveled his gun and took aim, ready to shoot; for some reason, he had a fiendish scowl on his face like he was getting enjoyment out of what he was about to do. His partner just happened to look over his shoulder in a nick of time and grasped his partner's wrist.

"Don't do it!" his voice halted.

Oblivious to everything, a sound deep in Trigga's throat erupted as he swallowed hard and hung his head. He dragged his feet like they were attached to bricks as he trudged over to where Mase lay in a fetal position, naked except for the rope tied around his hands and feet. Trigga fell to his knees by his brother's mutilated body, and his cell phone dropped from his hand to the ground with a thump. He leaned over Mase's face, which was partially lit by the fluorescent light of the moon and the stars above. There was silence behind him as everyone, even Burns and West, stopped to watch with curious eyes.

Over the time they had been tracking Trigga, Lloyd, and Mase's movements, they had not only longed to bring them to justice, but they'd also found themselves wrapped up in the drama of their lives. Seeing someone as strong, domineering, and untouchable as Trigga finally appearing to be vulnerable was enough to make them delay in rushing him.

Trigga knelt down at Mase's side, all the while fighting the gall of emotions that threatened to consume him like a tidal wave of gut wrenching hurt and despair.

"Mase..." he whispered pensively as in the back of his mind, he wondered why did they have to torture him like that.

The right side of his face was nearly missing, exposing his cheekbone and back teeth like a skeletal corpse. There was a hole in his face from his temple down to his chin the size of a small football, like someone had just snatched the skin off his face to the bone, or maybe his brother had been severely burned with some type of hot instrument.

His right eye was nearly hanging out the socket grotesquely. Red ants, rodents, and most likely rats had been scavenging, devouring his face and eyeballs along with other parts of his body. Trigga could tell by the large chunks of flesh that were missing from his brother's lower extremities. Even his penis had large bite marks in it.

"Ohhh, God ohh, God..." Trigga groaned, choked up. He fought to suppress a sob, and instead, wiped at a nest of large, angry red ants that had found refuge and food in Mase's eye socket. The bugs scattered, and some got on Trigga's hand. He brushed them off.

As soon as his hand raked at the bugs on his brother's face, he was startled just like everyone else when Mase gasped in a barely audible whisper with his one good eye open, trying to speak.

"Tri...gga...." Mase croaked in a dry whisper as the disturbed ants began to scurry across his face and body in a frenzy.

"Holy muthafuckin' gotdammit Virgin Mary! The guy is alive," Detective West said. His face had paled white as a sheet. The entire time they had been watching in disbelief. His partner just stared with his mouth agape, like he was tongued tied, speechless. So was Gunplay.

Trigga hung his head in despair as his shoulders rocked; it was obvious he was crying.

"I love... you... man," Mase muttered as his chest moved with a hole in it the size of a fist where he had been shot, and from the looks of it and other wounds, Mase had been shot several times and miraculously, he was still alive on a single thin thread of life.

As Trigga looked at his brother...his twin brother, who he'd been prepared to murder, kill on the spot, he never fathomed him being tortured and brutalized like this; no human being deserved this type of cruelty. Mase's face and body was scarred for life.

"Tri...gga...kill.... me..."

"What?" Trigga asked surprised, and placed his face close to his brother's mouth to listen.

"Don't...wanna live... not like this... pleeeaaazz," Mase began to cry as the bugs scurried across his face, and it suddenly dawned on Trigga what Mase was talking about. If Mase were to pull through and somehow live, which Trigga doubted, Mase's face and body would look like some type of grisly, ugly creature. Trigga understood; as it was, chicks had never found his brother attractive and would call him ugly.

A few feet away, there was a large cinder block, a concrete stone about thirty pounds and large enough to crush Mase's skull, taking him out his misery. Even though the cops standing nearby, Trigga was caught up in his feeling; he wasn't thinking rationally. Truth of the matter was, he didn't care.

Trigga stood, rising to his full height, and walked over awkwardly, picking up the large cinder block, prepared to smash his brother's skull to take him out his misery, to send him home with their mother.

Just as he held the block over his head...

"Okay, hold it right there! That is enough, asshole," West said.

Bloom! Bloom! Bloom!

Rat-tat-tat-tata-tata-tat-tat-tat-tat!

Before bludgeoning his brother to death, there was a barrage of bullets echoing in his ears, pulling his attention away from Mase's body. Trigga twisted around with his hand on his weapon and saw that three cars were pulling up to the property. All of the windows were down, and various kinds of guns were pushed out and taking aim right at him, Gunplay, the detectives, and anything else that was moving.

"Oh, shit! West, call for back up!" Burns yelled out as he tried to dive for cover with his weapon out. He shot a few shots off blindly; in the dark, it was hard to take proper aim.

"WEST! Call for back up! Do you hear me?" Burns yelled out again.

When he didn't receive an answer, he turned to his left and his eyes immediately fell on his partner's face. Burns' mouth fell in horror when he saw West's eyes, open wide in terrified horror, with a single bullet straight through his head. He was dead.

"Oh God! Oh God!" Burns mumbled as tears began to fill his eyes. "I knew it! I fuckin' knew we shouldn't have come—"

Rat-tat-tat-tata-tata-tat-tat-tat-tat!

The bullets thundered off even louder in his ears as the vehicles turned into the entrance of the ranch house, and continued their assault.

Gritting his teeth and willing himself to gather courage from God knows where, Burns reached over and grabbed the walkie-talkie out of West's cold, dead fingers. He'd grabbed it as soon as they had noticed the cars pulling up in front of the gate. Unfortunately, he'd been too late.

"The is Detective Burns reporting to base. Do you read me?" Burns waited for the reply as he watched Trigga and Gunplay fire away at the three cars which had pulled up.

Trigga had an AR-15 in his hand, and was tearing through any and everything ahead of him. He had rage in his eyes that could be seen even under the cloak of the night. Seeing his brother die before his eyes gave him renewed strength and fortified his fearlessness. For once, in the time since he'd been on the police force, Burns was grateful that someone he thought of as a thug and a criminal had a weapon in his hand. If it wasn't for Trigga and his friend, he would have surely been killed by now.

The dispatch responded and Burns sent in the request for backup as quickly as he could. Once he received confirmation that it was received, he picked up his weapon and began shooting off shots at any target he could see off in the distance. There wasn't much. Trigga and Gunplay had nearly finished them all off.

"Let's go," Trigga muttered when the bullets had ceased.

He and Gunplay took off running towards the cars while Burns lay in the high grass, watching them as if they had lost their minds. They hadn't properly checked the scene or anything...there could be more shooters out there. How could they be sure they had gotten them all?

For the first time in Burns' life, he was realizing that this wasn't the life for him. His partner was dead, and he was almost killed as well. If God allowed him to get out of this alive, he would move from out of homicides and the gang task unit and never go back.

"Shit!" Gunplay fumed as he checked all three vehicles, and the bodies that lay around them for one last time. "Every muthafuckin' nigga in here is dead. No fuckin' body to get info from!"

Trigga shook his head. "We don't need it."

Gunplay gave him a curious look, but didn't ask any questions when an expression crossed Trigga's face, which let him know that this was not the best time.

"What 'bout him?" Gunplay asked, holding his pistol up and raising it at Burns. "He's seen too much. We gotta get him, too."

Trigga did a half-turn to look at Burns. Burns shuddered, seeing murderous intent in his eyes, then he lowered his head and stared down at West's face, which was turning greyish as his wide open eyes stared off in the distance. Tears fell from Burns face as he mourned the death of his partner once more, while also preparing himself to join him.

"Naw, let 'im be," Trigga said, watching Burns cry over the loss of his partner. Trigga knew what that type of hurt felt like.

Walking over to where Burns stood hovering over West, Trigga reached down towards him, making him wince. He reached down and grabbed Burns' wallet out of his pocket and opened it.

"We gonna need someone on the inside," Trigga said to Gunplay with his eyes focused in on Burns, then he said to the detective, "You can let them know your partner is dead because Black killed him. Get everybody lookin' for him and call me if you find him before I do. If we good, then you good."

"Trigga, we gotta go. I hear them boys comin'," Gunplay warned as he listened off in the distance.

Trigga gave one last hard look at Burns before turning towards where his brother lay. Thinking that he saw movement, he started to walk over but then stopped suddenly when he heard Gunplay's voice. This time, he was speaking with more urgency and it grabbed Trigga's attention.

"They almost here."

Shaking his head to rid his mind of the false ray of hope that Mase was still alive, Trigga pulled away and ran over to where Gunplay was standing and waiting for him to get in the car. Trigga jumped in and cranked it up. Once the engine surged to life, he shot out onto the streets and started tearing down the road. They turned the corner just in a nick of time, just barely escaping the platoon of police cars that was arriving behind them.

CHAPTER TWENTY-SIX

THERE WAS ONLY ONE THING THAT COULD MAKE A STREET NIGGA leave the street life, and that was a woman worthy of giving up it all for.

As Trigga sat in front of the house that he'd gotten for Keisha, his mind pushed away the precariousness of his situation and he imagined coming home to her, in this very house, after working a long day at work. He thought of what it would feel like not to have to worry every second of the day that someone was after them or wanted to kill her, or harm his seed. Living a normal life without being cloaked by the terrors of his crimes was something he never envied, because he never thought it would be an option for him.

When you're in the streets, the only way out is either by death or serving a prison sentence. Every single day when Trigga woke up in the morning, he thanked God for another day because he knew that one day soon, some nigga would catch him slipping. The fact that he was even able to make it to where he was now was a miracle for somebody who'd been killing niggas since before he was thirteen years old.

"You a'ight, nigga?" Gunplay asked, emerging himself into Trigga's consciousness.

Trigga dropped his head and began fingering the object in his pocket, halfway making sure that it was there and halfway pushing himself to make the decision that he knew he had to make.

"Yeah," he responded, but it was obvious there was more he had to say so Gunplay waited.

"You ever think 'bout gettin' out and doin' some normal shit wit' Tavi?" Trigga asked, turning around to look at Gunplay.

There was a look of surprise on his face, but Trigga expected it. Never had he ever considered doing the things that he was now thinking about. He'd never had a reason. It was why Trigga kept his distance while niggas in the hood were finding chicks that would hold them down to hook up with. He'd seen how lonely his mother had been without his father around, and he didn't want to do that to a woman once the streets claimed him as their prize. That was still what was fucking with him now. If anything happened to him, he would be leaving Keisha and their child alone.

"Yeah, I mean I done thought 'bout dat shit...mostly when she gets to bitchin' 'bout it. But what da hell I'ma do if it ain't what I'm doin'? Ain't like I could be a stockbroker or some shit."

Both Trigga and Gunplay started laughing at his comment, but hidden under their chuckles was the hurtful realization that Gunplay was right.

"And Tavi loves how she livin' too much for a nigga to be on his dick and tryin' to figure out how to make it. I can't do that shit to her anyways. She deserves more for everythin' I done put her through."

Pressing his lips together firmly, Trigga nodded his head in agreement. Keisha deserved more too. He'd have to figure out a way to do both and keep her protected. At some point he could pull out, but he couldn't just yet. After he took care of Lloyd, he would work towards stacking enough bread to wash his money by investing in other business ventures that could sustain them. What he knew about Keisha was that she liked to be comfortable, but she wasn't flashy. He didn't need to give her the moon and the stars in order to make her happy, even though he would do all he could to give her the world.

Trigga opened the door and stepped out the car finally, firm in his decisions of what he needed to do. He couldn't get the image of his brother out of his mind. What happened to Mase could have easily happened to him, and one day it would if he didn't make any changes.

Gunplay got out of the car and met Trigga at the door as he waited for him to open it. Trigga unlocked it and pushed it open, then stepped out of the way for Gunplay to enter. After shooting him a look that asked if he was okay, he waited for Trigga to nod his head in response before he walked in ahead of him to find LeTavia, while snapping his fingers to make Athena follow him to the room. LeTavia was always the perfect end to his night and no matter what he put her through, he needed her when he came in from the streets. She knew it, but he knew it even more. He had to feel her warmth next to him.

Running a hand over his face before sighing heavily, Trigga tried to calm his nerves and get his shit together before he walked into the house. He was hiding it well, but losing Mase was fucking with him hard. Although he had betrayed him, he couldn't bring himself to celebrate in his death because deep down, he didn't want him dead. The compassion that Trigga had for Mase had started many years back when they were children, and it was something that he couldn't shake all that easily.

"*Mommy, why is he crying? Please, don't hurt him anymore!*" *Maurice begged when he walked in the room and saw Mase balled up in his bed in the fetal position, crying silently to himself.*

"*Shut up! Don't worry 'bout him, he's gettin' what he deserves for being bad!*"

"*What did he do?*"

"*Ms. Ostell caught him jumping out of her daughter's window when she got home dis evenin'! I taught his lil ass 'bout bein' grown!*" *his mama huffed as she placed her hands on her hips and peered at Mase through the open door.*

"*No—but that wasn't Mase,*" *Maurice started, hanging his head.*

He had thought that he'd been able to escape without being caught. Now he saw that he hadn't been so lucky.

"That wasn't Mase, Mama. That was me."

His mama's face softened as she looked at Maurice with compassionate eyes. She clicked her tongue in her mouth in a comforting way, and walked over to him with her hands out to pull him into her warm embrace.

"You so kind and lovin' to your brother, but I kno' it wasn't you. Mase already told me he was da one who did it. You're such a good boy...always tryna protect your brotha," she cooed as she held him and ran her hand up and down his back to calm him.

Maurice's eyes filled with tears as he watched his brother cry on the bed with his hands between his legs. Maurice shot him an apologetic look when Mase's eyes fell upon his, but Mase only responded by turning over, wincing in pain with every movement, and placing his back to him as he continued to cry.

It wasn't until recently that he'd become aware of what his mother did to Mase when he wasn't around, and it was only because he'd come home early from basketball practice one day and stumbled upon the sight of his mother holding Mase down while she laid a hot, steel rod across his penis, just long enough to make the skin blister almost immediately.

Astonished and afraid that she would do it to him next if he said anything, Maurice backed away slowly and never spoke of what he saw.

The brain has an interesting way of dealing with trauma. In Mase's case, he dealt with his trauma in passive aggressive ways and silently inflicted revenge on the ones who had any dealings in his pain. In Maurice's case, he dealt with it by repressing it altogether. Since that day, he'd never again thought of what he'd seen and had convinced himself that he had no idea what the black and bubbled markings on Mase's penis were from when he saw them in the gym one day.

For all intents and purposes, he hadn't seen what had occurred *that day between Mase and his mother, and since he didn't tell anyone about it, he assumed no one knew. But what he didn't know was that Mase knew. Mase had seen him at the door right before he backed away, and knowing that his brother was aware of the punishment he received but never did anything to stop it infuriated him. So he dealt with things like he always did...he let his hatred and jealousy of Maurice lay in his heart and fester over time, as he silently planned for the day where he would make Maurice pay.*

Trigga shook off the memory that had been playing and replaying in his mind, over and over since he'd seen his brother die in his arms, and walked into the quiet and dimly lit house. He knew it was that memory that made him feel responsible for Mase, no matter what he'd done. Mase took a lot of shit back in the day just so that he could have a better life, and as soon as their mother had been killed and Trigga took the lead role in the family, he made sure that he took care of Mase every step of the way. He felt that he owed Mase that much for never being there for him before.

"Baby? Are you okay?" Keisha asked as she walked up to him slowly.

He had been so into his thoughts that she'd crept up on him easily while he stood in the kitchen, searching for the bag of weed that he kept in there for times like these. Nothing like a few tokes on a good ass blunt to calm a nigga's nerves.

"I will be," he told her after he grabbed a bud from out the bag, and then started pulling the plastic off the blunt.

"Let me do that," Keisha said, grabbing the blunt from his fingers.

She started to pull it apart, dumped out its contents, and then laid it flat on the countertop. Trigga watched with fascination as she plucked the bits of weed out and laid it in between the folds of the blunt, careful not to include any seeds. Then she wrapped it back up, slowly and carefully, using her expert tongue to seal each bit, and she wound it around.

When she was done, she handed it to Trigga with a sly smile on her face as she watched him inspect it carefully.

"Humph," he hummed with approval as he placed it between his lips without lighting it, as if he was trying to assess if it felt right in his mouth.

Then he pulled it out and said, "I shouldn't be surprised. Square chicks always like to do hood shit."

"*Square* chicks? Da hell you mean by that? I'm no square chick!" Keisha laughed as she crossed her arms in front of her and watched Trigga slip the blunt back between his lips, holding it at the side of his mouth.

"Square chicks...if you ain't never held nothin' between yo' pussy for a nigga or cooked no crack in the kitchen, you just might be a square," he said to her with a chuckle.

Keisha thought back to all the things she'd done for Lloyd: holding his dope, almost shooting Dior...all things that Trigga didn't know about, and she prayed he never would. Not that she didn't trust him or she thought he would leave, but in spite of everything, she wanted to remain innocent in his eyes.

Leaning on the edge of the entrance to the kitchen, Keisha stared at Trigga, her love growing more and more by the second.

"Well, from what I hear, hood niggas like us square chicks," Keisha teased, unlinking her arms and placing her hands on her shapely hips. Trigga's eyes lowered slowly to her thin waist, and then slid down to where her hands lay on her rounded hips. She'd almost gained back all of her weight, and she was looking sexy as hell as she teetered from foot to foot with a smirk on her face.

"Yeah," Trigga smiled, licking his lips. "I do love my square chick. Bring ya ass over here right quick."

Ducking her head to the side as she walked to him, her heart flipped when Trigga opened up his arms to pull her in. She fell into him easily, resting her head on his chest as he rubbed her back and cradled her lovingly in his arms.

Keisha closed her eyes and tried to block out the thoughts that were hammering in her mind. She had told LeTavia that she would wait, but something about this moment seemed right. She had to tell him what was going on with the baby. Hearing about what was going on with their child might be what she needed to get him to understand that his place was at home with his family.

"Tri—Maurice," Keisha started. The way that Trigga's name rolled off her tongue felt foreign to her, but she wanted to get used to it. Trigga was the name reserved for his enemies. When he was home, he wasn't that to her. She wanted their home to be a place of peace, almost like a haven, hidden and tucked far beyond the reaches of the evils of the world. After speaking with LeTavia for a bit, she was beginning to realize that she couldn't expect Trigga to change when she'd pushed herself into his world. A lesser man might have seen her as an unwanted casualty of war and left her for dead way back in the beginning when they'd first met. But he didn't. Although he didn't know her from anyone, he risked his life to save hers consistently, and for that she owed him her loyalty, love, and respect.

"Yes?" Trigga asked with his eyebrow crinkled as he thought over whether or not he could get used to Keisha using his government name.

He'd gotten so accustomed to the way 'Trigga' rolled off her row of perfect teeth and soft, pink tongue, but he knew there was a reason that she wasn't using it just now, and he knew it was because of her need to distance him from the reality of his lifestyle.

"I need to tell you something. It's about the baby."

Keisha swallowed hard, urging herself to gather courage to let him know what was going on as he stared at her with concerned eyes. The blunt dropped between his lips and pointed towards her toes. Trigga grabbed it and dropped it on the countertop so he could focus all of his attention on her.

Tears came to her eyes, but she bit her lip to keep them away. She had to be strong and think positively. It was the only way to make sure that Trigga did the same.

"The baby has a hole...in his heart. It's called a congenital birth defect." Keisha paused when she heard Trigga take in a sharp breath.

When she looked at him, the look in his eyes crushed her soul.

He was so devastated, and she could see it in his expressive eyes, although he was struggling to keep his face straight. Then she thought she saw a shimmer of something in his eyes but he turned away from her, blocking her stare.

"I—I—I didn't mean to; I mean...L—Lloyd made me take the drugs. I didn't have a choice, I didn't know I was putting the baby at risk, I..." Keisha grabbed on to Trigga's arm to turn him back around, but he shook her off roughly, which almost broke her heart. Although she knew that she was to blame, not once did she ever expect that Trigga would place the weight of their baby's bad health solely on her head.

"I'm sorry, I never meant for this to happen to our baby, I—"

"It's not you!" Trigga said sharply, turning around. "It's not you! It's me!"

Wide-eyed, Keisha gawked at Trigga with her lips parted and a stark frown creating a hood over her clouded eyes. He was pressing his finger into his chest as he continued to declare to her that she wasn't the issue, he was. Keisha shook her head and walked closer to him to combat his words.

"No, it was because of the drugs in my system..."

"It was not, Keesh! I will not let you take the blame for some shit that ain't yo' fault. Ain't nobody gonna take the blame for some shit I did anymore," he said, more to himself than to her. Then turning to face Keisha, Trigga said, "Mase had the same condition with his heart and he's my twin. If the baby got it, it ain't because of you...it's because of me."

Keisha fell backwards into the seat that was behind her as Trigga paced back and forth in the living room, right in front of her. The weight that she'd been holding on her shoulders for all this time was gone, but it was now on Trigga, which made it no better.

The more I try to protect her, the more I hurt her, Trigga thought to himself as he paced the room.

Finally, he sat down across from Keisha and looked into her eyes. She wasn't saying anything, but she didn't have to. Everything that she could have ever said was already in his thoughts. It was turmoil to experience a love so magnificent and so pure, but also so devastating. Exhaling heavily, Trigga ran his hands over his face, and then stared wistfully at the wall ahead of him.

"Maybe you should just go," he said finally. "I'll make sure you got mo' money than you'll ever need and shit...but I—I can't let you be around me yet. I can't deal with this shit right now."

"What?!"

Enraged, Keisha stood up and stared at Trigga as he looked up at her as if he was sure in his standing that he was making a good decision. However, there was hurt and pain filling his eyes. There was no way he meant what he was saying.

"How could you say that?!"

"How could I say that?" Trigga punched his hand into the palm of the other, and then jumped up. "What da fuck you mean, Keesh?! You ain't built for this shit, but being wit' a nigga like me don't do nothin' but put you through it! Since you been wit' a nigga, you almost got killed TWICE! You been shot, got your ass beat, almost been raped, been kidnapped...that ain't no normal shit, Keesh! You living the life of a muthafuckin' gangsta bitch and you ain't one!"

Shocked into silence, Keisha stared at him as her mind went back to when Luxe had called her exactly that. A gangsta bitch. Even when Luxe had said it, Keisha wanted to yell out 'no, that's not me!'. That wasn't her, and this wasn't the kind of life she wanted. It was just what she'd fallen into.

"Can't you see this shit, Keesh? You been beggin' me to get out this life. But I can't and I won't...not yet anyways. But every second, I'm reminded about the fact that all I'm doin' is causin' you pain. Even now...you pregnant wit' a baby that's goin' through shit because of me! He ain't even here and I'm already not able to protect it! Just like I've never been able to protect you!"

"You have been able to protect me!" Keisha shot back, walking over to where he sat. "Don't you understand that I wouldn't even be here if it hadn't been for you? You've always been there for me...and the times you weren't was because I pushed you away. I don't feel safe unless you're around, and I'm not goin' anywhere. Don't you see that's why I want you to stay? Why I beg you to get out of this shit? It's because I need you! I don't want to think of a life without you in it, and what you do makes me afraid that I just may have to."

By the time Keisha finished speaking, she was sitting in Trigga's lap with her arms wrapped around his head as he held onto her tightly, with his head against her beating chest. What hurt most about the things that Trigga had said was that every part of it was exactly what she'd been thinking, but never wanted him to know. She was a college student, an overall good girl who had found herself in crazy situations from dealing with thugs and bad boys. But for the most part, she wasn't equipped for the things that they were dealing with, and often she wondered how life would have been if she had gotten with someone more like Chris, the college boy who Trigga had scared away at the bus stop.

But when she responded to Trigga, she realized how true her words were. She needed him much more than she thought he needed her. No matter what, she couldn't let him leave. She would never be happy.

"Stay with me," she whispered against the top of his head as he lay quietly on her chest.

Trigga didn't respond, but she felt him relax in her arms and his embrace tightened around her waist as he held her. Then suddenly, he lifted her gently and placed her on the seat next to him. When their eyes met, an array of emotions transferred between them, but none more powerful than the love they felt for each other.

The hum of the refrigerator was the only thing that could be heard as Keisha watched Trigga's face intently. He seemed to be fighting an internal battle, but she prayed that he had listened to her words and was no longer considering splitting their family apart. Two seconds later, she saw that Trigga had planned just the opposite when he dropped down to one knee right before her eyes.

All of the light in the room seemed to shine upon Trigga's face as he looked gingerly at Keisha. His mind spoke doubt as he wondered what kind of man with the heart of a gangsta could make a good husband, but his heart affirmed that he could do what was needed to take care of his family the way they needed to be cared for.

"I don't kno' shit 'bout bein' married or bein' a father. I ain't never had a father, and I killed the only man who I knew my mama ever fucked wit'." Trigga paused, and Keisha waited with wide eyes for him to continue. "I ain't shit in most people's eyes. I'm a street nigga who ain't never known anything but the streets. And I ain't never thought I would be anything more...never wanted anything more. But now that I kno' you, I do want more."

He paused once more, and Keisha batted the tears from her eyes with the back of her hand. She hadn't realized that she was crying until that moment. Trigga's words were so pure and honest; more so than anything that he'd ever said, and she could feel every word.

"Keisha Mikayla O'Neal, I promise that I will give you everythin' your heart desires if you'll just stick wit' a nigga. Just let me get shit straight, and I'll give it all up to be wit' you. I ain't perfect and you kno' dat shit, but I have perfect love for you and our shorty. If you'll ride for me, I promise I'll live for you until the day I die. So—" he took a deep breath and let it out before continuing, "—will you be my wife?"

Nodding her head slowly, Keisha held out her hand and allowed Trigga to slide a beautiful princess-cut diamond ring on her finger. It wasn't huge and flashy, because Trigga knew it wasn't her style. Instead, it was only a mere 2 carats and shined brightly throughout the room, catching every ray of light that shined through it.

Overcome with emotion, Keisha wrapped her arms around Trigga's neck as he pulled her into a deep kiss. Lifting her up in his arms, he pinned her against the wall and pushed up her silk nightgown that only came down long enough to nearly cover her bodacious thighs, as she clamped her legs around his waist. In that instance, Trigga forgot about any and everyone in the house as he explored Keisha's mouth with his tongue while cupping her ass in his hands. She was the most beautiful woman on Earth, and now she was his.

Trigga unbuckled his jeans as soon as he was able to tell that Keisha had no underwear on. He was ready to enter her and from the way she was panting heavily while he ran his hands all over her body, she was ready too. Not one to waste any time, Trigga lowered her gently, right onto his erection. Keisha responded by wrapping her legs even tighter around him, enveloping him in her love as she moaned softly in his ear.

The sound of her singing her song of pleasure into his ears was too much to handle, and he couldn't hold back. Gripping her tightly, he pushed forcefully into her but clenched tightly on his teeth, forcing himself to add a degree of gentility to his thrusts. Keisha's head fell back and her lips parted as she reveled in the feeling of the purest form of love that anyone could ever feel. The feel of Trigga's warm flesh rubbing against her most sacred spot excited her past the point of an orgasm, although that was sure to come.

"Don't stoooop," Keisha moaned when she felt Trigga pull back, thinking that he was going to stop, but in reality he was trying to make sure he wasn't putting too much pressure on her.

When she squeezed him tighter with her legs, he pushed in harder, watching her face the entire time to take notice of even the smallest hint of pain.

But all he saw was her pleasure.

Grinding even harder into her, Trigga continued to watch her face and increased his thrusts with every pleasure-filled gasp that escaped her lips until he was all out fucking her, thrashing hard and vigorously as her back lay pinned against the wall. Keisha dug her claws into his back and grinded her hips against his manhood, encasing him in the purest form of ecstasy he'd ever felt.

This was it. This was love. In that moment, he knew he'd give her anything. For always.

"Oh my God!" Keisha shrieked when they began to calm down from their high.

Trigga's eyes were closed as he felt his heart banging in his chest. He was still caught up in the rapture of her, and he didn't want to come down. He didn't want to let go, but he knew when he opened his eyes that he would focus on her face, and the reality of his situation would come crashing back to his consciousness. The image of her reminded him of how precious she was to him, how vulnerable she made him, and how much he knew and understood he wouldn't stop doing whatever he had to do to ensure that she would never feel pain.

"Let me run your water for a bath," Trigga told her as he lowered her to the floor and watched her fix her nightgown across her wide hips. "Tomorrow we are going to the doctor, so you need to get some sleep. We gotta go early because I gotta work at night."

Pulling her lips into her mouth, Keisha didn't object to anything he said as she normally did when he mentioned working. She just nodded her head and followed him to the room. When they passed by the room Gunplay and LeTavia were in, light moans of passionate lovemaking could be heard from the hall.

In this life, every day that your nigga made it home was a blessing, and like LeTavia said she did for Gunplay, Keisha made a mental note to remind Trigga of that when he returned home every night.

CHAPTER TWENTY-SEVEN

"You have reached the voicemail box of 2-1-4..."

"Dammit, Austin!"

Dior hung up the phone and blew out a sharp breath of frustration after hearing the voicemail come on once again. Her parents had taken Karisma for the afternoon to give Dior some much needed time alone. She thought that maybe she could call Austin and ride around with him for a bit to escape the four walls she'd been secluded to for the last few weeks, but once again he didn't answer the phone.

The strangest feeling was overcoming Dior and she had been trying her best to ignore it. The all too familiar feeling of jealousy was taking over as she started to be reminded of how she felt back in the day, sitting at home blowing up Lloyd's phone while he hung out with the next bitch. Austin wasn't her man and she was trippin', calling his phone back to back until he would turn it off.

Since finding out he was in town, she'd been trying to get him to visit her and he always stated he would, but still hadn't dropped by. The last time she spoke to him, she heard a chick's voice in the background but when she asked him about it, he ignored her and proceeded to end the call. Since then he had been ignoring her calls, which infuriated her, adding steadily to her jealous rage.

Picking up the phone, she dialed Austin's number one last time. Sure enough, it went straight to voicemail.

"I kno' you gettin' my muthafuckin' phone calls! So I guess this where we at, huh? I'm only worth shit when you want somethin', right? So what about if I tell Lloyd that it was you who organized that hit on Queen's crew and had her brother killed so that she could get Lloyd and his team out the way for you? I bet you wouldn't like dat shit, huh? I'm the bitch who gave you the info you needed to do the shit you out there doin' now! Just remember that shit when you out there fuckin' around wit' your bitch!"

With that, Dior smashed her finger on the button to end the call and fell back into the rocker that her mother had bought her to rock Karisma to sleep in. Dior swayed back and forward in it a few times, thinking about what she'd done as her anger slowly dissipated. By the time the fire inside her had cooled down to a wavering flame, the reality of what she'd done set in and she grabbed the phone again to call Austin. Biting on the edge of her lip, she tried to suppress the anxious feeling of terror that was nibbling at the nape of her neck while she waited for the voicemail to pick up.

"Austin," she said in a calm tone, "I—I didn't mean that. I was just angry. You kno' you been sayin' you was comin' out here, and I've been lonely and shit. Wit' Ken dead a—and...you're the only one I got to talk to. I'm sorry."

Exasperated and jittery from the thought of what she'd done, Dior hung up the phone and tried to take a few breaths to calm the banging of her heart in her chest. She'd let her emotions get the best of her and made a stupid mistake. Austin wasn't one to be fucked with and to top it off, he was crazy as hell. That was part of what made him so damn sexy.

"Shit!" Dior cursed as she stood to her feet with ease.

More and more, her strength had been returning to her each day. She was almost at 100% if it weren't for her emotional disarray from all the bullshit going on with Austin. She had to get him out of her mind, but what she was going through was normal for a woman who had been in a relationship for over a decade. She was used to having the attention of a man, or at least being in a position where she should have been given a man's attention. So when one nigga fell through, she readily clung to the next. Austin was a flirt and charming, with a sexy thug swag that made him irresistible, so it was easy to fall. Now she was seeing that he must have not felt the same for her.

Dior walked in the kitchen and bit on her bottom lip as she looked out the window at her car parked in her parents' driveway. They kept the keys on the key rack in the kitchen and never drove it, keeping hope alive that one day she would be able to drive it again herself. Dior grabbed the keys and picked up her cell phone.

"Yes? Everythin' ah'right?" Dior's mother's voice chimed through the speakers of the phone, immediately putting her at ease.

"Yes, Mama. What are you and daddy doin'?"

"We are 'bout to take Lil Mama for some ice cream and then spend some time at the park 'fore we go visit Sister Carole from the church. She said she made somethin' for her."

Dior smiled into the phone as she listened to her mother talk. Her parents were definitely making up for all the lost time with Dior by spoiling their grandchild. Their religious beliefs and status had made her father pretty much disown her when she married Lloyd, but now that they were apart, it was like old times when she was still their beloved daughter.

"Okay, well a friend of mine is takin' me out of the house for a few hours. If I'm not home when you get here, I'm okay."

"Oh?!" Dior's mother asked, her voice elevating in pitch with her question. "This wouldn't happen to be that 'man friend' you been sneakin' 'round whisperin' to on the phone, huh chile?"

Dior let out a dry laugh.

I wish, she thought to herself, thinking about how nice it would have been to see Austin after weeks of texting and flirting on the phone.

"Um...no, but I'll be back soon."

"Okay, baby."

Dior hung up the phone quickly and grabbed the keys off the rack, then walked to the door. She didn't know exactly where she was going or what she planned to do, but she had to get out of the house and get her mind off Austin.

"DIS BITCH IS BUGGIN'," Austin muttered to himself as he listened to Dior's message.

Laying back in the bed, he put his hand behind his head and thought to himself about the threats she'd given him.

It's a shame. I liked Dior, Austin thought to himself as he stared at the ceiling.

She had to go, and there was no question about it. She'd come to her senses and claimed that she was only kidding, but it was too late because the threats had already been said, and Austin couldn't let that kind of shit walk.

"Who is buggin'?" NeTasha asked, stirring from beside him.

After almost running into Trigga at the club the other night, she had tried to break it off with Austin, but he made it very obvious that he wasn't having that.

NeTasha was sleeping peacefully when she stirred awake, the alarming sensation that she was being watched making her heartbeat increase as her eyes fluttered open. When she was able to make out the horrific outline of a dark figure sitting in front of her, she almost jumped straight out of the bed, clutching the covers around her neck to cover her naked body. She reached out and yanked on the chain hanging from the lamp near her to illuminate the room.

"AUSTIN! What the hell are you doing in here?!" NeTasha yelled out with her hand on her chest to settle her beating heart.

"The fuck you doin'? Tryna avoid a nigga?" Austin asked, his

brow furrowed as he spoke. He ran his tongue slowly over his top row of teeth as he waited for her to answer.

"No, I—I—I just don't know if I can deal wit' your lifestyle. I get scared and I..." her voice trailed off as she tried to search for an excuse that didn't lead him to the fact that she was really scared out of her mind that he would find out about her and Trigga.

"Listen, shawty...the safest place for you to be is wit' a nigga like me. A lot of niggas done seen you wit' me and they kno' you my lady. If you leave me, it's a guarantee it ain't gon' be good for ya. Ya feel me?" he told her in a tone that made her shudder. She wasn't sure if it was a warning or a threat from the way he said it.

"Okay," NeTasha said slowly, knowing she had no choice. She swallowed the lump in her throat and tried to fight away the fearful expression from on her face.

And then suddenly, a sincere and charming smile spread across Austin's face as he shed his dangerous alter-ego and became the man she'd fallen for that day in the restaurant. NeTasha frowned as she waited for what he was about to say and do. He was so unpredictable.

"Look outside," he said to her, nodding his head towards the window.

Taking a deep breath, NeTasha shot him a hesitant glance and then stood up to walk over to her window. When she pulled apart the blinds, what she saw almost made her pass out right onto the floor. It was an all-white Mercedes coup convertible, with a big red ribbon tied over the top of it.

NeTasha turned around and looked at Austin as he walked up beside her and placed the key fob in her hand.

"It's yours," he said, and she melted.

"Huh?" Austin asked. He sat up, scrolling through Dior's text messages in his phone until he settled on the one he'd been looking for.

NeTasha turned around to face him. "You said someone was buggin'. Who?"

Austin looked up at her with a blank face, and then something passed before his eyes, like a shadow.

"I wasn't talkin' to you," was his response as he dodged her question. He said it in a way that wasn't rude or rough; it was matter of fact, and she knew to drop the issue.

Austin pressed the button to forward the message that Dior had sent him a few days back to someone he knew would appreciate it.

Aye, lil cuz. I found yo' old bitch.

Austin sent the text to Lloyd, along with the address that she'd sent him when she was begging for him to come through. He had made sure that every text he sent her didn't allude to anything going on between them. He flirted a little, but just enough so that he could always say that he was trying to get her to send the address to him so he could give it to Lloyd.

This was always the plan with Dior, to use her until he didn't need her anymore. She was bad as hell, but she could never be anyone Austin truly fucked with because she would turn on a nigga too quickly. When she had first hooked up with Lloyd, she had been loyal but the money had made her greedy, and a greedy, disloyal chick wasn't worthy of his dick.

Austin dropped his phone and turned over to wrap his arm around NeTasha, the one he knew was worthy of everything he wanted to give her. He kissed her on her neck and then followed up with a soft, slow lick before biting gently on her shoulder. Pleasure and then pain. That was his style, and she seemed to love it. They were a perfect match.

"Open your legs," he said. "I wanna suck on it."

"I can't...my period still on," NeTasha murmured, pulling her legs up and slightly moving away from him.

Austin sat up and shot her a look, then his eyes went to the ceiling as he thought to himself.

"Shit...How many days has it been?" he asked, counting them off in his head.

"Two," NeTasha told him, avoiding his gaze.

He let out a sharp breath and then fell back on the bed. "Fuck, so it's heavy or light?"

"Heavy," she said quickly.

Almost too quickly, Austin's eyebrow rose and she hurried to explain.

"It—it will be lighter tomorrow and then by day five, it's off," she rambled out quickly, hoping that he believed the lie.

She was trying to buy time. She needed to figure out how the hell she was going to have sex and make sure that he still thought she was a virgin. If he found out that she had been lying all this time, and especially if she found out who she'd lost it to, she knew that he wouldn't hesitate to kill her.

"Okay...so three more days and then I get to sample that pussy, huh?" Austin asked with a smile that almost made her heart flutter.

NeTasha nodded her head. Austin shrugged and then pulled her body close to him, spooning her in the small bed that they lay in. It was a full size bed but to Austin, it might as well have been a twin. He hadn't slept in anything smaller than a California King since he started wiping his own ass.

"We gotta talk 'bout dis apartment," he said suddenly after thinking about how uncomfortable he was in the small ass bed.

"What about it?" NeTasha asked him, feeling herself falling back to sleep.

"I think I'ma use it fo' a stash spot. Tomorrow, we gon' look at some houses. I'ma move you into a bigger crib."

A feeling of joy mixed with tiny shards of anxiety washed over NeTasha as she allowed Austin's words to flutter through her mind. It was nice having someone try his hardest to give her the world for once.

But at what cost?

CHAPTER TWENTY-EIGHT

THE FLUORESCENT LIGHTS ABOVE THEM SHINED, AS A MOTH captured in its irradiant glow fluttered about in a last attempt to find an exit into the incandescent allure of the white lights. Keisha watched as Trigga stood up for what felt like the tenth time since they'd been sitting in the doctor's office and walked around agitated, occasionally inspecting all of the instruments and gadgets throughout the room. Standing in front of where she sat on top of the examination table, he let his eyes look over her to make sure that she was fine, and then his curiosity got the best of him and he pulled out a tool from the side of the table.

"Da fuck is this?" he asked, holding up the speculum with a bizarre look on his face as he examined it.

Batting her eyes a few times before she realized what Trigga was holding in his hands, Keisha gasped and then started to laugh. She placed her hand on her belly, which looked rounder than normal in her tight-fitted tank top, as she continued to laugh at the confused expression on his face.

"You might want to take that away from your face!" Keisha said between laughs, trying to catch her breath. "That's what the doctor puts inside a woman to open her up."

Horrified to the fullest, as if something that had been in the woman before was going to launch itself onto his face, Trigga jumped back and almost dropped the object onto the floor, right as the doctor walked in with her long, dark red hair falling in long tendrils of smooth curls around her shoulders.

"Hi, I'm Dr. Grize—"

She stopped short when her eyes focused in on what Trigga had in his hands. Trigga twisted up his face and pushed it in her direction.

"Aye, we gon' need you to use somethin' else. She ain't deep enough for this shit," Trigga informed the doctor to Keisha's horror.

She covered her face in utter embarrassment as the doctor looked back and forth between the both of them while she tried to gauge whether Trigga was serious, but the twisted scowl on his face spoke to his seriousness.

"Um...I—I, uh..." the doctor searched for the correct words to say as her face grew to be nearly as red as her hair. "I assure you that I won't be putting this all the way up there so...she doesn't have to be quite so deep, er, I mean..." she stopped and shook her head as she placed the tool back to where Trigga had pulled it from.

"Well, hi, I'm Dr. Grizelda. Keisha, I've already met you and...I guess this is the 'DP'?" she asked cheerfully as she attempted to start over from the beginning.

"DP?" Trigga asked with a frown. He gave Keisha a look, as if he seriously doubted the sanity of the doctor.

"DP means 'dear partner', baby," Keisha explained with a smile. She'd been searching through the pregnancy forums online the past few days to pass the time, so she knew all of the acronyms.

"No, I'm her 'dear husband'," Trigga corrected which made Keisha roll her eyes, although she had a smile on her face. She looked down at her beautiful ring, and felt her heart swell with the love she felt.

"Okay, well now that we got that understood, we can talk. Since I just examined you not even that long ago, I'm guessing that you want to speak about the test results we received for the baby."

Both Keisha and Trigga nodded their heads as they waited for her to continue.

"Well, your baby has what we call a congenital heart defect, meaning he has a tiny hole in his heart. It's a defect that occurs early in development for a number of reasons. It can be genetic—" Keisha squeezed Trigga's hand to comfort him when she felt him tense up, "—but it can also occur if the mother suffers a virus or infection during the baby's early development—" Now it was Trigga's turn to squeeze Keisha's hand when he felt her tense up.

"We don't know just yet how this may affect the baby. He may be absolutely normal and just need doctor appointments to monitor it, he may need medication or...in some cases, babies develop Down Syndrome. It is hard to say, but it's not the end of the world. You both seem like a very loving couple, and I'm sure you can get through anything...even this."

Keisha's eyes were moist with tears, but she blinked them away and then cleared her throat.

"Can we...can we see the baby?"

Dr. Grizelda's eyes lit up at the idea and she nodded her head slightly, a small smile gracing her thin lips.

"Yes, you can. Let me wash up and we can set it up."

Minutes later, Dr. Grizelda had pushed up Keisha's blouse under her breasts and was spreading the blue gel all over her small, round belly.

"You have such a tiny belly, but I'm surprised that you're showing so well to not be that far along. Must be a big baby!"

Keisha turned to look at Trigga, who was rubbing his hands together and nodding happily with a slick smirk on his face.

"Yeah, dats what I'm talkin' about! Baby boy 'bout to be on *swole* just like his pops!" Trigga smiled down at Keisha while flexing his muscles, as if to illustrate his words. She laughed, and he bent down to kiss her on the forehead.

Suddenly, the whooshing, rhythmic thumping of a strong beating heart erupted into the semi-quiet room, pulling Keisha and Trigga's attention to the screen.

"That's him," Trigga whispered out in an affirmative way, rather than as a question. "That's my boy."

"Your girl," Keisha corrected him as she stared at her baby on the screen. Their baby.

"He's perfect," Trigga uttered as he watched the movement.

From where he stood, he couldn't see anything but the flawless combination that he and Keisha had made. A baby that would be the perfect mixture of her good and his strength. Leaning down, he looked into Keisha's eyes and smiled. When she looked back at him, she saw that his eyes had filled with tears of happiness, but they didn't fall.

"It's okay to cry when it's from happiness," Keisha whispered as she reached out and rubbed his hand.

Trigga snorted and shook his head at her. "Do I look like a cryin' ass nigga?"

She couldn't help but burst into giddy laughter.

―――――――

TRIGGA WALKED SLIGHT AHEAD of Keisha as they walked down the hall from the doctor's office toward the elevator. Keisha stared at the back of Trigga as he walked in front of her, his eyes panning the space around them as if he were looking for something.

Like magic, the elevator doors opened ahead of them right as they approached, and a man dressed in a white jacket walked off holding a stack of papers.

"Stay here," Trigga commanded Keisha quietly, and then walked away without offering any additional explanation.

Keisha watched curiously as Trigga walked behind the man and tapped him on the shoulder. The white man with pale skin and blond hair turned around quickly and focused on Trigga as he listened intently to what he had to say, then suddenly a smile graced his face as his eyes shot back to Keisha, who was frowning as she watched the two men speak.

The hell is he up to? Keisha thought to herself.

After wrapping up the brief conversation, Trigga walked back over to her and grabbed her by the hand. He pressed the button to open the elevator doors and stepped on, pulling her on behind him. The doors closed and Trigga pressed the button for the second floor instead of the lobby, which further confused her.

"Where are we going?" Keisha asked finally after Trigga didn't bother giving her any explanation.

"You'll see," was all he said.

The elevator chimed once they'd reached the second floor, and the doors opened. With a frown on her face and her lips pushed out in a soft pout, she followed Trigga as he led her to their next destination.

"Let's step in here," he said once they'd made it to a door off to the side from where the other patient's rooms were.

Keisha looked around, and then glanced at the sign on the door.

Chapel.

"The chapel?" Keisha asked, slowly beginning to guess at what Trigga was up to.

Trigga looked at her as he pulled the door open, a sly smile on his face and a twinkle in his soft eyes. He nodded his head and waited for her to walk in, a gentle way of giving her the option to decide if she was ready or not. Returning his smile, Keisha walked in without hesitating a second longer. She was sure. She'd been sure.

The dim lighting in the room, which was only lit by candles, provided the perfect atmosphere for what was about to take place. Keisha looked down and ran her hand over the beautiful knee-length white skirt that Trigga had picked for her to wear that morning, along with her white crop top, wondering if he'd had this moment in mind the entire time.

The door opened behind them and Keisha turned slightly to see who was joining them.

A priest.

"Dr. Manchello told me that my services were needed...this time for a pleasant reason, I was informed."

The older black man walked over and stood right in front of Trigga, extending his hand for him to shake it. Keisha looked at him with tears in her eyes as the idea of what was about to happen was finally setting in.

"I'm Reverend Crenshaw, and I'm here to perform your ceremony," he smiled deeply, which made wrinkles form around his gentle eyes. He made both of them relax immediately.

Trigga shook his hand, and then watched as the man extended his hand to Keisha and shook hers as well. He wouldn't ever tell a soul, but he could feel the tingly of anxiety rise up in the pit of his stomach. He was about to do something he didn't think he'd ever do. The only thing that comforted him was the fact that he knew the time was right, and he was with the only person he would ever think of taking this step with. Keisha was the one for him, and he wanted to make that permanent. For as long as they lived.

"There is some paperwork the two of you need to sign before we get started," Reverend Crenshaw stated, pulling out a folder from behind him that Keisha hadn't seen before.

As soon as they finished going over the paperwork, the doors opened once again. Keisha turned around and saw Gunplay and LeTavia walking through the doors, donning the largest smiles on their faces known to man.

"What's up, nigga? You 'bout to really do this shit, huh?" Gunplay laughed, dapping Trigga up.

"De'Shaun! Don't you see the preacher right there?" LeTavia chided as she hugged Keisha and rolled her eyes. "I apologize for him, preacher man."

"You ain't gotta do nothin' for me!" Gunplay shot back. "I got this!" He turned to the preacher and gave him an apologetic look. "My bad, man."

The preacher gave him a curt nod with his lips pulled in a straight line as he shook his head slowly, and then turned to Trigga.

"Okay, let's get started."

Less than ten minutes later, Keisha was looking into Trigga's eyes as took a deep sigh and prepared to say her vows. This was the moment that she'd thought about so many times, but never knew exactly what she should say but standing there, the words came to her as easily as if she'd rehearsed them.

"Maurice Bivens...aka 'Trigga'," she added with a short chuckle. "I love you more than life itself. The worst night of my life turned out to be the best because I met you. We've never had a simple, peaceful moment in our entire lives, and I thought that I couldn't live like that. I thought that I couldn't take being a part of the path that we've been walking, but the truth is the only thing that I can't take is being without you.

Today, I vow myself to you. I vow my life to you, and I vow my love to you. There is no one or nothing that can change how I feel about you, and nothing can take away my loyalty. Whatever you choose for us and wherever you lead me, I promise I will go. You got a lot of worries, but whether I will be by your side when you wake up will never be one of them. I love you. Forever and always, I'm yours."

By the time Keisha said her last word, tears of happiness and sincerity had filled her eyes to the point that she could barely make out Trigga's face until they fell down her cheeks, and when she was able to focus in on his eyes, she saw nothing there but the love that he reflected from hers.

"Keisha..." Trigga paused as he tried to find the words that he wanted to say to show her what was in his heart. "No one ever loved you like I love you. No one has ever felt that love, and no one has ever given that love. Before I even really knew you, I was willing to die for you. And I didn't know why back then, but I didn't know a lot of shit back then."

The reverend shifted and cleared his throat, but Trigga ignored him and continued on.

"What I do know is that I want to spend my entire life loving you. And I want that to be a long, healthy, peaceful, simple life..."

He clenched his jaw as he thought about what he was saying. Truth was, he knew Keisha didn't mean anything by it but her saying that the time she'd spent with him had never been simple or peaceful hurt him. That's all he wanted for her and his child. He wanted them happy and at peace. He didn't want her to spend her time always looking over her shoulder for danger, or wondering if he wouldn't come home at night. He wanted to give her what he knew deep down that she wanted, but wouldn't ask.

Glancing back at Gunplay, Trigga watched as he nodded his head slightly, almost as if he were giving him the courage for what he knew Trigga was choosing to do.

"My focus from now on is you and the baby, and nothing else. It's only us from now on out. I am going to spend every moment of my life making you happy, and being the man you need. Until death do us part."

Trigga pressed his lips together and exhaled heavily before turning to the reverend to let him know that he had finished what he wanted to say. Keisha didn't understand just yet what all he meant, but she would.

He was done. From now on, he didn't want to focus on anything or anyone if it wasn't her or the baby. Fuck everything else.

"By the power vested in me," the reverend said as Keisha's smile grew wider and wider in anticipation. "I know pronounce you husband and wife."

Trigga pulled Keisha into his arms as Gunplay and LeTavia hooted in the background and cupped her round, fat ass in his hands as he pulled her into a deep, passionate kiss, as if no one else was there.

"DAMN!" Gunplay laughed as he watched. LeTavia swatted him on his arm and sucked her teeth.

"De'Shaun! The preacher man!" she scolded him.

Gunplay folded his arms in front his chest as he smiled and watched Trigga suck on Keisha's lips, while still cupping his hands around her backside.

"Trig don't care about no preacher man," he laughed as LeTavia rolled her eyes. "My nigga done took the plunge and got that ball and chain!"

"Let me get you out of here," LeTavia said, pushing him gently towards the door. "A'ight, we'll see ya'll later. I gotta get this idiot out of here so he might have a chance at heaven."

"Alright," Keisha laughed as she watched them walk away before turning back to Trigga, who hadn't taken his eyes off her.

"How's it feel to be married, Mrs. Bivens?" Trigga asked with a smirk as he ran his tongue sexily over his top row of teeth.

Keisha shuddered as she watched him. She couldn't wait to get home and get a refresher course on everything that tongue could do.

"It'll feel even better when we get home, Mr. Bivens."

"A'ight, let's go then. Thanks Rev," Trigga said. He walked over and handed the reverend a stack of money. "This is for the favor, much appreciated. I would like to take you out or something, but I can't at the moment."

He turned to Keisha, who was waiting with a smile across her face, and winked at her before grabbing her hand in his.

"I have to go start living my life with my wife."

CHAPTER TWENTY-NINE

AN HOUR AFTER LEAVING HER MOTHER'S HOUSE, DIOR FOUND herself in familiar territory perusing the streets of Atlanta, for reasons she couldn't even explain. It was stupid to be in Lloyd's city but after being married to him for so long, she knew his whereabouts and she knew where not to go if she didn't want to run into him. So running into him was the least of her worries.

Who she did want to run into was Austin.

From what he had said when he first landed in Atlanta, he was staying at the W hotel downtown, and that's exactly where she seemed to be headed. When Dior finally reached the building and saw the sign that told her she'd reached her destination, she couldn't bring herself to turn in.

What am I gonna say to him if I see him? Dior thought to herself as she sat in the left lane with her blinker on.

She didn't have the slightest idea what she could say to Austin to explain why she was at his hotel. What she wanted to do was repeat her apology in person, and pray he would understand that she would never betray him like she'd so easily done Lloyd. Lloyd deserved everything she'd done to him, but Austin didn't. But somehow as she stared at the building, she wondered to herself if doing this would be worth it. Austin didn't seem like the type to like surprises.

Beeeeeeeeeeep! Beeeeep!

Dior gripped the steering wheel tightly as a car horn honked behind her, urging her to make an immediate decision. The sun shined into her eyes as she glanced in the rearview mirror to look at the driver behind her, while her mind tried to come to a conclusion on what she should do.

Then suddenly, almost as if it were an ominous sign, the cars shifted in the other lane which allowed her to see three vultures attacking their dead prey on the side of the street. Dior felt a creeping feeling rise up her spine as she sat hypnotized, watching the birds tear away at the flesh of the carcass of the freshly killed animal, as if they were starving for the nourishment of the deceased doe that lay wide-eyed on the side of the road.

I gotta go, Dior decided emphatically as she jerked the wheel in the other direction, and took a turn down a side street.

She drove in silence, thinking heavily on what she'd seen back in front of the hotel. What bothered her most is that vultures were something you didn't see in the city, though it was common in the country where her family lived. In the city you would see vultures of the human variety, people like Austin, who preyed on the weaknesses of other; but rarely did you see the actual bird.

"He played me," she muttered to herself as she drove. "He played me just like Lloyd did."

The more Dior thought about it, the more enraged she became. Lloyd and Austin were still alive and breathing, while the one man who had never wronged her, Kenyon, was dead. Falling for Kenyon hadn't been part of the plan, but it had happened anyways. And as usual, Lloyd made sure to put an end to her happiness. Although she didn't know for sure, Dior was positive that Lloyd was to blame for what happened to him. If only he had left when she wanted him to instead of turning into a rat. Dior knew Queen would be coming after

Kenyon at some point, and she tried to urge him to follow their plan and leave for that reason, but he didn't listen.

Now he is dead, Dior thought. *Before Queen could even have her men get to him, Lloyd got him first. I hate him.*

Stopping at a stoplight, the sun seemed to dim and the overcast of darkness made Dior check out her surroundings. It felt familiar to her, but she couldn't quite place why.

Then it came to her. She was right around the corner from the hospital. Maybe it was time for her to go ahead and let Dr. Stephens know she could walk, and had been able to for quite some time.

With a sigh, Dior pulled into the parking lot of the hospital and started to circle around as she looked for a parking spot. It was a crowded day, and there weren't many places to park, but that wasn't abnormal for a hospital right in the city.

"Oh, wait!" Dior exclaimed when she remembered something that would help her with her parking woes. Her handicap plaque.

Reaching down, Dior grabbed it from out of the dashboard and placed it where it should be right on the rearview mirror. When she placed her hands on the steering wheel and pulled her attention back to the parking lot, what she saw in front of her almost made her scream aloud.

"That bitch!" Dior sneered as she stared at the woman who was coming out of the hospital doors.

She was walking hand-in-hand with an extremely attractive, toasted caramel-complexioned man, who was dressed in a low-key but effortlessly sexy way with expensive sneakers on that perfectly matched his casual attire.

"Hoe done came up. She fuckin' around wit' someone else's man since her thottin' ass can't get her own!"

Dior continued to glare at Keisha as she walked next to Trigga, giggling and smiling as if her life was better than she could have wished it to be. She looked almost angelic, so happy that she had a heavenly glow around her face. And then when Dior's eyes dropped down to her belly, she could see why.

"She's pregnant?!"

Flashbacks of what had happened over six months ago flashed through her brain as she watched Trigga help Keisha step down off the curb, as if her little ole baby bump was making it hard for her. He was tending to her carefully and with so much love, just as Dior had wished Lloyd did when she was pregnant.

Tears came to Dior's eyes as she thought about the day she had busted in on Keisha and Lloyd back at his condo that he used for fucking his tramps. It was the day that Keisha had tried to kill her and her baby. Karisma was in her belly, and Keisha held a gun to it while in a rage, prepared to take her and her child's life.

In that moment, Dior knew she would attempt to do the same.

SCREEEEEECCCCCCHHHHH! ERRRRRRRKKKKK!

Dior mashed the gas as hard as she could, making the car jump as the engine roared and it jolted off towards where Keisha and Trigga stood.

A wide smile spread across Dior's face, which was so twisted in maniacal glee that she could barely be recognized. She was going to finally get the satisfaction she deserved by finishing something that Keisha started. The day that she busted in on Keisha and Lloyd was the day that started it all. If it hadn't been for her busted, trashy ass, everything that had subsequently went wrong in Dior's life would have never occurred.

And for that, she would pay.

CHAPTER THIRTY

TRIGGA AND KEISHA WALKED OUT OF THE HOSPITAL HAND-IN-hand, still caught up in the feeling of euphoria of being able to see their first born and now officially being man and wife. The sun shined high in the sky, which hurt Keisha's sensitive eyes. She squinted and held her hand up to her forehead to block out some of its majestic rays. The bright light was already making her head hurt and she was beginning to feel a little dizzy, but she didn't want to tell Trigga that. He was still smiling...more than he had in months. Maybe even since she'd met him.

"Aye, I'ma need yo' ass to stop calling Jr. a 'she', a'ight?" he commanded as he held the door open for her to walk out.

"How you know he ain't a she?" Keisha giggled when Trigga gave her a wide-eyed look.

"I know because I ain't makin' no 'she-hes' in this bitch! Fuck you mean, 'how I know he ain't a she'?! Because HE ain't!"

Keisha continued to laugh, and shook her head from side to side. She looked out at the parking lot with her hand to her forehead, still blocking out the sun as she searched for Trigga's car. Then her breath caught in her chest when her eyes fell on something.

Dior? she thought to herself as she squinted at a car that was steadily approaching the entrance of the hospital.

The woman ducked down suddenly, and Keisha continued to stare with her lips parted as she waited to ensure that she hadn't seen who she thought she had. Lloyd's wife was one of the last people on Earth that she wanted to run into at the moment.

"Keesh? You a'ight?" Trigga asked, wrapping his hand around her back and giving her a soft nudge.

Keisha looked at him and nodded, then shot another look over at the woman in the car, but the sun was so bright that she couldn't get past the glare of the windshield. Shrugging off the feeling of paranoia that was plaguing her, she turned back to Trigga and gave him a weak smile.

"I'm good...I just feel a little light-headed. Yo' lil girl already causing me grief," Keisha sighed.

"You mean my lil nigga," Trigga corrected. "Lemme help you."

Trigga reached out and grabbed her by the elbow to help her down the curb, and Keisha chuckled before playfully batting him away.

"Maurice, I think I can get down this lil ass curb by myself!" Keisha laughed as she stepped down, but Trigga jerked her towards him in a joking manner, then scooped her up under his arm.

"Girl, bring yo' ass over here and let a real nigga help you. You must ain't never had a muthafucka do some cheesy shit for you before!" he joked.

Pausing for a second, Keisha ignored the way the sunlight made her eyes burn and stared right into Trigga's grey eyes, which reflected the light in a way that took away the hard, threatening expression that was normally set in his face. This was the perfect moment.

If only it could last forever.

"Keesh, I wanna explain something I said in my vows" Trigga began suddenly, then paused. He exhaled heavily and when his eyes returned to hers, she could feel the sincerity radiating from his stare. Her heart skipped a beat as she waited for what he was about to say.

"I know you deserve better, and I want to give you better…" Trigga paused and ran his hand over his face. "This street thing… chasing Lloyd…following Queen's orders…I'm done with all that shit. It's over. I lost everything, and now I got a second chance. I finally got everything I didn't know I wanted." Keisha felt a flutter in her heart but she was frozen with shock as she listened intently, hanging on to his every word.

"What you've been through almost killed me. I almost lost you and our baby. I've already lost my brother and my mother. The streets ain't done shit for either one of us but take away things and people we loved. I…" He paused as he struggled with his next words. "I—I have some money saved and it's enough for us to live on…I was thinking about opening a club and just livin' out our lives on some peaceful shit, na'mean?" he smirked and pinched her cheek as he waited for her to respond.

I do is what Keisha wanted to tell him. Her heart spoke the words before her lips could even begin to move. Everything that Trigga was saying was everything that she'd hoped for in all the time they'd been together. To have a normal life with the man she loved, away from the streets and away from danger…there was nothing more that she could ever ask him for.

The answer to his question was 'yes'. Keisha knew exactly what he meant, and she was just about to tell him that when she saw his facial expression shift from one of absolute contentment to sheer terror. Keisha's mouth dropped open and her eyes opened wide as she tried to read the alarm on his face.

SCREEEEEECCCCCCHHHHH! ERRRRRRRKKKKK!

The sound of tires coming to a screeching start not far behind her made Keisha's heart leap from her chest, and seemingly lodge itself in her throat, stopping her from being able to complete the simple task of breathing. She felt Trigga's hand clutch hard down on her arm, to the point that she instantly felt bruised. His mouth opened wide, and all sound around her muted in that instance before she could hear his words.

"KEISHA! MOOOOOOOOOOOOOVVE!" he yelled out so loudly that the bass of his voice vibrated in her head, and bounced back and forth between her ears.

Screaming from near and from far shook her very bones as she staggered around quickly towards the sound of squealing tires, and the smell of burnt rubber behind her.

And that's when she saw it.

It was a car, and it was coming right for her.

Opening her mouth horrified, she screamed; it was as if she felt the pain before the large automobile had a chance to crush her and her unborn child. She could feel herself being pulled and recognized Trigga was screaming her name as he made a futile last second move to pull her arm. Keisha stumbled backwards in an ill-fated attempt to move out of the way, but she was too late.

Suddenly, a force stronger than anything she had felt before clamped down on both arms and jerked her to her left. Her head flew to that side and when she opened her eyes, she was staring into Trigga's. His expression was blank, although his eyes were glazed over and filled with love, almost as if he were telling her goodbye for the last time.

Time stopped as her life flashed before her, making seconds feel like hours as she stared into his eyes for what felt like forever. She was cradled in the peace and tranquility of his stare.

And then, in the next instant, she was being slung backwards like a half-pound ragdoll, effortlessly and forcefully flung out of the way of danger. Squeezing her eyes shut to brace herself from the fall, Keisha landed with a loud resounding 'thump' on the sidewalk, scraping the back of her thighs in a way that she knew would draw blood in the process.

The pain ripped through her, but it was nothing like the painful agony she felt when she opened her eyes.

"TRIGGGGGGGAAAAAAAAAA!" Keisha screamed out in a way that was reserved for women who were experiencing the anguish of having their heart crushed.

But there was nothing she could do. With her hands pressed into the sides of her face and her mouth open wide as she screamed words that only God could translate, she watched the car sail right for Trigga at an unmercifully fast speed that was impossible to escape.

SCREEEEEEEEECCCCH!

BOOM!

To be continued...in Keisha & Trigga 4: The Finale!

PART FOUR IS OUT NOW!

THE EPIC SAGA HAS COME TO AN END...BUT HAS JUSTICE BEEN served?

After finding love in the midst of the most treacherous circumstances, Keisha and Trigga decide to leave everything behind them and focus on their marriage and new baby. But when Trigga overhears interesting news regarding the baby's paternity, it leaves him doubting the loyalty of the only woman he's loved. After all they've endured to be together, will this new challenge ruin them?

Lloyd, still the thorn in everyone's side, is more merciless than he's ever been being that he's a street nigga with absolute nothing to lose. But luck strikes when someone comes to his aid to finally nail Keisha and Trigga for good. But it's the last person anyone would suspect.

Austin's intentions when it comes to his cousin's empire slowly begin to come to the light and the more they are revealed to Lloyd, the more he is unwilling to let Austin run free in his streets. When Lloyd calls on his infamous Ground Patrol to teach Austin a lesson, he feels that he's finally rid himself of his conniving cousin for good.

The problem is, Austin has never been one to not get his way. And, just as he plans to show NeTasha, if he claims something as his, he won't stop until it is. Even if that means joining with an unlikely ally.

MORE GUNPLAY & LETAVIA!

Want to learn more about Gunplay & LeTavia? Read 'Shawty Want a Thug' now!

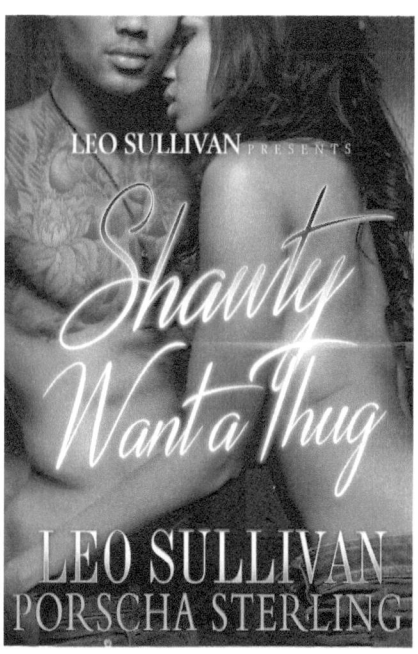

THANKS FROM LEO SULLIVAN

First I would like to thank God for giving me the ability to write with longevity and creativity that has allowed me to touch the lives of millions. I would also like to thank the readers that have supported me from back in the day. This has been a long journey and I am happy to have had you along for the ride.

I would also like to thank my family, which are too many to name and if I miss someone I will be on your most wanted list. Not this time, I love you all. I want to thank my staff and writers, the entire Sullivan Productions LLC Films and Literary family.

I also want to thank the very talented and beautiful Porscha Sterling. Trust when I tell you, this book was truly a labor of love and could not be possible if it was not for Porscha's hard work and dedication. I loved writing about the sinister, dark characters like Lloyd and his crew. Porscha has wanted to kill him since the last book so, what happens in this next installment was interesting and I hope you all enjoyed it. As for the series in its entirety, as a writer I write until the story tells itself and is finished. Thus, the saga continues.

As for the loyal readers, I do read all your reviews and social media comments. In fact, they motivate me. So keep those reviews coming and I promise to keep writing and giving you my very best.

Lastly, be on the look out for my movies, *Life Without Hope* and *Summer Madness*, coming soon.

You can follow me on Facebook or Instagram.

LEO SULLIVAN

THANKS FROM PORSCHA STERLING

Keisha & Trigga is quickly turning into my favorite series!

HUGE THANKS to every reader of this series! There is so much in this series that you guys are allowing us to do that pushes the envelope beyond anything that I've done in other series. I'm happy that you all enjoy it as much as I do!

To Leo, thank you for being an extraordinary writing partner! It's wonderful to write with someone whose strength lies in areas that I feel are my weakest because I learn so much. The only thing I really wish for when it comes to my writing is for people to enjoy it and for me to experience growth. You help me with both of those goals! We had such...*ahem*... 'strong discussions' (not arguments LOL) over where to take these characters but I think every 'strong discussion' led to a great result.

HUGE thanks to every author signed to Royalty Publishing House. You guys trust me with your dreams and I don't take that lightly. I'm proud of every one of you and thankful that you continue to have faith in me. #Royalty4Life

Feel free to contact me on Facebook, Instagram or Twitter!

Porscha Sterling

FIND OUT MORE ABOUT QUEEN

To read about QUEEN of the QUEEN'S CARTEL, check out THE COCAINE QUEEN by Porscha Sterling! Exclusively available on the LiT Reading App.

READ MORE ON THE LIT READING APP!

Read more books like this one **for less**! Check out some other new releases on the LiT Reading App. Go to www.litreadingapp.com to learn more!

JOIN OUR MAILING LIST!

Text **LEOSULLIVAN** to **22828** to join our mailing list!
To submit a manuscript for our review, email us at
submissions@leolsullivan.com

To submit a manuscript for our review, email us at
leosullivanpresents@gmail.com